The Woman Who Thought She Was a Planet

and Other Stories

Also by Vandana Singh
Younguncle Comes to Town
Younguncle in the Himalayas

The Woman Who Thought She Was a Planet

and Other Stories

VANDANA SINGH

PENGUIN BOOKS

ZUBAAN
K-92 Hauz Khas Enclave, New Delhi 110 016, India

in collaboration with

PENGUIN BOOKS
Published by the Penguin Group
Penguin Books India Pvt Ltd, 11 Community Centre, Panchsheel Park, New Delhi 110 017, India
Penguin Group (USA) Inc., 375 Hudson Street, New York, New York 10014, USA
Penguin Group (Canada), 90 Eglinton Avenue East, Suite 700, Toronto, Ontario, M4P 2Y3, Canada (a division of Pearson Penguin Canada Inc.)
Penguin Books Ltd, 80 Strand, London WC2R 0RL, England
Penguin Ireland, 25 St Stephen's Green, Dublin 2, Ireland (a division of Penguin Books Ltd)
Penguin Group (Australia), 250 Camberwell Road, Camberwell, Victoria 3124, Australia (a division of Pearson Australia Group Pty Ltd)
Penguin Group (NZ), 67 Apollo Drive, Rosedale, North Shore 0632, New Zealand (a division of Pearson New Zealand Ltd)
Penguin Group (South Africa) (Pty) Ltd, 24 Sturdee Avenue, Rosebank, Johannesburg 2196, South Africa

Penguin Books Ltd, Registered Offices: 80 Strand, London WC2R 0RL, England

First published by Penguin Books India and Zubaan Books 2008
This anthology copyright © Zubaan 2008

The copyright for individual stories vests with the author

All rights reserved

10 9 8 7 6 5 4 3 2 1

This is a work of fiction. Names, characters, places and incidents are either the product of the author's imagination or are used fictitiously and any resemblance to any actual person, living or dead, events or locales is entirely coincidental.

ISBN 9788189884048

Typeset by FACET Design, D-9 Defence Colony, New Delhi

Printed at Baba Barkhanath Printers, Haryana

This book is sold subject to the condition that it shall not, by way of trade or otherwise, be lent, resold, hired out, or otherwise circulated without the publisher's prior written consent in any form of binding or cover other than that in which it is published and without a similar condition including this condition being imposed on the subsequent purchaser and without limiting the rights under copyright reserved above, no part of this publication may be reproduced, stored in or introduced into a retrieval system, or transmitted in any form or by any means (electronic, mechanical, photocopying, recording or otherwise), without the prior written permission of both the copyright owner and the above-mentioned publisher of this book.

For my sister, Ruchika,
and my brother, Ashok, remembering
the *kagaz ki kashti,* the *barish ka pani.*

CONTENTS

1.	Hunger	1
2.	Delhi	19
3.	The Woman Who Thought She Was a Planet	39
4.	Infinities	55
5.	Thirst	89
6.	Conservation Laws	109
7.	Three Tales from Sky River	130
8.	The Tetrahedron	139
9.	The Wife	168
10.	The Room on the Roof	180
	A Speculative Manifesto	200
	Acknowledgements	204

Hunger

SHE WOKE UP early as usual. The apartment, with its plump sofas like sleeping walruses, the pictures on the walls slightly and mysteriously askew, pale light from the windows glinting off yesterday's glasses she'd forgotten on the coffee table — the apartment seemed as though it had been travelling through alien universes all night and had only now landed in this universe, cautiously letting in the unfamiliar air. Outside the birds were stirring, parakeets in the neem trees, mynahs strutting on the roadsides, their calls mingling with the beep-beep-beep of a car backing in the parking area below.

How strange everything was! In the dream last night it had been the most natural thing in the world to be dancing with a tree, to be nibbling gently at the red fruit hanging from its branches as they swayed. Vikas hadn't been with her in that dream, and she had felt slightly guilty dancing with someone else, even in a dream, even if that someone had been a tree. But it had seemed so natural, so familiar, that in that moment she'd been convinced, finally, that she had found her home planet. And just as she'd started feeling at home, her eyes had opened, and there she was, lying in a strange bed next to a strange beast that she slowly recognized as her very dear husband, Vikas.

And where have *you* been? she wanted to ask him, but he was asleep. If she told him her dream, he would laugh and threaten to find a shrink. Not for you, Divya, he would say, but for me. He liked to say that she was beyond redemption, reading those trashy science fiction novels. But sometimes she wanted to ask him, quite seriously, how to explain the way she felt in the mornings: that even the most familiar thing felt strange, that she had to — almost — learn the world anew. Try explaining that! she said to Vikas' imaginary shrink.

Their daughter lay asleep in her room, curled like an embryo among the sheets. She was twelve today, there was going to be a big party. What was she, Divya, doing, standing in the doorway of the child's room, thinking about alien universes! The child herself — how much longer a child? So strange, so different from the squalling, wrinkled little creature she had first held in her arms twelve years ago! Her face still so young, so innocent, and yet on the inside she was developing layers, convolutions; she was becoming someone that Divya as yet did not know. Divya sighed and went out of the room, drifting through the apartment, touching and straightening things as though to make sure they were there, they were fine. She picked up the glasses from the coffee table and went into the kitchen, which (being on the north-west side of the apartment) was still in darkness. With the usual trepidation she turned on the light.

As light flooded the room, mice fled to dark corners. Divya stepped gingerly in. The kitchen was never hers at night but belonged, for that duration, to the denizens of another world. There were cockroach cocktail parties and mouse reunions, and (in the monsoons) conferences of lost frogs. In the kitchen sink, the *nali-ka-kida*, the drain insects, whatever they were, waited hopefully for darkness, waving their feelers. None of the other creatures — mice and muskrats and frogs — bothered Divya like the cockroaches and *nali-ka-kida*. But it unnerved her that she had somehow, quite unknowingly, surrendered ownership of the kitchen at night.

She put the glasses noisily in the sink. Kallu the crow flew down to the window-sill from the neem tree outside, and cawed at her. His presence was a relief. She gave him a piece of the *paratha* that she had been saving up from last night to eat later. The *parathas* were fat, stuffed with spiced potatoes and peas, the best that the cook Damyanti had ever made. For a moment Divya wanted desperately to curl up in bed with the parathas and a book with a title like *The Aliens of Malgudi* or *Antariksh ki Yatra*. The day stretched before her, rife with impossibilities — to get all that food cooked, the whole house cleaned, and then to entertain the families of Vikas's colleagues without a faux pas… It simply couldn't be done. She wasn't made for such things — she was from another planet, where you danced with trees and ate *parathas* and read trashy science fiction novels.

But it had to be done. "Take me with you, Kallu," she told the crow, but he only cawed sardonically at her and flew heavily off. She sighed and began to wash the glasses. If only Vikas hadn't got that big promotion, she thought, feeling guilty for thinking so. Now he was junior vice-president, which was not at all as exciting as a president of vices ought to be — and they had to move amongst the upper echelons of the company, VPs and CEOs, whose houses were completely air-conditioned and whose windows all shut, so that mice and cockroaches and frogs would have to line up and come in at the main entrance, with the permission of the doorkeeper, like everybody else. The most innocent of things, like children's birthdays, were now minor political extravaganzas with the women all made-up, clinking with expensive jewellery, sniping gently at each other while calling each other 'darling,' and the men talking on like robots about stocks and shares.

She went to the back door and found the newspaper on the landing. As she straightened she smelled it — a stench rolling down from the top of the stairs. The pungent, sharp, stale odour of urine.

The old man was responsible for the smell. He lived on the top landing, which was little used because it led to the rooftop terrace. Divya looked at the door of the servants' flat. It was shut tight. So was the door of the apartment opposite hers, where the morose and silent Mr Kapadia lived.

She took a deep breath and knocked loudly on the servants' quarters' door, where Ranu, Mr Kapadia's cook, lived with her husband.

The woman herself opened the door. She turned her nose up at the smell.

"All right, all right," she spat, before Divya could say a word. She turned and yelled for her husband. "Wash the stairs, you lazy lout, that good-for-nothing fellow has wet his bed again!" She looked at Divya, hands on hips, nostrils flared.

"Satisfied?"

"Why don't you let the old man use the bathroom in the night?" Divya said angrily. "The poor fellow is your father-in-law — treat him with some respect! And listen, make sure the stairs stay clean all day. We have people coming over."

In answer Ranu slammed the door. Divya went back into the house, feeling sick. She wondered if the old fellow was ill again. She let him run little errands for her, like getting the milk from the milk-booth in the mornings, for which she would give him a little money or food. He was a small, emaciated, bird-like man, with a slurred speech that had resulted from some disease of his middle age. Sometimes he would tell her stories of his bygone days and she would nod at intervals although she hardly understood any of it, except a word here or there, like *bicycle*, or *river*, or *tomato chutney*, which, put together, made no sense at all. In her more fanciful moments she had thought that perhaps the old fellow was an alien, speaking to her in an exotic tongue or in code, delivering a message that she had to try to decipher. But he was just an old man down on his luck, with no place to go but the nest of rags at the top of the stairs, subject always to the whims and frightful temper of his daughter-in-law. Divya resolved that later on she would find out if the fellow had fallen ill. He hadn't come by yesterday for the milk. She would have to send Vikas to the milk-booth today.

Divya was hungry.

She had been cleaning all morning and had skipped lunch. By the afternoon, the house was sparkling. She hadn't known what to do with most of the things that they had accumulated — the piles of books on the floor all over the house, the loose photographs on every surface like schools of dead fish, the magazines sliding off stacks in the bathroom. But she had found in herself unexpected reserves of cunning — she'd hidden piles of books behind the beds in the bedrooms, given the magazines to the *kabari* man without asking Vikas if he wanted to keep any of them, collected the photos and put them in a plastic bag in the clothes cupboard. The cleaning woman, who was lazier than a street dog in the sun, loved parties and had worked with great enthusiasm to make the floors shine, knowing that some of the good food would come her way later on.

Late afternoon, Divya was standing in front of the stove, stirring the *matar-paneer*. There was sweat gathering on her forehead, under the hairline, and steam rising off the big *karahi* as the peas bubbled in their sauce of onions, ginger, tomatoes, cumin and coriander. Big chunks of *paneer* like white barges in the gravy, and the aroma! The aroma was enough to make the head swim. Divya had never been so hungry, and was regretting not having had lunch. She was paying for it now: her stomach rumbled, her mouth watered, she felt faint with desire. It should have been easy to munch something while cooking.

But the fact was that she was afraid of the cook. Damyanti was a small, stern woman who stood no nonsense from her employers. She took great pride in her creations and had, Divya thought, an unreasonable code of conduct: you did not eat before your guests, you did not filch from the serving dishes, and there was no need to taste the food unless you wanted to insult the cook. Damyanti had already scolded her once for trying to throw away the carrot-tops.

"You've left so much of the carrots on this, I can easily take it home and put it in a *sabzi;* and the greens can go to Karan's cow. Don't you know what happens to those who waste food?"

The reason Damyanti could bully her employers and get away with it was because her cooking was sublime. The fact that she had condescended to stay and cook for much of the afternoon meant that Divya was, by tacit agreement, completely under her thumb.

"What happens?" Divya asked, trying to sound unconcerned.

"People who waste food end up being reborn as *nali-ka-kidas*," said Damyanti, setting hot onion *pakoras* into a cloth-lined serving dish. Divya shivered. Imagine that, having those horrible, long feelers, living in dark drains, emerging at night to eat the leavings of others!

The *matar-paneer* was done; Damyanti was setting up the big *dekchi* for the rice, putting in the ghee, the cardamom, a cinnamon stick, cloves. It smelled like heaven. Divya clutched the wall with one hand. The thought occurred to her that she should let the party go to hell, dismiss Damyanti and sit on the kitchen floor, surrounded by vats of fragrant dishes, and fall upon them in a frenzy. She collected herself. Maybe she should simply go get the *parathas* she had been saving in the fridge. They would taste divine, even cold. She had surely never been so hungry as now!

But Damyanti (coming to get the *dhania* leaves) caught her at the fridge, with her hand clutching a piece of *paratha* half-way to her mouth.

Chee chee! she said. "Don't you know what happens to the woman who eats during cooking? Do you want to make all the food *jootha?*"

Divya never found out what terrible fate would have resulted from her almost-lapse because at that precise moment, Vikas came in with the cake, laughing and trying to fend Charu off because she wanted to see what it looked like. Divya had to put the *parathas* back and make room in the fridge for the enormous cake. Vikas touched Divya's dishevelled hair as she turned away — she suppressed a desire to bite his hand.

"Are you going to face the guests like this, Divu? They'll be here in an hour! Go dress!"

"I have to get the *chholey* cooking," she said irritably, following Damyanti into the kitchen. There was a knock on the back door.

"I'll see who it is" Charu said, flying off resplendent in a new blue dress, happy because the cake was her favourite kind, triple chocolate. Divya went back into the kitchen, got the other *karahi* on the stove, put in the oil and the spices and onions. When Damyanti's back was turned for half a second she popped a piece of *paneer* into her mouth from the dish of *matar-paneer*, and burnt her tongue. She could hear Charu talking to someone at the door, running into the house and back to the door again; she heard the soft, hesitant, mangled words of the old man upstairs. So he was up and about, the old fraud! Pissing in his bed, stinking up the stairs, giving her a headache first thing in the morning. And she had had to get the milk herself earlier, because Vikas had to go out to get the drinks. Tears welled up in her eyes. If only she could eat something! How absurd this was, to be afraid to eat in your own house!

She was about to purloin another piece of *paneer*, burnt tongue or no, when Vikas came in.

"Divya, you'll never believe what I saw in our room. A mouse! Really, when will you stop feeding every living creature in the area. They think our house is a hotel! And we have all these people coming… where did you put the rat poison?"

He had got it last week, a small blue vial of death that she hadn't been able to bring herself to use. It stood on the highest shelf in their bathroom.

"It wasn't there," he said when she told him this. "Divya, really!"

He knew she didn't like using the poison, but the traps hadn't worked either. Vikas had taken the traps to the park every morning and let the mice out, but they had wasted no time in returning. Stricter measures had been called for.

What Divya remembered was this: she was ten years old, and had been visiting an aunt's house in the summer. It was an old bungalow, ridden with denizens of all kinds, including an army of mice. Her uncle had set poisoned food all over the house and killed off the army. Divya had a vivid memory of the tiny corpses, their bodies twisted with the final agony, all over the house. Then, a day or two later, there had been the smell in her room, which had finally been traced to a nest behind the big wooden cupboard. Twelve baby mice, pink and hairless, had died of starvation after the adults had been killed. All the time Divya had been reading her mystery books and sipping her lemonade, those babies had been slowly dying. She had cried for days.

"Vikas, this is no time to be setting out rat poison," she said, but he was already distracted by the *pakoras*. "Smells good," he said wistfully, leaning over the glass-covered dish.

Before Divya could utter a word, Damyanti had put two pakoras and some tamarind chutney on a plate and handed it to him, all the while smiling approvingly as Vikas ate. Divya stared at him, and then at her, speechless with indignation.

"But…," she started to say, when she heard the fridge door open and shut and there was Charu walking past the kitchen door in her blue dress, holding Divya's precious *parathas* in her hand.

In an instant she was in front of her daughter, confronting her, snatching the *parathas* away. She stared at Charu, breathless with anger.

"What are you doing with my *parathas*?"

Charu stared back, eyes wide with confusion.

"I was just giving it to the old man, he said he was hungry, Ma…"

There was a roaring in Divya's ears. She felt momentarily dizzy.

"Tell him we can't spare any," she said, more harshly than she had intended. "Don't you have better things to do? Where are the presents you were wrapping for your friends? Did you get enough for the other children, too?"

An expression she could not identify flickered over the child's face. Divya knew Charu was not happy about the other children, the strangers who would be coming to the party. Apart from Charu's three friends there would be a fourteen-year-old boy, the nephew of Vikas's new boss, Mr Lamba, and an eleven-year-old girl, daughter of the Pathanias. But all that – the sulks and protestations — had been over and done with, or so Divya thought. She saw the tears rise in Charu's eyes.

"It's my birthday," the child said, fiercely. "You're not supposed to scold me on my birthday!"

At that moment, Divya was aware that certain knots had come into being in the smooth tapestry of her life, knots she would not necessarily know how to untangle, but there was Vikas calling out that the Chaturvedis were already here, and Charu was already at the door, talking to the old man. Damyanti took the *paratha*s from Divya's limp fingers and pushed her, not ungently, in the direction of the bedroom.

"Get ready for your guests, I'll do the *chholey*," she said, and Divya went to change her sari and wash her face, and put on some lipstick, feeling dazed, feeling as though something momentous had happened or was about to happen. The book she was reading, *The Aliens of Malgudi*, lay on the dressing table; she stared wistfully at the lurid cover, with the spaceship and the buxom space-bandit, Viraa. The plot had to do with Viraa discovering aliens disguised as humans, living in the town of Malgudi. They were from some planet light-years away. Divya wondered how she was going to survive.

As for the Chaturvedis, she should have remembered from the gossip that they always came at least half an hour early, possibly because Mrs Chaturvedi — an inveterate gossip and interlocutor — liked to have her victims to herself before the others came.

The party was in full swing. Divya dashed from kitchen to drawing room, from guest to guest, until the world became a blur of silk saris and lipsticked mouths opening and closing, the clink of glasses; the flow of myriad streams of conversations, none of which made any sense to her. In the kitchen she took a moment to wipe her brow. Just then Mrs Lamba loomed large in the kitchen doorway, resplendent in green silk.

"My dear, what a lot of trouble! Look at you, all sweating! You should have got the whole thing catered. I will give you my caterer's telephone number. He does some very nice European-style *hors d'oeuvres*…"

"Aha, but, Mrs. Lamba, you must try these *pakoras*…" Mrs Raman said brightly, munching away behind her. Mrs Lamba condescended to nibble at one.

"Not bad," she said in a surprised tone. Damyanti, wiping the serving dish for the *chholey*, glared at her.

Vikas came in wanting more glasses. There weren't enough at the bar. The Saikias and the Bhosles were here. And where was the fruit juice for the children?

Over the next hour or so, Divya caught a few glimpses of her daughter. Charu wouldn't look at her. The girl's laugh was higher than usual — she was in the middle of her little circle of friends. At the periphery were the eleven-year-old daughter of the Pathanias and the fourteen-year-old nephew of the Lambas. Divya went over to make sure they weren't feeling left out. No, Charu was nothing if not kind-hearted — she had served birthday cake to everyone, and now the two had been invited to play a computer game in Charu's room along with the inner circle of friends, and they were all trooping off together. The Lambas' nephew looked frankly bored; the Ramans' daughter cast a despairing glance at her parents as she left the room.

So much unhappiness, Divya thought suddenly. She was feeling better, with some *pakoras* in her stomach, but now a wave of anguish swept through her. She looked at the women, clustered together, their face paint standing out garishly in the light. It was one of those moments when everyone had run out of conversation at the same time, like actors taking a break from their roles. Mrs Lamba's fleshy face looked haggard, Mrs Raman's, nervous. In that moment she had a sudden shock of recognition, a fellow-feeling she could not explain. Then Mrs Chaturvedi leaned toward Mrs Lamba with a conspiratorial look, and the buzz of conversation resumed. What were they hatching now? Whose reputation was being built up, or destroyed? By contrast the men seemed less sinister, talking in loud voices about the latest financial news — they were like little puppets, moving and twitching to order, while the women, with Mrs Lamba at the centre, controlled the strings. Why had Divya had that sudden moment of empathy with the women — no, empathy was too strong a word — but why she had felt what she felt, she did not know.

She had a sudden longing for the days when Vikas was still a junior manager in the company and birthdays, and life itself, were less complicated. Then, she could ensure everyone's happiness. Charu could be comforted with a hug. But look at her now, with that veil over her eyes, taking a tray of soda to her room for her friends. She didn't like the way I snapped at her, Divya thought. On her birthday too! She's getting all sensitive and dignified now. Every year she steps away from me, one step. Two steps. And look at Vikas! He looked the genial host, pouring the drinks, laughing at Mr Lamba's jokes, but she could see the strain on his face. Her poor Vikas, growing up, growing old. Worried about creating the right impression. The old Vikas had enjoyed making cartoons of his superiors, shared jokes with her about how stupid office politics was. She felt sorry for him, having to laugh at those jokes of Mr Lamba's.

What was the point of it all?

As the evening wore on, she knew that she had achieved some degree of success. Damyanti had left around the middle of the evening and she had managed the serving of the dinner mostly on her own, with some help from Mrs Bhosle and Mrs Raman, two ladies on the outer perimeter of Mrs Lamba's circle. Whether it was Damyanti's cooking or whether Mrs Lamba had been feeling indulgent, she felt as though she had passed some kind of test, that she had crossed an invisible barrier and was now one of Them. She didn't like it, didn't like pretending to like it. She wasn't as good at acting as the other women. But for Vikas... she looked across at him, and he raised his head and met her gaze, and in his look was relief and humour and the reassurance that the evening would soon be over... yes, she would do it for him. At least for another half an hour, or however long it took for the last glasses to be set down, the last goodbyes said.

Then she heard a child scream.

The children had been running around, playing some kind of crazy game, after having sat still through dinner. The Lambas' nephew, Ajeet, had started them on it, Divya thought, against Charu's wishes. But he had the authority of being fourteen and having travelled all over the world with his parents (his speech was peppered with references to London and New York and Sydney), and he was already beginning to develop an air of studied cynicism, a man of the world. Divya could sense Charu being pulled in, and repelled, and pulled in, and repelled, and had suffered for her daughter, who still would not look at her. She wanted to tell her that the world wouldn't care for her hurt feelings, that she needed to be stronger and less vulnerable to everyday hurts if she were to survive; she wanted to tell her that kind of men that grew from boys like Ajeet were bad news, all preening, fake charm and pretended indifference… look at him, manipulating the younger ones just because he was bored and wanted whatever entertainment the situation had to offer…

In the split second after the scream Divya established that it was not her Charu, and that the sound came from outside the apartment, from the vicinity of the back door. She was already moving toward it, and so was Vikas, and Mrs Pathania, whose daughter it was who had screamed. At the back door she saw that the children were clustered at the top of the stairs that led to the terrace; there was a faint smell in the air, not urine. The landing was very quiet, with only one light burning over the stairway, and the servants quarters' door (she noted as she ran up the stairs) was locked.

The children moved aside to let her see; Mrs Pathania's daughter was already half-falling down the stairs into her mother's arms. What Divya saw was the old man curled up in a nest of rags, clutching his throat with both hands, quite dead. His hooked nose, protruding from his too-thin face, gave him the appearance of a strange bird; his heavy-lidded eyes were open and staring at some alien vista she could not imagine. At the same time she was aware that Vikas was gently ushering the children down the stairs, and the Lambas were coming up to look. She started to say, "He's sick, poor man, I'll get the doctor," for the sake of the children, but the boy Ajeet interrupted her.

"He's dead," he said scornfully. He gave her defiant half-grin. "I kicked his foot, so I know."

At the precise moment before the Lambas reached the landing, Divya saw two things: the piece of paper in the dead man's hand, and the blue vial of rat poison standing quite close to his ragged pillow. In that instant she had swooped down and gathered both items, covering them with the *pallu* of her sari. She turned to face the Lambas. Mrs Lamba gave a high-pitched cry and fell against her husband, who, not being built to handle the weight, tottered against the wall. Mrs Bhosle took over, muttering words of comfort and calling for brandy, giving Divya an unexpectedly sympathetic look. Mr Lamba drew himself up to his full height. Divya noticed that the tip of his nose was quite pale.

"What is the meaning of this! Who is this fellow?"

"The father-in-law of my neighbour's servant," Divya said. "They don't feed him—"

"I don't care who he is," Mr Lamba said. "How can you tolerate having riff-raff living in your building? The man could be dangerous! Or have a disease! Like AIDS!"

Mrs Lamba shook herself loose from Mrs Bhosle's grip. She pointed an accusing finger at Divya.

"What will I tell my sister when she gets back from London? Her son has been subjected to this… this unspeakable sight! The poor boy! And you call yourself a hostess. Wife of a vice-president!"

She turned to the other guests standing in shocked silence on the steps.

"Let us leave this horrible place… these… people," she said. "They have no standards." She turned to Divya, shook a finger in her face. "Never have I been so insulted in all my life!"

Divya looked from the dead body of the man to the upturned faces. Mrs Bhosle shook her head, but nobody said anything to contradict Mrs Lamba.

"Yes, please leave," Divya said firmly. Charu had begun to sob against her father's chest. Poor Vikas — he looked completely shocked. Mrs Bhosle and Mrs Raman helped everyone find purses and shawls, and then ushered them all out. Divya did not say any goodbyes except to thank Mrs Bhosle and Mrs Raman for their help. Already, as the party was going down the stairs, she could hear Mrs Chaturvedi's high, whining voice, eagerly discussing the incident. The ladies would feast off it for many parties and dinners to come.

While they waited for the police to arrive, Charu cried against her mother's shoulder, her sobs shaking her whole body. Divya could do nothing but hold her. Waves of guilt washed over her. If only she could go back to that moment in time, when the old man had knocked on the door and Charu had been taking the *parathas* to him! Perhaps the *parathas* would not have saved him (the damned things were still in the fridge) — but who could tell? The poor man, to die like that! It wasn't fair — to raise your son and grow old, and be turned out to starve... Nor was it fair that she, Divya, was to be punished for one moment of carelessness, one instant where she had forgotten the right thing to do — and that this oversight should carry so much weight that it outweighed all her earlier acts of kindness to the old man, the giving of food, and the chance to earn a little money and respectability. Had none of that counted for anything? Would she now have to tiptoe through the world, watching for any lapse, any moment of forgetfulness? If the punishment was to be hers alone, she could bear it — but how cruel of the world, to punish a child instead: Charu in her new blue dress, who had learned on the day she turned twelve that Death lived in the world, and in time it would devour everyone she loved. And that it was possible to die alone and unloved. How does a child of twelve recover from that?

That moment... she kept returning to it in her mind. If only she hadn't been so hungry at the time! If Damyanti hadn't given Vikas those *pakoras*, or if Vikas hadn't been asking her about the rat poison...

The rat poison. A cold terror swept over Divya. How had the rat poison got to the old man's bedside?

She heard Vikas pacing to and fro in the drawing room, waiting for the police.

She had put the blue vial back on the bathroom shelf, behind the shampoo. The little square of stiff paper that had been in the dead man's hand she had put in the little dresser drawer where she kept her jewellery. It was a black and white picture — she hadn't had time to look at it properly. Now she made Charu sip some water.

"He was an old man, Charu," Divya said. "He was ill. Nothing we could have done would have saved him."

And so we lie to our children, she thought bitterly.

Charu choked on the water, coughed.

"He said the rats were running all over him at night…"

Divya held her breath. 'Did you give him the rat poison?'

Charu nodded. "He said the rats were really big and he was afraid of getting bitten…"

Divya steadied herself, patted the child's hair.

"Listen, Charu, what you did was fine, but I don't want you to mention it to anyone. All right? Don't say anything about what the old man said or what you did. Let Papa and me talk to the policemen."

Charu's eyes went wide.

"Oh mama, do you think… oh, do you think…"

"No, no, child, quiet now. Everything is going to be fine."

Two policemen came, took notes, banged on the servant's door and on Mr Kapadia's as well, but there was no answer. It was Saturday and Ranu and her husband were out — if Mr Kapadia was in, he didn't care. The policemen didn't seem to care either. They nodded when Divya talked about how Ranu and her family had neglected the old man, but shrugged when she asked if they would be brought to task.

'If we launched an investigation each time some old fellow dies of starvation, we would be overwhelmed,' said one. They got up and left the family to the silence, the splendid ruins of the birthday party.

Hunger

During a visit to the bathroom, Divya got a chance to look at the picture the old man had been holding when he died. It was a black and white photo, creased with age, and it was nearly impossible to make out whose picture it was. Divya would look at it many times in the next few months and wonder if the person was a woman or an animal or something entirely different.

Divya slept next to Charu that night, something she had not done in many years. They both slept fitfully. Divya felt sorry for Vikas, alone in the big bed in the next room. It would soon be time to worry about what would happen to his job. How strange that their fates should be tied to one old man whom nobody had known, whose speech nobody had understood. (Except for Charu — she realized, with a shock, that Charu must have been able to understand him to carry out his last request). Simply by dying, the old man would change their daughter's view of the world, and affect Vikas's career and the delicate network of social connections and links in which he existed, and change Divya herself in ways that she was yet to discover. She wondered what the old fellow had been trying to tell her these past years, in his broken voice; she should have listened more closely. She should have... she should have...

The old man lay in the centre of her whirling thoughts like an enigma. Some of the tears she wept that night were for him, but as sleep slowly came to her she realized that she had never known his name.

In the weeks and months that followed, Vikas gave up his job, changed companies and began to plan a move to a different apartment in a different part of town. His new job was not as prestigious or as well-paying as the old one had been, and Divya could tell that he was unhappy. He began to play around with an old hobby, photography, disappearing for hours sometimes on weekends, and coming back to plunge into the darkroom he had set up in a storeroom in the flat. He refused to talk about the terrible incident, which bothered Divya because before this she had been able to talk to him about everything. Charu had the resilience of youth; she appeared to recover quite quickly, although her school performance suffered in the months following the incident. But Divya could tell that something had changed within the child. There was a sadness about her eyes that Divya could sense even when Charu was laughing with her friends. Charu had always been a soft-hearted girl, but after the incident she could no longer bear any kind of cruelty, nor could she, as a consequence, watch the news without tears. Divya worried how Charu would live in the world, whether she would learn to adapt enough to survive its horrors. She feared also that Charu blamed her for the whole thing, but apart from the inevitable distancing that growth brings, there was no indication of this. There were times when the girl would come upon her mother and give her a fierce, deep hug for no reason at all, and Divya felt Charu was trying to tell her something in some other language, and that she was able to comprehend it in that other language as well.

But the change in Divya herself was perhaps the most peculiar. She had, like most mothers, always been sensitive to the needs of those she loved, but now she was able to anticipate them even before there was any evidence of them. She knew, for instance, that Charu would have her period tomorrow, and that the cramps would be bad; consequently she refused to let Charu go to school that day. She knew in the morning if Vikas was going to have a bad day at work, and when Kallu the crow landed on her kitchen window with an injured wing, she knew it before he had alighted.

When she went out, however, the gift or curse that had been left for her by the old man's death took its strangest form. When she looked upon the faces of strangers they appeared to her like aliens, like the open mouths of birds, crying their need. But most clearly she could sense those who were hungry, whether they were schoolchildren who had forgotten their lunch or beggars under the bridge, or the boot-boy at the corner, or the emaciated girl sweeping the dusty street in front of the municipal building.

Even in the great tide of humanity that thronged the pavements, amidst busy office-goers and college students with cellphones, or in the shadows of the high-rises and luxury apartment blocks, she could sense the hungry and forgotten, great masses of them, living like cockroaches in the cracks and interstices of the new old city. Their open mouths, gaping and horrific with need, at first frightened her, but then she began to carry about with her a few *parathas*, which she handed out to the hungry without a word, in the hope that the keening chorus of despair that nobody but she was able to hear would lessen a little. Although this didn't happen, she found herself unable to stop handing out *parathas* to the needy. Meanwhile, she continued to read her science fiction novels because, more than ever, they seemed to reflect her own realization of the utter strangeness of the world. Slowly the understanding came to her that these stories were trying to tell her a great truth in a very convoluted way, that they were all in some kind of code, designed to deceive the literary snob and waylay the careless reader. And that this great truth, which she would spend her life unravelling, was centred around the notion that you did not have to go to the stars to find aliens or to measure distances between people in light-years.

Delhi

TONIGHT HE IS INTENSELY aware of the city: its ancient stones, the flat-roofed brick houses, threads of clotheslines, wet, bright colours waving like pennants, neem tree-lined roads choked with traffic. There's a bus going over the bridge under which he has chosen to sleep. The night smells of jasmine, and stale urine, and the dust of the cricket field on the other side of the road. A man is lighting a *bidi* near him: face lean, half in shadow, and he thinks he sees himself. He goes over to the man, who looks like another layabout. "My name is Aseem," he says. The man, reeking of tobacco, glares at him, coughs and spits, *"kya chahiye?"* Aseem steps back in a hurry. No, that man is not Aseem's older self; anyway, Aseem can't imagine he would take up smoking *bidis* at any point in his life. He leaves the dubious shelter of the bridge, the quiet lane that runs under it, and makes his way through the litter and anaemic streetlamps to the neon-bright highway. The new city is less confusing, he thinks; the colours are more solid, the lights dazzling, so he can't see the apparitions as clearly. But once he saw a milkman going past him on Shahjahan road, complete with humped white cow and tinkling bell. Under the stately, ancient trees that partly shaded the streetlamps, the milkman stopped to speak to his cow and faded into the dimness of twilight.

When he was younger he thought the apparitions he saw were ghosts of the dead, but now he knows that is not true. Now he has a theory that his visions are tricks of time, tangles produced when one part of the timestream rubs up against another and the two cross for a moment. He has decided (after years of struggle) that he is not insane after all; his brain is wired differently from others, enabling him to discern these temporal coincidences. He knows he is not the only one with this ability, because some of the people he sees also see him, and shrink back in terror. The thought that he is a ghost to people long dead or still to come in this world both amuses and terrifies him.

He's seen more apparitions in the older parts of the city than anywhere else, and he's not sure why. There is plenty of history in Delhi, no doubt about that — the city's past goes back into myth, when the Pandava brothers of the epic *Mahabharata* first founded their fabled capital, Indraprastha, some three thousand years ago. In medieval times alone there were seven cities of Delhi, he remembers from a well-thumbed history textbook — and the eighth was established by the British during the days of the Raj. The city of the present day, the ninth, is the largest. Only for Aseem are the old cities of Delhi still alive, glimpsed like mysterious islands from a passing ship, but real, nevertheless. He wishes he could discuss his temporal visions with someone who would take him seriously and help him understand the nature and limits of his peculiar malady, but ironically, the only sympathetic person he's met who shares his condition happened to live in 1100 AD or thereabouts, the time of Prithviraj Chauhan, the last great Hindu ruler of Delhi.

He had been walking past the faded white colonnades of some building in Connaught Place when he saw her: an old woman in a long skirt and shawl, making her way sedately across the car park, her body rising above the road and falling below its surface in parallel with some invisible topography. She came face-to-face with Aseem. They both stopped. Clinging to her like gray ribbons were glimpses of her environs — he saw mist, the darkness of trees behind her. Suddenly, in the middle of summer, he could smell fresh rain. She put a wondering arm out toward him but didn't touch him. She said: "What age are you from?" in an unfamiliar dialect of Hindi. He did not know how to answer the question, or how to contain within him that sharp shock of joy. She, too, had looked across the barriers of time and glimpsed other people, other ages. She named Prithviraj Chauhan as her king. Aseem told her he lived some nine hundred years after Chauhan. They exchanged stories of other visions: she had seen armies, spears flashing, and pale men with yellow beards, and a woman in a metal carriage, crying. He was able to interpret some of this for her before she began to fade away. He started toward her as though to step into her world, and ran right into a pillar. As he picked himself off the ground he heard derisive laughter. Under the arches, a shoeshine boy and a man chewing betel leaf were staring at him, enjoying the show.

Once he met the mad emperor, Mohammad Shah. He was walking through Red Fort late one afternoon, avoiding clumps of tourists and their clicking cameras. He was feeling particularly restless; there was a smoky tang in the air, because some gardener in the grounds was burning dry leaves. As the sun set, the red sandstone fort walls glowed, then darkened. Night came, blanketing the tall ramparts, the lawns through which he strolled, the shimmering beauty of the Pearl Mosque, the languorous curves of the now distant Yamuna that had once flowed under this marble terrace. He saw a man standing, leaning over the railing, dressed in a red silk *sherwani*, jewels at his throat, a gem studded in his turban. He smelled of wine and rose attar, and he was singing a song about a night of separation from the Beloved, slurring the words together.

Bairan bhayii raat sakhiya...

Mammad Shah piya sada Rangila...

Mohammad Shah Rangila, early 1700's, Aseem recalled. The emperor who loved music, poetry and wine more than anything, who ignored warnings that the Persian king was marching to Delhi with a vast army...

"Listen, king," Aseem whispered urgently, wondering if he could change the course of history, "You must prepare for battle. Else Nadir Shah will overrun the city. Thousands will be butchered by his army…"

The king lifted wine-darkened eyes. "Begone, wraith!"

Sometimes he stops at the India Gate lawns in the heart of modern Delhi and buys ice-cream from a vendor, and eats it sitting by one of the fountains that Lutyens built. Watching the play of light on the shimmering water, he thinks about the British invaders, who brought one of the richest and oldest civilizations on earth to abject poverty in only two hundred years. They built these great edifices, gracious buildings and fountains, but even they had to leave it all behind. Kings came and went, the *goras* came and went, but the city lives on. Sometimes he sees apparitions of the *goras*, the palefaces, walking by him or riding on horses. Each time he yells out to them: "Your people are doomed. You will leave here. Your Empire will crumble." Once in a while they glance at him, startled, before they fade away.

In his more fanciful moments he wonders if he hasn't, in some way, caused history to happen the way it does. Planted a seed of doubt in a British officer's mind about the permanency of the Empire. Despite his best intentions, convinced Mohammad Shah that the impending invasion is not a real danger but a ploy wrought against him by evil spirits. But he knows that apart from the Emperor, nobody he has communicated with is of any real importance in the course of history, and that he is simply deluding himself about his own significance.

Still, he makes compulsive notes of his more interesting encounters. He carries with him at all times a thick, somewhat shabby notebook, one half of which is devoted to recording these temporal adventures. But because the apparitions he sees are so clear, he is sometimes uncertain whether the face he glimpses in the crowd, or the man passing him by on a cold night, wrapped in shawls, belong to this time or some other. Only some incongruity — spatial or temporal — distinguishes the apparitions from the rest.

Sometimes he sees landscapes, too, but rarely — a skyline dotted with palaces and temple spires, a forest in the middle of a busy thoroughfare, and, strangest of all, once an array of tall, jewelled towers reaching into the clouds. Each such vision seems to be charged with a peculiar energy, like a scene lit up by lightning. And although the apparitions are apparently random and don't often repeat, there are certain places where he sees (he thinks) the same people again and again. For instance, while travelling on the Metro he almost always sees people in the subway tunnels, floating through the train and the passengers on the platforms, dressed in tatters, their faces pale and unhealthy as though they have never beheld the sun. The first time he saw them, he shuddered. "The Metro is quite new," he thought to himself, "and the first underground train system in Delhi. So what I saw must be in the future…"

One day, he tells himself, he will write a history of the future.

The street is Nai Sarak, a name he has always thought absurd. New Road, it means, but this road has not been new in a very long time. He could cross the street in two jumps if it weren't so crowded with people, shoulder to shoulder. The houses are like that too, hunched together with windows like dull eyes, and narrow, dusty stairways and even narrower alleys in between. The ground floors are taken up by tiny, musty shops containing piles of books that smell fresh and pungent, a wake-up smell like coffee. It is a hot day, and there is no shade. The girl he is following is just another Delhi University student looking for a bargain, trying not to get jostled or groped in the crowd, much less have her purse stolen. There are small, barefoot boys running around with wire-carriers of lemon-water in chipped glasses, and fat old men in their undershirts behind the counters, bargaining fiercely with pale, defenseless college students over the hum of electric fans, rubbing clammy hands across their hairy bellies, while they slurp their iced drinks, signalling to some waif when the transaction is complete, so that the desired volume can be deposited into the feverish hands of the student. Some of the shopkeepers like to add a little lecture along the lines of "Now, my son, study hard, make your parents proud…" Aseem hasn't been here in a long time (since his own college days in fact); he is not prepared for any of this, the brightness of the day, the white dome of the mosque rising up behind him, the stone walls of the old city engirdling him, enclosing him in people and sweat and dust. He's dazzled by the white *kurtas* of the men, the neat beards and the prayer caps; this is of course the Muslim part of the city, Old Delhi, but not as romantic as his grandmother used to make it sound. He has a rare flash of memory into a past where he was a small boy listening to the old woman's tales. His grandmother was one of the Hindus who never went back to Old Delhi, not after the madness of Partition in 1947, the Hindu-Muslim riots that killed thousands, but he still remembers how she spoke of the places of her girlhood: *parathe-walon-ki-gali*, the lane of the *paratha*-makers, where all the shops sell freshly-cooked flatbreads of every possible kind, stuffed with spiced potatoes or minced lamb, or fenugreek leaves, or crushed cauliflower and fiery red chillies; and Dariba Kalan, where after hundreds of years they still sell the best and purest silver in the world, delicate chains and anklets and bracelets. Among the crowds that throng these places he has seen the apparitions of courtesans and young men, and the blood and thunder of invasions, and the bodies of princes hanged by British soldiers. To him the old city, surrounded by high, crumbling stone walls, is like the heart of a crone who dreams perpetually of her youth.

The girl who's caught his attention walks on. Aseem hasn't been able to get a proper look at her — all he's noticed are the dark eyes, and the death in them. After all these years in the city he's learned to recognize a certain preoccupation in the eyes of some of his fellow citizens: the desire for the final anonymity that death brings.

Sometimes, as in this case, he knows it before they do.

The girl goes into a shop. The proprietor, a young man built like a wrestler, is dressed only in cotton shorts. A masseur is working his back, kneading and sculpting the slick, gold muscles. The young man says: "Advanced Biochemistry? Watkins? One copy, only one copy left." He shouts into the dark, cavernous interior, and the requisite small boy comes up, bearing the volume as though it were a rare book. The girl's face shows too much relief; she's doomed even before the bargaining begins. She parts with her money with a resigned air, steps out into the noisy brightness, and is caught up with the crowd in the street like a piece of wood tossed in a river. She pushes and elbows her way through it, fending off anonymous hands that reach toward her breasts or back. He loses sight of her for a moment, but there she is, walking past the mosque to the bus-stop on the main road. At the bus-stop she catches Aseem's glance and gives him the pre-emptive cold look. Now there's a bus coming, filled with people, young men hanging out of the doorways as though on the prow of a sailboat. He sees her struggling through the crowd toward the bus, and at the last minute she's right in its path. The bus is not stopping but (in the tantalizing manner of Delhi buses) barely slowing, as though to play catch with the crowd. It is an immense green and yellow metal monstrosity, bearing down on her, as she stands rooted, clutching her bag of books. This is Aseem's moment. He lunges at the girl, pushing her out of the way, grabbing her before she can fall to the ground. There is a roaring in his ears, the shriek of brakes, and the conductor yelling. Her books are scattered on the ground. He helps pick them up. She's trembling with shock. In her eyes he sees himself for a moment: a drifter, his face unshaven, his hair unkempt. He tells her: don't do it, don't ever do it. Life is never so bereft of hope. You have a purpose you must fulfill. He's repeating it like a mantra, and she's looking bewildered, as though she doesn't understand that she was trying to kill herself. He can see that he puzzles her: his grammatical Hindi and his fair English labels him middle-class and educated, like herself, but his appearance says otherwise. Although he knows she's not the woman he is seeking, he pulls out the computer printout just to be sure. No, she's not the one. Cheeks too thin, chin not sharp enough. He pushes one of the business cards into her hand and walks away. From a distance he sees that she's looking at the card in her hand and frowning. Will she throw it away? At the last minute she shoves it into her bag with the books. He remembers all too clearly the first time someone gave him one of the cards. "Worried About Your Future? Consult Pandit Vidyanath. Computerized and Air-Conditioned Office. Discover Your True Purpose in Life." There is a logo of a beehive and an address in South Delhi.

Later he will write up this encounter in the second half of his notebook. In three years he has filled this part almost to capacity. He's stopped young men from flinging themselves off the bridges that span the Yamuna. He's prevented women from jumping off tall buildings, from dousing themselves with kerosene, from murderous encounters with city traffic. All this by way of seeking her, whose story will be the last in his book.

But the very first story in this part of his notebook is his own…

Three years ago. He is standing on a bridge over the Yamuna. There is a heavy, odorous fog in the air, the kind that mars winter mornings in Delhi. He is shivering because of the chill and because he is tired, tired of the apparitions that have always plagued him, tired of the endless rounds of medications and appointments with doctors and psychologists. He has just written a letter to his fiancée, severing their already fragile relationship. Two months ago he stopped attending his college classes. His mother and father have been dead a year and two years respectively, and there will be no one to mourn him, except for relatives in other towns who know him only by reputation as a person with problems. Last night he tried, as a last resort, to leave Delhi, hoping that perhaps the visions would stop. He got as far as the railway station. He stood in the line before the ticket counter, jostled by young men carrying holdalls and aggressive matrons in bright saris. "Name?" said the man behind the window, but Aseem couldn't remember it. Around him, in the cavernous interior of the station, shouting, red-clad porters rushed past, balancing tiers of suitcases on their turbaned heads, and vast waves of passengers swarmed the stairs that led up across the platforms. People were nudging him, telling him to hurry up, but all he could think of were the still trains between the platforms, steaming in the cold air, hissing softly like warm snakes, waiting to take him away. The thought of leaving filled him with a sudden terror. He turned and walked out of the station. Outside, in the cold, glittering night, he breathed deep, fierce breaths of relief, as though he had walked away from his own death.

So here he is, the morning after his attempted escape, standing on the bridge, shivering in the fog. He notices a crack in the concrete railing, which he traces with his finger to the seedling of a pipal tree, growing on the outside of the rail. He remembers his mother pulling pipal seedlings out of walls and the paved courtyard of their house, over his protests. He remembers how hard it was for him to see, in each fragile sapling, the giant full-grown tree. Leaning over the bridge he finds himself wondering which will fall first — the pipal tree or the bridge. Just then he hears a bicycle on the road behind him, one that needs oiling, evidently, and before he knows it some rude fellow with a straggly beard has come out of the fog, pulled him off the railing and on to the road. "Don't be a fool, don't do it," says the stranger, breathing hard. His bicycle is lying on the roadside, one wheel still spinning. "Here, take this," the man says, pushing a small card into Aseem's unresisting hand. "Go see them. If they can't give you a reason to live, your own mother wouldn't be able to."

The address on the card proves to be in a small marketplace near Sarojini Nagar. Around a dusty square of withered grass, where ubiquitous pariah dogs sleep fitfully in the pale sun, there is a row of shops. The place he seeks is a corner shop next to a vast jamun tree. Under the tree, three humped white cows are chewing cud, watching him with bovine

Delhi

indifference. Aseem makes his way through a jangle of bicycles, motor-rickshaws and people, and finds himself before a closed door, with a small sign saying, only, "Pandit Vidyanath, Consultations." He goes in.

The Pandit is not in, but his assistant, a thin, earnest-faced young man, waves Aseem to a chair. The assistant is sitting behind a desk with a PC, a printer, and a plaque bearing his name: Om Prakash, BSc. Physics, (Failed) Delhi University. There is a window with the promised air-conditioner (apparently defunct) occupying its lower half. On the other side of the window is a beehive in the process of completion. Aseem feels he has come to the wrong place, and regrets already the whim that brought him here, but the beehive fascinates him, how it is still and in motion all at once, and the way the bees seem to be in concert with one another, as though performing a complicated dance. Two of the bees are crawling on the computer and there is one on the assistant's arm. Om Prakash seems completely unperturbed; he assures Aseem that the bees are harmless, and tries to interest him in array of bottles of honey on the shelf behind him. Apparently the bees belong to Pandit Vidyanath, a man of many facets, who keeps very busy because he also works for the city. (Aseem has a suspicion that perhaps the great man is no more than a petty clerk in a municipal office). Honey is ten rupees a bottle. Aseem shakes his head, and Om Prakash gets down to business with a noisy clearing of his throat, asking questions and entering the answers into the computer. By now Aseem is feeling like a fool.

"How does your computer know the future?" Aseem asks.

Om Prakash has a lanky, giraffe-like grace, although he is not tall. He makes a deprecating gesture with his long, thin hands that travels all the way up to his mobile shoulders.

"A computer is like a beehive. Many bits and parts, none is by itself intelligent. Combine together, and you have something that can think. This computer is not an ordinary one. Built by Pandit Vidyanath himself."

Om Prakash grins as the printer begins to whir.

"All persons who come here seek meaning. Each person has their own *dharma*, their own unique purpose. We don't tell future, because future is beyond us, Sahib. We tell them why they need to live."

He hands a printout to Aseem. When he first sees it, the page makes no sense. It consists of x's arranged in an apparently random pattern over the page. He holds it at a distance and sees, indistinctly, the face of a woman.

"Who is she?"

"It is for you to interpret what this picture means," says Om Prakash. "You must live because you need to meet this woman, perhaps to save her or be saved. It may mean that you could be at the right place and time to save her from some terrible fate. She could be your sister or daughter, or a wife, or a stranger."

There are dark smudges for eyes, and the hint of a high cheekbone, and the swirl of hair across the cheek, half-obscuring the mouth. The face is broad and heart-shaped, narrowing to a small chin.

"But this is not very clear... It could be almost anyone. How will I know..."

"You will know when you meet her," Om Prakash says with finality. "There is no charge. Thank you sir, and here are cards for you to give other unfortunate souls."

Aseem takes the pack of business cards and leaves. He distrusts the whole business, especially the bit about no charge. No charge? In a city like Delhi?

But despite his doubts he finds himself intrigued. He had expected the usual platitudes about life and death, the fatalistic pronouncements peculiar to charlatan fortune-tellers, but this fellow, Vidyanath, obviously is an original. That Aseem must live simply so he might be there for someone at the right moment: what an amusing, humbling idea! As the days pass it grows on him, and he comes to believe it, if for nothing else than to have something in which to believe. He scans the faces of the people in the crowds, on the dusty sidewalks, the overladen buses, the Metro, and he looks for her. He lives so that he will cross her path some day. Over three years he has convinced himself that she is real, that she waits for him. He's made something of a life for himself, working at a photocopy shop in Lajpat Nagar, where he can sleep on winter nights, or making deliveries for shopkeepers in Defence Colony, who pay enough to keep him in food and clothing. Over three years he has handed out hundreds of the little business cards, and visited the address in South Delhi dozens of times. He's become used to the bees, the defunct air-conditioner, and even to Om Prakash. Although there is too much distance between them to allow friendship (a distance of temperament, really), Aseem has told Om Prakash about the apparitions he sees. Om Prakash receives these confidences with his rather foolish grin and much waggling of the head in wonder, and says he will tell Pandit Vidyanath. Only, each time Aseem visits there is no sign of Pandit Vidyanath, so now Aseem suspects that there is no such person, that Om Prakash himself is the unlikely mind behind the whole business.

Sometimes he is scared of finding the woman. He imagines himself saving her from death or a fate worse than death, realizing at last his purpose. But after that what awaits him? The oily embrace of the Yamuna?

Or will she save him in turn?

One of the things he likes about the city is how it breaks all rules. Delhi is a place of contradictions — it transcends thesis and anti-thesis. Here he has seen both the hovels of the poor and the opulent monstrosities of the rich. At major intersections, where the rich wait impatiently in their air-conditioned cars for the light to change, he's seen bone-thin waifs running from car to car, peddling glossy magazines like *Vogue* and *Cosmopolitan*. Amid the glitzy new high-rises are troupes of wandering cows, and pariah dogs; rhesus monkeys mate with abandon in the trees around Parliament House.

He hasn't slept well. Last night the police raided the Aurobindo Marg sidewalk where he was sleeping. Some foreign VIP was expected in the morning so the riff-raff on the roadsides were driven off by stick-wielding policemen. This has happened many times before, but today Aseem is smarting with rage and humiliation: he has a bruise on his back where a policeman's stick hit him, and it burns in the relentless heat. Death lurks behind the walled eyes of the populace, but for once he is sick of his proximity to death. So he goes to the only place where he can leave behind the city without actually leaving its borders — houses and crowded roads, within Delhi's borders, there lies an entire forest: the Delhi Ridge, a green lung. The coolness of the forest beckons to him.

Only a little way from the main road, the forest is still, except for the subdued chirping of birds. He is in a warm, green womb. Under the acacia trees he finds an old ruin, one of the many nameless remains of Delhi's medieval era. After checking for snakes and scorpions, he curls up under a crumbling wall and dozes off.

Some time later, when the sun is lower in the sky and the heat not as intense, he hears a tapping sound, soft and regular, like slow rain on a tin roof. He sees a woman — a young girl — on the paved path in front of him, holding a cane before her. She's blind, obviously, and lost. This is no place for a woman alone. He clears his throat and she starts.

"Is someone there?"

She's wearing a long blue shirt over a *salwaar* of the same colour, and there is a shawl around her shoulders. The thin material of her *dupatta* drapes her head, half-covering her face, blurring her features. He looks at her and sees the face in the printout. Or thinks he does.

"You are lost," he says, his voice trembling with excitement. He's fumbling in his pockets for the printout. Surely he must still be asleep and dreaming. Hasn't he dreamed about her many, many times already? "Where do you wish to go?"

She clutches her stick. Her shoulders slump.

Delhi

"Naya Diwas Lane, good sir. I am travelling from Jaipur. I came to meet my sister, who lives here, but I lost my papers. They say you must have papers. Or they'll send me to Neechi-Dilli with all the poor and the criminals. I don't want to go there! My sister has money. Please, sir, tell me how to find Naya Diwas."

He's never heard of Naya Diwas Lane, or Neechi Dilli. New Day Lane? Lower Delhi? What strange names. He wipes the sweat off his forehead.

"There aren't any such places. Somebody has misled you. Go back to the main road, turn right, there is a marketplace there. I will come with you. Nobody will harm you. We can make enquiries there."

She thanks him, her voice catching with relief. She tells him she's heard many stories about the fabled city, and its tall, gem-studded minars that reach the sky, and the perfect gardens. And the ships, the silver *udan-khatolas*, that fly across worlds. She's very excited to be here at last in the Immaculate City.

His eyes widen. He gets up abruptly but she's already fading away into the trees. The computer printout is in his hand, but before he can get another look at her, she's gone.

What has he told her? Where is she going, in what future age, buoyed by the hope he has given her, which (he fears now) may be false?

He stumbles around the ruin, disturbing ground squirrels and a sleepy flock of jungle babblers, but he knows there is no hope of finding her again except by chance. Temporal coincidences have their own unfathomable rules. He's looked ahead to this moment so many times, imagined both joy and despair as a result of it, but never this apprehension, this uncertainty. He looks at the computer printout again. Is it mere coincidence that the apparition he saw looked like the image? What if Pandit Vidyanath's computer generated something quite random, and that his quest, his life for the past few years has been completely pointless? That Om Prakash or Vidyanath (if he exists) are enjoying an intricate joke at his expense? That he has allowed himself to be duped by his own hopes and fears?

But beyond all this, he's worried about this girl. There's only one thing to do: go to Om Prakash and get the truth out of him. After all, if Vidyanath's computer generated her image, and if Vidyanath isn't a complete fraud, he would know something about her, about that time. It is a forlorn hope, but it's all he has.

He takes the Metro on his way back. The train snakes its way under the city through the still-new tunnels, past brightly lit stations where crowds surge in and out. At one of these stops he sees the apparitions of people, their faces clammy and pale, clad in rags; he smells the stench of unwashed bodies too long out of the sun. They are coming out of the cement floor of the platform, as though from the bowels of the earth. He's seen them many times before; he knows they are from some future he'd rather not think about. But now it occurs to him with the suddenness of a blow that they are from the blind girl's future. Lower Delhi — Neechi Dilli — that is what this must be: a city of the poor, the outcast, the criminal, in the still-to-be-carved tunnels underneath the Delhi that he knows. He thinks of the Metro, fallen into disuse in that distant future, its tunnels abandoned to the dispossessed, and the city above a delight of gardens and gracious buildings, and tall spires reaching through the clouds. He has seen that once, he remembers. The Immaculate City, the blind girl called it.

By the time he gets to Vidyanath's shop, it is late afternoon, and the little square is filling with long shadows. At the bus-stop where he disembarks there is a young woman sitting, reading something. She looks vaguely familiar; she glances quickly at him but he notices her only peripherally.

He bursts into the room. Om Prakash is reading a magazine, which he sets down in surprise. A bee crawls out of his ear and flies up in a wide circle to the hive on the window. Aseem hardly notices.

"Where's that fellow, Vidyanath?"

Om Prakash looks mildly alarmed.

Delhi

"My employer is not here, sir."

"Look, Om Prakash, something has happened, something serious. I met the girl of the printout. But she's from the future. I need to go back and find her. You must get Vidyanath for me. If his computer made the image of the girl, he must know how I can reach her."

Om Prakash shakes his head sadly.

"Panditji speaks only through the computer." He looks at the beehive, then at Aseem. "Panditji cannot control the future, you know that. He can only tell you your purpose. Why you are important."

"But I made a mistake! I didn't realize she was from another time. I told her something and she disappeared before I could do anything. She could be in danger! It is a terrible future, Om Prakash. There is a city below the city where the poor live. And above the ground there is clean air and tall minars and *udan-khatolas* that fly between worlds. No dirt or beggars or poor people. Like when the foreign VIPs come to town and the policemen chase people like me out of the main roads. But Neechi Dilli is like a prison, I'm sure of it. They can't see the sun."

Om Prakash waves his long hands.

"What can I say, Sahib?"

Aseem goes around the table and takes Om Prakash by the shoulders.

"Tell me, Om Prakash, am I nothing but a strand in a web? Do I have a choice in what I do, or am I simply repeating lines written by someone else?"

"You can choose to break my bones, sir, and nobody can stop you. You can choose to jump into the Yamuna. Whatever you do affects the world in some small way. Sometimes the effect remains small, sometimes it grows and grows like a pipal tree. Causality as we call it is only a first-order effect. Second-order causal loops jump from time to time, as in your visions, sir. The future, Panditji says, is neither determined nor undetermined."

Aseem releases the fellow. His head hurts and he is very tired, and Om Prakash makes no more sense than usual. He feels emptied of hope. As he leaves, he turns to ask Om Prakash one more question.

"Tell me, Om Prakash, this Pandit Vidyanath, if he exists — what is his agenda? What is he trying to accomplish? Who is he working for?"

"Pandit Vidyanath works for the city, as you know. Otherwise he works only for himself."

He goes out into the warm evening. He walks toward the bus stop. Over the chatter of people and the car horns on the street and the barking of pariah dogs, he can hear the distant buzzing of bees.

At the bus-stop the half-familiar young woman is still sitting, studying a computer printout in the inadequate light of the streetlamp. She looks at him quickly, as though she wants to talk, but thinks better of it. He sits on the cement bench in a daze. Three years of anticipation, all for nothing. He should write down the last story and throw away his notebook.

Mechanically, he takes the notebook out and begins to write.

She clears her throat. Evidently she is not used to speaking to strange men. Her clothes and manner tell him she's from a respectable middle-class family. And then he remembers the girl he pushed away from a bus near Nai Sarak.

She's holding the page out to him.

"Can you make any sense of that?"

The printout is even more indistinct than his. He turns the paper around, frowns at it and hands it back to her.

"Sorry, I don't see anything."

She says:

"You could interpret the image as a crystal of unusual structure, or a city skyline with tall towers. Who knows? Considering that I'm studying biochemistry and my father really wants me to be an architect with his firm, it isn't surprising that I see those things in it. Amusing, really."

She laughs. He makes what he hopes is a polite noise.

"I don't know. I think the charming and foolish Om Prakash is a bit of a fraud. And you were wrong about me, by the way. I wasn't trying to... to kill myself that day."

Delhi

She's sounding defensive now. He knows he was not mistaken about what he saw in her eyes. If it wasn't then, it would have been some other time — and she knows this.

"Still, I came here on an impulse," she says in a rush, "and I've been staring at this thing and thinking about my life. I've already made a few decisions about my future."

A bus comes lurching to a stop. She looks at it, and then at him, hesitates. He knows she wants to talk, but he keeps scratching away in his notebook. At the last moment before the bus pulls away, she swings her bag over her shoulder, waves at him and climbs aboard. The look he had first noticed in her eyes has gone, for the moment. Today, she's a different person.

He finishes writing in his notebook, and with a sense of inevitability that feels strangely right, he catches a bus that will take him across one of the bridges that span the Yamuna.

At the bridge he leans against the concrete wall looking into the dark water. This is one of his familiar haunts; how many people has he saved on this bridge? The pipal tree sapling is still growing in a crack in the cement — the municipality keeps uprooting it but it is buried too deep to die completely. Behind him there are cars and lights and the sound of horns, the jangle of bicycle bells. He sets his notebook down on top of the wall, wishing he had given it to someone, like that girl at the bus-stop. He can't make himself throw it away. A peculiar lassitude, a detachment, has taken hold of him and he can think and act only in slow motion.

He's preparing to climb on to the wall of the bridge, his hands clammy and slipping on the concrete, when he hears somebody behind him say "Wait!" He turns. It is like looking into a distorting mirror. The man is hollow-cheeked, with a few days' stubble on his chin, and the untidy thatch of hair has thinned and is streaked with silver. He's holding a bunch of cards in his hand. A welt mars one cheek, and his left sleeve is torn and stained with something rust-coloured. The eyes are leopard's eyes, burning with a dreadful urgency. "Aseem," says the stranger who is not a stranger, panting as though he has been running, his voice breaking a little. "Don't..." He is already starting to fade. Aseem reaches out a hand and meets nothing but air. A million questions rise in his head but before he can speak the image is gone.

Aseem's first impulse is a defiant one. What if he were to jump into the river now, what would that do to the future, to causality? It would be his way of bowing out of the game that the city's been playing with him, of saying: I've had enough of your tricks. But the impulse dies. He thinks, instead, about Om Prakash's second-order causal loops, of sunset over the Red Fort, and the twisting alleyways of the old city, and death sleeping under the eyelids of the citizenry. He sits down slowly on the dusty sidewalk. He covers his face with his hands; his shoulders shake.

After a long while he stands up. The road before him can take him anywhere, to the faded colonnades and bright bustle of Connaught Place, to the hush of public parks, with their abandoned cricket balls and silent swings, to old government housing settlements where, amid sleeping bungalows, ancient trees hold court before somnolent congresses of cows. The dusty by-lanes and broad avenues and crumbling monuments of Delhi lie before him, the noisy, lurid marketplaces, the high-tech glass towers, the glitzy enclaves with their citadels of the rich, the boot-boys and beggars at street corners... He has just to take a step and the city will swallow him up, receive him the way a river receives the dead. He is a corpuscle in its veins, blessed or cursed to live and die within it, seeing his purpose now and then, but never fully.

Staring unseeingly into the bright clamour of the highway, he has a wild idea that, he realizes, has been bubbling under the surface of his consciousness for a while. He recalls a picture he saw once in a book when he was a boy: a satellite image of Asia at night. On the dark bulge of the globe there were knots of light; like luminous fungi, he had thought at the time, stretching tentacles into the dark. He wonders whether complexity and vastness are sufficient conditions for a slow awakening, a coming-to-consciousness. He thinks about Om Prakash, his foolish grin and waggling head, and his strange intimacy with the bees. Will Om Prakash tell him who Pandit Vidyanath really is, and what it means to "work for the city?" He thinks not. What he must do, he sees at last, is what he has been doing all along: looking out for his own kind, the poor and the desperate, and those who walk with death in their eyes. The city's needs are alien, unfathomable. It is an entity in its own right, expanding every day, swallowing the surrounding countryside, crossing the Yamuna which was once its boundary, spawning satellite children, infant towns that it will ultimately devour. Now it is burrowing into the earth, and even later it will reach long fingers towards the stars.

What he needs most at this time is someone he can talk to about all this, someone who will take his crazy ideas seriously. There was the girl at the bus-stop, the one he had rescued in Nai Sarak. Om Prakash will have her address. She wanted to talk; perhaps she will listen as well. He remembers the printout she had shown him and wonders if her future has something to do with the Delhi-to-come, the city that intrigues and terrifies him: the Delhi of *udan-khatolas*, the "ships that fly between worlds," of starved and forgotten people in the catacombs underneath. He wishes he could have asked his future self more questions. He is afraid because it is likely (but not certain, it is never that simple) that some kind of violence awaits him, not just the violence of privation, but a struggle that looms indistinctly ahead, that will cut his cheek and injure his arm, and do untold things to his soul. But for now there is nothing he can do, caught as he is in his own time-stream. He picks up his notebook. It feels strangely heavy in his hands. Rubbing sticky tears out of his eyes, he staggers slowly into the night.

The Woman Who Thought She Was a Planet

RAMNATH MISHRA'S LIFE changed forever one morning, when, during his perusal of the newspaper on the veranda, a ritual that he had observed for the last forty years, his wife set down her cup of tea with a crash and announced:

"I know at last what I am. I am a planet."

Ramnath's retirement was a source of displeasure to them both. He had been content to know his wife from a distance, to acknowledge her as the benign despot of the household and mother of his now-grown children, but he had desired no intimacy beyond that. As for Kamala herself, she seemed grumpy and uncomfortable with his proximity — her façade of the dutiful Indian wife had dropped after the first week. Now he lowered his newspaper, scowling, prepared to lecture her sternly for interrupting his peace, but instead his mouth fell open in silent astonishment.

His wife had got to her feet and was unwinding her sari.

Ramnath nearly knocked over his chair.

"What are you doing — have you lost your mind?" He leaped at her, grabbing a scrap of blue cotton sari with one hand and her arm with the other, looking around wildly to see if the servants were around, or the gardener, or whether the neighbours were peeping through the sprays of bougainvillea that sheltered the veranda from the summer heat. His wife, arrested in his arms, glared at him balefully.

"A planet does not need clothes," she said with great dignity.

"You are not a planet, you are crazy," Ramnath said. He propelled her into the bedroom. Thankfully, the washerwoman had left and the cook was in the kitchen, singing untunefully to the radio. "Arrange your sari for heaven's sake."

She complied. Ramnath saw that tears were glistening in her eyes. He felt a stab of concern mingled with irritation.

"Have you been feeling ill, Kamala? Should I phone Dr Kumar?"

"I am not ill," she said. "I have had a revelation. I am a planet. I used to be a human, a woman, a wife and mother. All the time I wondered if there was more to me than that. Now I know. Being a planet is good for me. I have stopped taking my liver pills."

"Well, if you were a planet," Ramnath said in exasperation, "you would be an inanimate object circling a star. You would probably have an atmosphere and living things crawling about you. You would be very large, like Earth or Jupiter. You are not a planet but a living soul, a woman. A lady from a respectable household who holds the family honour in her hands."

He was gratified that he had explained it so well because she smiled at him and smoothed her hair, nodding. "I must go see to lunch," she said in her normal voice. Ramnath went back to reading his newspaper on the veranda, shaking his head at the things a man had to do. But he could not concentrate on the prime minister's latest antics. It came to him suddenly that it could be a rather frightening thing not to know the person with whom he had lived for forty years. Where had she been getting such strange ideas? He remembered the scandal when, many years ago, a great-aunt of his had gone mad, locked herself in the outdoor toilet of the ancestral home and begun shrieking like a sarus crane in the mating season. They had finally got her out while curious neighbours thronged the courtyard, muttering with false sympathy and shouting encouragement. He remembered how quiet she had seemed after they helped her over the broken door, how there had been no warning before she bent her head, apparently in meek surrender, and bit her husband on his arm. She had ended up in the insane asylum in Ranchi. What terrible dishonour the family had suffered, what indignity — a mad person in a respectable upper middle-class family — he shuddered suddenly, set down his newspaper and went to call Dr Kumar. Dr Kumar would be discreet, he was a family friend…

But when he went into the drawing room, it was dark — somebody had closed the curtains, shutting out the morning light. Disturbed by the unnatural silence — the cook had stopped singing — he groped blindly towards the light-switch, which was closer to him than any of the windows. "Kamala!" he called, irritated to find his voice trembling. Abruptly, a curtain at the other end of the room was drawn violently back, letting in a burst of sunshine that hurt his eyes. There stood his wife, naked, facing the sun with her arms spread wide. She began to turn slowly. There was a beatific expression on her face. The sunlight washed her ample body, the generous terraces and folds of flesh that cascaded down to her sagging belly and buttocks. Ramnath was transfixed with horror. He ran up to the curtain, drew it closed, put his hands on his wife's plump shoulders and shook her hard.

"You have gone mad! What will the neighbours think? What did I do to deserve this!"

He dragged her to the bedroom and looked around for her sari. The blouse, petticoat and sari lay in crumpled folds on the bed. This in itself was disturbing because she was usually obsessive about tidiness. He realized that he had no idea how to put the sari on her. He saw the nightgown hanging neatly folded on the mosquito-netting bar, and grabbed it. His wife was struggling in his arms.

"Are you completely shameless? Put this on!"

After a while he managed to get the nightgown on her, but it was back-to-front. That didn't matter. He sat her down on the bed.

"Stay here and don't move. I am going to call the doctor. Has the cook gone out?"

Her nod reassured him, but she would not look at him. As Ramnath went into the drawing room, he hesitated, then turned on the light instead of drawing open the curtains. He was irritated to find that a part of his body had responded to her nakedness and his struggle with her. Resolutely he put all distracting thoughts aside and went to the phone.

Dr Kumar was out attending to a hospital emergency. Ramnath thought unkind thoughts about his friend. "Tell him he *must* phone the moment he returns — it is a matter of great urgency," he told the servant. He slammed down the phone. He went back to the bedroom. His wife was lying down, apparently asleep.

All that day Ramnath kept guard over his wife. By lunch she had changed back into her sari and combed her hair. The cook served them a stew of chick-peas simmered in a sauce of onions, cumin, ginger and chillies. There was basmati rice which they kept only for special occasions, and tiny fried eggplants stuffed with tomatoes and spices. Ramnath, having no idea what his wife's favourite dishes were, had asked the cook to make whatever she liked, hoping that food would distract her from this insanity. But she picked at her food absently, a dreamy look on her face. It was obvious that her thoughts were miles away. Ramnath felt a surge of anger and self-pity. What had he done to deserve this? He had worked hard for forty years or more, risen up to the ranks of a senior bureaucrat in the state government. He had fathered two sons. Now it occurred to him that it would have been nice to have a daughter, somebody whom he could call on at times like this. His mind did a quick survey of elderly female relatives — but they were either all dead, or lived in other towns and villages. Why didn't that damned doctor phone?

Ramnath's day was completely ruined. In the evenings he liked to go to the senior club and play chess with other retirees, but today he dared not leave his wife. She, for her part, spoke only when spoken to. She seemed outwardly calm, instructing the cook and dusting the pictures and bric-a-brac in the drawing room herself, but occasionally he would catch her gazing dreamily into a private world, a smile on her lips. He phoned the doctor again but the damn fool had come home only briefly, dressed for a party and left without receiving the urgent message.

That night was one of the worst that Ramnath had ever experienced. His wife tossed in her sleep, straining against some invisible restraining force like a moored ship trying to break free. Ramnath himself was beset by nightmares of planets and matronly naked women. He woke several times, looking warily at his wife as she slept fitfully, her graying hair all over the pillow, half-covering her open mouth. A wisp of hair blew out of her mouth with her breath, and it seemed to him as though it took on the aspect of some awful living thing. He brushed the hair off her face, trying not to tremble. In the moonlight from the window, her face was like the surface of the moon: pitted and cratered, fissured with age. She looked like a stranger.

The next morning his wife was rather subdued. She did not go out in the middle of the day to visit Mrs Chakravarti or Mrs Jain, as she used to do. She let the phone ring until Ramnath, maddened by her indifference, picked up the receiver and shouted into it, only to be embarrassed by the cool voice of Mrs Jain. "My wife is not well," he said, immediately regretting it. Mrs Jain, all concern, showed up ten minutes later with Mrs Chakravarti, bearing fruits and a special herbal concoction that Mrs Chakravarti's mother-in-law had made. For a minute Ramnath felt like telling them to go away and leave him in peace, but their matronly figures resplendent in crisp, starched cotton saris, their perfumed, hennaed hair tied so neatly into buns, their air of righteous sisterly concern quite defeated him. Kamala came out of the bedroom, where she had been lying down, greeted them with surprised pleasure and led them all back into the room. Ramnath, thus displaced, sat and fretted on the hot veranda, first refusing and then accepting the cook's offer of home-made lemon water. Inside the bedroom the women were all sprawled on the bed like beached whales, sipping lemon water and talking and giggling. He could not tell what they were gossiping about. But slowly he became comforted by the notion that his wife was at least acting normally. Perhaps having her friends over was a good thing. Perhaps he could manage a visit to the club this evening.

As soon as the women left, Kamala reverted to her old air of quiet indifference. Meanwhile Dr Kumar called. The idiot insisted on asking exactly what the matter was with Mrs Mishra. Ramnath, feeling his wife's eyes on him, did not know what to say. "It's a lady matter," he said finally, embarrassed. "I can't explain over the phone. Can you come?"

Dr Kumar came that evening and stayed to dinner. He checked Kamala's blood pressure, listened to her heart. His assistant, a taciturn young man, withdrew blood for further testing. During all this Kamala was serene, hospitable, asking after the doctor's family with sweet concern. It occurred to Ramnath that she had already acquired the infamous cunning of the insane, which enables them to conceal their madness at will.

"You must be mistaken, Mishra-ji," the doctor said on the phone two days later. "Everything is normal — she is, in fact, much healthier than before. If she has been behaving strangely, it is probably mental. Not always the sign of disease. Women are odd — they act strangely when they are hankering after something. She should go out, maybe go visit one of your sons. Grandchildren would do her good."

But Kamala refused to leave town. At last Ramnath, acting on the doctor's advice, persuaded her to walk with him in the evenings, hoping that the open air would do her good. He kept a steely eye on her — if she as much as touched the free end of her sari hanging over her shoulder, he would grunt warningly and slap her hand. The narrow lanes of their neighbourhood were lined with amaltash trees heavy with cascades of golden flowers. In the playground the older boys finished the last round of cricket in the failing light, while smaller children squatted in the dust, playing with marbles, ignoring wandering cows and sedate, elderly citizens taking the air. Neighbours sitting on the verandas of their bungalows called out greetings. Torn between hope and dread, Ramnath frequently and surreptitiously examined his wife's face for signs of incipient madness. She remained calm and sociable, although as they walked on it seemed as though she were falling into a trance, interrupted only by sighs of deep rapture as she gazed at the sunset.

In the week that followed, Kamala attempted twice to take off her clothes. Both times Ramnath managed to restrain her, although the second time she almost managed to escape from him. He caught her just as she was about to run out into the driveway in nothing but a petticoat and blouse, in full view of street vendors, cricket-playing children and respectable elderly gentlemen. He wrestled her into the bedroom and tried to slap some sense into her, but she continued to struggle and weep. At last, frustrated, he pulled half a dozen saris out from the big steel cupboard and flung them on the bed.

"Kamala," he said desperately, "even planets have atmospheres. See here, this gray sari, it looks like a swirl of clouds. How about it?"

She calmed down at once. She began to put on the gray sari although the fabric, georgette, was unsuitable for summer.

"At last you believe me, Ramnath," she said. Her voice seemed to have changed. It was deeper, more powerful. He looked at her, aghast. She had addressed him by his name! That was all very well for the new generation of young adults, but respectable, traditional women never addressed their husbands by their names. He decided not to do anything about it for now. At least she was clothed.

At night Ramnath lay wrestling with doubts and fears. A breeze blew in through the open window, stirring the mosquito netting. In the starlight his wife, the room, everything looked alien. He propped himself on one elbow and looked at the stranger beside him. A thought came to him that if he could get her confined to the asylum in Ranchi without a scandal, he would do it. But she had that idiot Kumar charmed. The way she had asked so nicely about his ailing mother, congratulated him on his recent membership of a prestigious medical organization. Kumar had known the family for years — and, it occurred to Ramnath, had always had a soft spot for his wife. Who would have thought she'd had so much cunning in her? Now, as he watched her sleep, her hair in disarray and her mouth open like some hideous cavern, it occurred to him how easy his life would be if she would simply die. He was ashamed of the thought as soon as it formed but he could not take it back. It called to him and seduced him and resounded in his head until he was convinced that if he could not have her committed, he would have to kill her himself. He could not live like this.

Every night it became a ritual for him to look at her and imagine the different ways he could commit murder. He had been shocked at himself at first — him, a fine, upstanding ex-bureaucrat contemplating something as hideous as the murder of the mother of his sons — but there was no denying that the thought, the fantasy, he told himself, gave him pleasure. A secret, shameful sort of pleasure, like sex before marriage, but pleasure nonetheless.

He began to count the ways. Suffocation with a pillow while she slept would be the easiest, but he had no idea if the forensics people could infer from that what had happened. Strangulation had the same problem. Poison — but where to procure it? And now that she had stopped taking her liver pills he could no longer perform some artful substitution. Damn the woman!

One night, as he watched her sleeping, he put his hand very gently on her neck. She stirred a little, frightening him, but he made himself keep his hand there, feeling the pulse in her throat. He began to stroke her neck with his thumb. Abruptly she coughed and he jerked his hand away in terror. But she did not wake. She was coughing up something dark from her mouth. For a moment he thought it was blood, that he should call the doctor; his next thought was that perhaps she was dying of her own accord. Maybe it had been enough to wish it so strongly. She coughed again and again but she did not wake. Now the dark stuff had gathered about her mouth, on her chin, like a jelly. To his horror he saw that the darkness was not blood but composed of small, moving things. One stood up on its hind legs for a moment, surveying him, and he drew back in horror. It was insectoid, alien, about as tall as his index finger. There was an army of those things coming out of her mouth.

The mosquito netting was tucked under the bed on all sides — he pushed at it, trying to tear it with his hands, but they were upon him before he could get out of the bed. He tried to cry out but all he could manage was a whimper. They covered his body, crawling inside his clothes, beating and biting at him with short, sharp appendages. He tried to brush them off but there were too many of them. They made a sound like crickets singing, but softer. He howled in despair, calling to Kamala to save him, but she lay peacefully beside him as the things came out of her. After a while he fainted.

Much later he opened his eyes, with some difficulty — they were sticky with dried tears. A pale morning light came in through the window. There was no sign of the creatures. There was a large tear in the mosquito netting and a mosquito was humming in his ear. His wife lay sleeping beside him. Perhaps what he had experienced had been a nightmare, he told himself, that it was his conscience punishing him for his impious thoughts. But he knew that the soreness all over his body, the marks of bites and the bruises, were real. He turned fearfully towards his wife. Abruptly her eyes snapped open.

Hai bhagwan! She was looking at the tear on his white sleepshirt, the pinpricks of blood. He flinched as she reached out a hand to touch the tiny wounds. They had spared his face. More cunning, he thought. "Why didn't you wake me? I would have told them — they would have understood, not hurt you."

"What are those things?" he whispered.

"Inhabitants," she said. "I'm a planet, remember?"

The Woman Who Thought She Was a Planet

She smiled at the look on his face.

"Don't be afraid, Ramnath." Again, the free use of his name! Was she possessed? Should he consult an astrologer? An exorcist? He, a rational man, reduced to this!

"Don't be afraid," she said again. "The younger ones probably want to find a place to colonize. If you ever want to be a satellite, Ramnath, let me know. The little animals are good for a planet. They have restored my health."

"Do you want to go visit your mother?" he whispered. "You haven't been home for a while. I will make all the arrangements…"

He had not let her go home to her ancestral village for the past five years — there was always something going on that needed her attention. The marriage of their sons, his retirement and the fact that *somebody* had to run the house and supervise the servants.

"Oh Ramnath," she said, her eyes softening. "You were never this generous before. I think you have quite changed. No, I don't want to leave you, not yet."

She bathed his wounds with Dettol and warm water. She watched over him solicitously as he ate his breakfast. Later, her distracted look returned as she moved about the house, dusting and rearranging things mechanically. Ramnath felt the need to escape.

"Do you mind if I go to the club this evening?"

"No, of course not," she said amiably. "Go enjoy yourself."

When he went to his club he made a private and very expensive phone call to his older son.

"But Papa, I just heard from Ma. She sounded quite normal. Are you sure you are feeling well? … No, I can't come now, there is a very important case at court. My senior partner has put me in charge…"

The younger son was in Germany on an engineering assignment. Defeated, Ramnath immersed himself in a game of chess with an acquaintance who beat him easily.

"Losing your touch, sir?" said the younger man annoyingly.

When Ramnath got home, he felt he was returning to prison. The house was quite silent except for the cook singing in the kitchen. It occurred to him to tell the fellow to shut up. But where was his wife?

"She went to the park, Sahib," the cook said.

He wondered whether to go after her. But five minutes later she was coming up the driveway clutching a balloon. She waved and smiled at him quite shamelessly. He saw with relief that she was clothed. She was eating an ice-cream bar.

"I had such fun, Ramnath," she told him. "I played with the little ones. I bought them all balloons. I haven't had a balloon in such a long time."

Later, after the cook had retired, he spoke to her.

"Kamala, those... things, those creatures inside you... I think we should get you checked up. It is not right to keep all this from Dr Kumar. You have a terrible disease..."

"But, Ramnath, I have no sickness. I am well, very well. After years."

"But..."

"And the things, as you call them are not things but my own creation. They came from me, Ramnath."

She slapped his face playfully.

"You look pulled down and grumpy," she said, pinching his thin cheek. "My little animals would do you so much good, Ramnath, if only you would rid yourself of your prejudice."

He backed away from her, outraged and horrified.

"Never! Kamala, I am going to sleep on the sofa. I cannot..."

"As you wish," she said indifferently.

That night he lay awake for a long time. He could hear the crickets singing outside the window, but was too nervous to get up and shut out the sound. All the small night-time sounds — the whisper of the curtain in the breeze, the asthmatic squeak of the ceiling fan, the rustle of the leaves of the bougainvillea outside — all this made him think of the insect-like creatures. Once he woke up and fancied that some of them were standing on the top of the narrow sofa, looking down at him and gesturing in a very human way, as he lay there, helpless. He began to edge off the sofa, his heart hammering wildly, but a sudden gust of wind filled the curtains so they billowed out like ghostly sails, letting in the moonlight — and he saw that there was nothing on the top of the sofa after all. At last he fell asleep, exhausted.

Over the next few days, Ramnath kept hold of his sanity with great difficulty. He wondered whether he should renounce the world and retire to the Himalayas. Perhaps the gods he had so casually dismissed the past few years were getting their revenge now. He still toyed with the idea of murder, although it seemed impossible now, at least at close range. Looking at his wife over dinner, he began to wonder for the first time about her. What was she really like? What did she want that he had not given her? How had he come to this?

"Kamala," he said one day. He was in a strange mood. He had lit an incense stick in front of the household gods that morning. The scent of sandalwood still pervaded the house. It made him feel humble, virtuous, as though he was at last letting go of his ego and surrendering to the divine. "Tell me, what is it like… to have those… animals inside you…"

She smiled. Her teeth were very white.

"I hardly feel them most of the time, Ramnath," she said. "I wish you would agree to be colonized. It would do you good and it would help them — the younger ones have been clamouring for a new world. I hear them singing sometimes, chirping sounds like crickets. It is a language I am beginning to understand."

He thought he heard it faintly then, too.

"What are they saying?"

She frowned, listening. She sighed.

"A planet needs a sun, Ramnath," she said evasively. "My journey is just beginning."

Vandana Singh

After this interchange he noticed an increased restlessness in his wife. She kept going out to the garden to sun herself in the forty degree centigrade heat, among the wilting guava trees. In the house she moved from room to room, making little chirping sounds and humming tunelessly to herself. Ramnath felt his pious resolve shatter. Irritated, he spent that evening at his club.

The next evening, remembering his duty, Ramnath dragged his wife out for a walk. She protested a little feebly but let him pull her into the street. By the time they reached the park a soft twilight had fallen. A few stars and a pale moon hung in the sky. Kamala lingered at the edge of the park.

"Come on," Ramnath said, impatient to continue walking.

But instead his wife gave a cry of pleasure and turned into the park, where in the semi-darkness a man was selling balloons. She began to run towards the balloon man, gesturing like an excited child. Embarrassed and annoyed, he followed her at a more dignified pace.

"More balloons," he heard her say. Coins tinkled. A small crowd of street urchins appeared from nowhere. He could hear the rhythmic squeak of a swing in the semi-darkness ahead.

Now she was handing balloons out to the gaggle of brats, who jumped and chattered excitedly around her.

"Me too, Auntie-ji!"

The balloons bobbed over their heads like dim little orbs in the moonlight. Ramnath pushed aside the children and grabbed his wife by the shoulder.

"Enough," he said impatiently. "You are spoiling these good-for-nothings!"

She shrugged off his hand. She let go of one of her balloons and watched it float lazily up into the starlit sky. A sudden gust of wind came up and dislodged the free end of her sari from her shoulder, baring her blouse. The balloon man stared at her ample cleavage.

"Adjust your sari for heaven's sake," Ramnath said in a desperate whisper. He looked around to see if anyone else was watching this spectacle and was horrified to see the ramrod figure of Judge Pandey walking towards them on the path through the park, his cane tap-tapping. Fearful that the judge would see him and associate him with this madwoman, Ramnath retreated into the inadequate shadow of an ashok tree. Fortunately Judge Pandey didn't see him. He saw what seemed to be a wanton looking woman and walked quickly past her in case anyone noticed him staring. Ramnath, sweaty with relief, emerged from the shadows and grabbed the end of his wife's sari that lay on the dusty ground. His wife had released three other balloons into the air and was watching them go up with childish pleasure. The children were shouting in their shrill voices.

"Let another one go, Auntie-ji!"

"Come home, Kamala," Ramnath said pleadingly. "This is madness!"

But instead of answering, Kamala let go of all the balloons, some seven or eight of them. They floated up into the sky. She stretched her arms out to them, her face full of a blissful yearning. Slowly and majestically she began to rise over the ground — an inch, two inches.

"What are you doing?" Ramnath said in a horrified whisper.

Three feet, four feet. Ramnath's mouth fell open. He pulled on the end of the sari he was holding but she continued to rise, turning slowly, trailing two yards, then five yards of cotton. Too late, Ramnath let go of the sari. His wife rose into the night air, her white petticoat filling with air like the sails of a ship.

"Oooh! Look what Auntie is doing!"

Some of the urchins had drawn back. The balloon man's face was a round circle of astonishment.

"Come back!" Ramnath shouted.

The children were yelling and pointing and jumping with glee. She was well up now, higher than the trees and houses. The balloons scattered above her like a flotilla of tiny escort ships. People were running out of their houses now, pointing and staring. Something white and ghostly came slipping down from the sky — her petticoat! Her blouse and undergarments were next. Ramnath stood transfixed with horror while the urchins cavorted about, trying to catch the garments in the darkness. Somebody — Mrs Jain, perhaps — began wailing. "*Hai Bhagwan*, that is Kamala, Kamala Mishra!"

The cry was taken up all around. With each shout Ramnath felt his family name and honour sinking into the ground. He tried to slink away, keeping to the shadows of trees like a thief, hoping nobody would recognize him. But then, on the road, Judge Pandey tapped him on the shoulder. The veteran judge's solemn, impassive face was the last thing he wanted to see.

"Most reprehensible, Mishra! Most reprehensible!"

Ramnath moaned and fled to his house, throwing dignity to the winds. All around people were saying his wife's name — the neighbours, the street urchins, the servants, the man selling roasted corn at the end of the street.

The house was dark and empty. No doubt the cook had gone to see the show as well. Ramnath felt he could face nobody after this. He stood in the middle of the dark drawing room, thinking wildly of escape, or suicide.

He went to the window and looked out apprehensively. There she was, a tiny, bright blob still rising into the sky. How dare she leave him like this!

It occurred to him that there was only one option — to take enough things from the house, leave by the late train and disappear. He could even change his name, he thought. Begin anew. The house was willed to his sons. He would not let his dishonour touch them. Let them all think he was dead!

She was out of sight now. For a moment he almost envied her, out there among the stars. He imagined, despite himself, the little alien creatures running over the wild terrain of her body, exploring the mountains, gullies and varied habitats of that mysterious and unknowable geography. What sun would she find? What vistas would she see? A sob caught in his throat. How would he manage now, with nobody to look after him?

A small sound caught his attention. Perhaps it was the cook returning, or the neighbours coming to feast on the remains of his dignity. There was no time. He rushed to the bedroom, turned on the light. Breathing hard, he started to pull things out of the steel cupboard, things he would need, like money, her jewellery, and clothes. It was then that he felt something on his shoulder.

He would have screamed if he had remembered how; the insectoids were already marching up his back, over his shoulder and into his terrified, open mouth.

Infinities

*An equation means nothing to me unless it expresses
a thought of God.*
Srinivasa Ramanujan, Indian mathematician (1887-1920)

ABDUL KARIM IS HIS NAME. He is a small, thin man, precise to the point of affectation in his appearance and manner. He walks very straight; there is gray in his hair and in his short, pointed beard. When he goes out of the house to buy vegetables, people on the street greet him respectfully. "Salaam, Master Sahib," they say, or "Namaste, Master Sahib," according to the religion of the speaker. They know him as the mathematics master at the municipal school. He has been there so long that he sees the faces of his former students everywhere: the autorickshaw driver Ramdas who refuses to charge him, the man who sells *paan* from a shack at the street corner, with whom he has an account, who never reminds him when his payment is late – his name is Imran and he goes to the mosque far more regularly than Abdul Karim.

They all know him, the kindly mathematics master, but he has his secrets. They know he lives in the old yellow house, where the plaster is flaking off in chunks to reveal the underlying brick. The windows of the house are hung with faded curtains that flutter tremulously in the breeze, giving passersby an occasional glimpse of his genteel poverty — the threadbare covers on the sofa, the wooden furniture as gaunt and lean and resigned as the rest of the house, waiting to fall into dust. The house is built in the old-fashioned way about a courtyard, which is paved with brick except for a circular omission where a great litchi tree grows. There is a high wall around the courtyard, and one door in it that leads to the patch of wilderness that was once a vegetable garden. But the hands that tended it — his mother's hands — are no longer able to do more than hold a mouthful of rice between the tips of the fingers, tremblingly conveyed to the mouth. The mother sits nodding in the sun in the courtyard while the son goes about the house, dusting and cleaning as fastidiously as a woman. The master has two sons — one is in distant America, married to a *gori bibi*, a white woman — how unimaginable! He never comes home and writes only a few times a year. The wife writes cheery letters in English that the master reads carefully, his finger under each word. She talks about his grandsons, about baseball (a form of cricket, apparently), about their plans to visit, which never materialize. Her letters are as incomprehensible to him as the thought that there might be aliens on Mars, but he senses a kindness, a reaching out, among the foreign words. His mother has refused to have anything to do with that woman.

The other son has gone into business in Mumbai. He comes home rarely, but when he does he brings with him expensive things — a television set, an air-conditioner. The TV is draped reverently with an embroidered white cloth and dusted every day but the master can't bring himself to turn it on. There is too much trouble in the world. The air-conditioner gives him asthma so that, too, remains silent, in the searing heat of summer. His son is a mystery to him — his mother dotes on the boy but the master can't help fearing that this young man has become a stranger, that he is involved in some shady business. The son always has a cellphone with him and is always calling nameless friends in Mumbai, bursting into cheery laughter, dropping his voice to a whisper, walking up and down the pathetically clean drawing-room as he speaks. Although he would never admit it to anybody other than Allah, Abdul Karim has the distinct impression that his son is waiting for him to die. He is always relieved when his son leaves.

Still, these are domestic worries. What father does not worry about his children? Nobody would be particularly surprised to know that the quiet, kindly master of mathematics shares them also. What they don't know is that he has a secret, an obsession, a passion that makes him different from them all. It is because of this, perhaps, that he seems always to be looking at something just beyond their field of vision, that he seems a little lost in the cruel, mundane world in which they live.

He wants to see infinity.

It is not strange for a mathematics master to be obsessed with numbers. But for Abdul Karim, numbers are the stepping stones, rungs in the ladder that will take him (Inshallah!) from the prosaic ugliness of the world to infinity.

When he was a child he used to see things from the corners of his eyes. Shapes moving at the very edge of his field of vision. Haven't we all felt that there was someone to our left or right, darting away when we turned our heads? In his childhood he had thought they were *farishte*, angelic beings keeping a watch over him. And he had felt secure, loved, nurtured by a great, benign, invisible presence.

One day he asked his mother:

"Why don't the *farishte* stay and talk to me? Why do they run away when I turn my head?"

Inexplicably to the child he had been, this innocent question led to visits to the Hakim. Abdul Karim had always been frightened of the Hakim's shop, the walls of which were lined from top to bottom with old clocks. The clocks ticked and hummed and whirred while tea came in chipped glasses and there were questions about spirits and possessions, and bitter herbs were dispensed in antique bottles that looked at though they contained djinns. An amulet was given to the boy to wear around his neck; there were verses from the Qur'an he was to recite every day. The boy he had been sat at the edge of the worn velvet seat and trembled; after two weeks of treatment, when his mother asked him about the *farishte*, he had said:

"They're gone."

That was a lie.

My theory stands as firm as a rock; every arrow directed against it will quickly return to the archer. How do I know this? Because I have studied it from all sides for many years; because I have examined all objections which have ever been made against the infinite numbers; and above all because I have followed its roots, so to speak, to the first infallible cause of all created things.

Georg Cantor, German mathematician (1845-1918)

In a finite world, Abdul Karim ponders infinity. He has met infinities of various kinds in mathematics. If mathematics is the language of Nature, then it follows that there are infinities in the physical world around us as well. They confound us because we are such limited things. Our lives, our science, our religions are all smaller than the cosmos. Is the cosmos infinite? Perhaps. As far as we are concerned, it might as well be.

In mathematics there is the sequence of natural numbers, walking like small, determined soldiers into infinity. But there are less obvious infinities as well, as Abdul Karim knows. Draw a straight line, mark zero on one end and the number one at the other. How many numbers between zero and one? If you start counting now, you'll still be counting when the universe ends, and you'll be nowhere near one. In your journey from one end to the other you'll encounter the rational numbers and the irrational numbers, most notably the transcendentals. The transcendental numbers are the most intriguing — you can't generate them from integers by division, or by solving simple equations. Yet in the simple number line there are nearly impenetrable thickets of them; they are the densest, most numerous of all numbers. It is only when you take certain ratios like the circumference of a circle to its diameter, or add an infinite number of terms in a series, or negotiate the countless steps of infinite continued fractions, do these transcendental numbers emerge. The most famous of these is, of course, pi, 3.14159..., where there is an infinity of non-repeating numbers after the decimal point. The transcendentals! Theirs is a universe richer in infinities than we can imagine.

In finiteness — in that little stick of a number line — there is infinity. What a deep and beautiful concept, thinks Abdul Karim. Perhaps there are infinities in us too, universes of them.

The prime numbers are another category that capture his imagination. The atoms of integer arithmetic, the select few that generate all other integers, as the letters of an alphabet generate all words. There are an infinite number of primes, as befits what he thinks of as God's alphabet...

How ineffably mysterious the primes are! They seem to occur at random in the sequence of numbers: 2, 3, 5, 7, 11... There is no way to predict the next number in the sequence without actually testing it. No formula that generates all the primes. And yet, there is a mysterious regularity in these numbers that has eluded the greatest mathematicians of the world. Glimpsed by Riemann, but as yet unproven, there are hints of order so deep, so profound, that it is as yet beyond us.

To look for infinity in an apparently finite world — what nobler occupation for a human being, and one like Abdul Karim in particular?

As a child he questioned the elders at the mosque: What does it mean to say that Allah is simultaneously one, and infinite? When he was older he read the philosophies of Al Kindi and Al Ghazali, Ibn Sina and Iqbal, but his restless mind found no answers. For much of his life he has been convinced that mathematics, not the quarrels of philosophers, is the key to the deepest mysteries.

He wonders whether the *farishte* that have kept him company all his life know the answer to what he seeks. Sometimes, when he sees one at the edge of his vision, he asks a question into the silence. Without turning around.

Is the Riemann Hypothesis true?

Silence.

Are prime numbers the key to understanding infinity?

Silence.

Is there a connection between transcendental numbers and the primes?

There has never been an answer.

But sometimes, a hint, a whisper of a voice that speaks in his mind. Abdul Karim does not know whether his mind is playing tricks upon him or not, because he cannot make out what the voice is saying. He sighs and buries himself in his studies.

He reads about prime numbers in Nature. He learns that the distribution of energy level spacings of excited uranium nuclei seem to match the distribution of spacings between prime numbers. Feverishly he turns the pages of the article, studies the graphs, tries to understand. How strange that Allah has left a hint in the depths of atomic nuclei! He is barely familiar with modern physics — he raids the library to learn about the structure of atoms.

His imagination ranges far. Meditating on his readings, he grows suspicious now that perhaps matter is infinitely divisible. He is beset by the notion that maybe there is no such thing as an elementary particle. Take a quark and it's full of preons. Perhaps preons themselves are full of smaller and smaller things. There is no limit to this increasingly fine graininess of matter.

How much more palatable this is than the thought that the process stops somewhere, that at some point there is a pre-preon, for example, that is composed of nothing else but itself. How fractally sound, how beautiful if matter is a matter of infinitely nested boxes.

Vandana Singh

There is a symmetry in it that pleases him. After all, there is infinity in the very large too. Our universe, ever expanding, apparently without limit.

He turns to the work of Georg Cantor, who had the audacity to formalize the mathematical study of infinity. Abdul Karim painstakingly goes over the mathematics, drawing his finger under every line, every equation in the yellowing textbook, scribbling frantically with his pencil. Cantor is the one who discovered that certain infinite sets are more infinite than others — that there are tiers and strata of infinity. Look at the integers, 1, 2, 3, 4… Infinite, but of a lower order of infinity than the real numbers like 1.67, 2.93 etc. Let us say the set of integers is of order Aleph-null, the set of real numbers of order Aleph-One, like the hierarchical ranks of a king's courtiers. The question that plagued Cantor and eventually cost him his life and sanity was the Continuum Hypothesis, which states that there is no infinite set of numbers with order *between* Aleph-Null and Aleph-One. In other words, Aleph-One succeeds Aleph-Null; there is no intermediate rank. But Cantor could not prove this.

He developed the mathematics of infinite sets. Infinity plus infinity equals infinity. Infinity minus infinity equals infinity. But the Continuum Hypothesis remained beyond his reach.

Abdul Karim thinks of Cantor as a cartographer in a bizarre new world. Here, the cliffs of infinity reach endlessly toward the sky, and Cantor is a tiny figure lost in the grandeur, a fly on a precipice. And yet, what boldness! What spirit! To have the gall to actually *classify* infinity…

His explorations take him to an article on the mathematicians of ancient India. They had specific words for large numbers. One *purvi*, a unit of time, is seven hundred and fifty-six thousand billion years. One *sirsaprahelika* is eight point four million *purvis* raised to the twenty-eighth power. What did they see that caused them to play with such large numbers? What vistas were revealed before them? What wonderful arrogance possessed them that they, puny things, could dream so large?

He mentions this once to his friend, a Hindu called Gangadhar, who lives not far away. Gangadhar's hands pause over the chessboard (their weekly game is in progress) and he intones a verse from the Vedas:

From the Infinite, take the Infinite, and lo! Infinity remains...

Abdul Karim is astounded. That his ancestors could anticipate Georg Cantor by four millennia!

That fondness for science, ... that affability and condescension which God shows to the learned, that promptitude with which he protects and supports them in the elucidation of obscurities and in the removal of difficulties, has encouraged me to compose a short work on calculating by *al-jabr* and *al-muqabala*, confining it to what is easiest and most useful in arithmetic.

Al Khwarizmi, eighth century Arab mathematician

Mathematics came to the boy almost as naturally as breathing. He made a clean sweep of the exams in the little municipal school. The neighbourhood was provincial, dominated by small tradesmen, minor government officials and the like, and their children seemed to have inherited or acquired their plodding practicality. Nobody understood that strangely clever Muslim boy, except for a Hindu classmate, Gangadhar, who was a well-liked, outgoing fellow. Although Gangadhar played *gulli-danda* on the streets and could run faster than anybody, he had a passion for literature, especially poetry — a pursuit perhaps as impractical as pure mathematics. The two were drawn together and spent many hours sitting on the compound wall at the back of the school, eating stolen jamuns from the trees overhead and talking about subjects ranging from Urdu poetry and Sanskrit verse to whether mathematics pervaded everything, including human emotions. They felt very grown-up and mature for their stations. Gangadhar was the one who, shyly, and with many giggles, first introduced Kalidasa's erotic poetry to Abdul Karim. At that time girls were a mystery to them both: although they shared classrooms it seemed to them that girls (a completely different species from their sisters, of course) were strange, graceful, alien creatures from another world. Kalidasa's lyrical descriptions of breasts and hips evoked in them unarticulated longings.

They had the occasional fight, as friends do. The first serious one happened when there were some Hindu-Muslim tensions in the city just before the elections. Gangadhar came to Abdul in the school playground and knocked him flat.

"You're a bloodthirsty Muslim!" he said, almost as though he had just realized it.

"You're a hell-bound kafir!"

They punched each other, wrestled the other to the ground. Finally, with cut lips and bruises, they stared fiercely at each other and staggered away. The next day they played *gulli-danda* in the street on opposite sides for the first time.

Then they ran into each other in the school library. Abdul Karim tensed, ready to hit back if Gangadhar hit him. Gangadhar looked as if he was thinking about it for a moment, but then, somewhat embarrassedly, he held out a book.

"New book... on mathematics. Thought you'd want to see it..."

After that they were sitting on the wall again, as usual.

Their friendship had even survived the great riots four years later, when the city became a charnel house — buildings and bodies burned, and unspeakable atrocities were committed by both Hindus and Muslims. Some political leader of one side or another had made a provocative proclamation that he could not even remember, and tempers had been inflamed. There was an incident — a fight at a bus-stop, accusations of police brutality against the Muslim side, and things had spiraled out of control. Abdul's elder sister Ayesha had been at the market with a cousin when the worst of the violence broke out. They had been separated in the stampede; the cousin had come back, bloodied but alive, and nobody had ever seen Ayesha again.

The family never recovered. Abdul's mother went through the motions of living but her heart wasn't in it. His father lost weight, became a shrunken mockery of his old, vigorous self — he would die only a few years later. As for Abdul — the news reports about atrocities fed his nightmares and in his dreams he saw his sister bludgeoned, raped, torn to pieces again and again and again. When the city calmed down, he spent his days roaming the streets of the market, hoping for a sign of Ayesha — a body even — torn between hope and feverish rage.

Their father stopped seeing his Hindu friends. The only reason Abdul did not follow suit was because Gangadhar's people had sheltered a Muslim family during the carnage, and had turned away a mob of enraged Hindus.

Over time the wound, if it did not quite heal, became bearable enough that he could start living again. He threw himself into his beloved mathematics, isolating himself from everyone but his family and Gangadhar. The world had wronged him. He did not owe it anything.

Aryabhata is the master who, after reaching the furthest shores and plumbing the inmost depths of the sea of ultimate knowledge of mathematics, kinematics and spherics, handed over the three sciences to the learned world.

The mathematician Bhaskara, commenting on the 6th century Indian mathematician Aryabhata, a hundred years later.

Abdul Karim was the first in his family to go to college. By a stroke of great luck, Gangadhar went to the same regional institution, majoring in Hindi literature while Abdul Karim buried himself in mathematical arcana. Abdul's father had become reconciled to his son's obsession and obvious talent. Abdul Karim himself, glowing with praise from his teachers, wanted to follow in the footsteps of Ramanujan. Just as the goddess Namakkal had appeared to that untutored genius in his dreams, writing mathematical formulas on his tongue (or so Ramanujan had said), Abdul Karim wondered if the *farishte* had been sent by Allah so that he, too, might be blessed with mathematical insight.

During that time an event occurred that convinced him of this.

Abdul was in the college library, working on a problem in differential geometry, when he sensed a *farishta* at the edge of his field of vision. As he had done countless times before, he turned his head slowly, expecting the vision to vanish.

Instead he saw a dark shadow standing in front of the long bookcase. It was vaguely human-shaped. It turned slowly, revealing itself to be thin as paper — but as it turned it seemed to acquire thickness, hints of features over its dark, slender form. And then it seemed to Abdul that a door opened in the air, just a crack, and he had a vision of an unutterably strange world beyond. The shadow stood at the door, beckoning with one arm, but Abdul Karim sat still, frozen with wonder. Before he could rouse himself and get up, the door and the shadow both rotated swiftly and vanished, and he was left staring at the stack of books on the shelf.

After this he was convinced of his destiny. He dreamed obsessively of the strange world he had glimpsed; every time he sensed a *farishta* he turned his head slowly toward it — and every time it vanished. He told himself it was just a matter of time before one of them came, remained, and perhaps — wonder of wonders — took him to that other world.

Then his father died unexpectedly. That was the end of Abdul Karim's career as a mathematician. He had to return home to take care of his mother, his two remaining sisters and a brother. The only thing he was qualified for was teaching. Ultimately he would find a job at the same municipal school from which he had graduated.

On the train home, he saw a woman. The train had stopped on a bridge. Below him was the sleepy curve of a small river, gold in the early morning light, mists rising faintly off it, and on the shore a woman with a clay water pot. She had taken a dip in the river – her pale, ragged sari clung wetly to her as she picked up the pot, set it on her hip and began to climb the bank. In the light of dawn she was luminous, an apparition in the mist, the curve of the pot against the curve of her hip. Their eyes met from a distance – he imagined what he thought she saw, the silent train, a young man with a sparse beard looking at her as though she was the first woman in the world. Her own eyes gazed at him fearlessly as though she were a goddess looking into his soul. For a moment there were no barriers between them, no boundaries of gender, religion, caste or class. Then she turned and vanished behind a stand of shisham trees.

He wasn't sure if she had really been there in the half-light or whether he had conjured her up, but for a long time she represented something elemental to him. Sometimes he thought of her as Woman, sometimes as a river.

He got home in time for the funeral. His job kept him busy, and kept the moneylender from their door. With the stubborn optimism of the young, he kept hoping that one day his fortunes would change, that he would go back to college and complete his degree. In the meantime, he knew his mother wanted to find him a bride…

Abdul Karim got married, had children. Slowly, over the years of managing rowdy classrooms, tutoring students in the afternoons and saving, paisa by paisa, from his meager salary for his sisters' weddings and other expenses, Abdul Karim lost touch with that youthful, fiery talent he had once had, and with it the ambition to scale the heights to which Ramanujan, Cantor and Riemann had climbed. Things came more slowly to him now. An intellect burdened by years of worry wears out. When his wife died and his children grew up and went away, his steadily decreasing needs finally caught up with his meager income, and he found for the first time that he could think about mathematics again. He no longer hoped to dazzle the world of mathematics with some new insight, such as a proof of Riemann's hypothesis. Those dreams were gone. All he could hope for was to be illumined by the efforts of those who had gone before him, and to relive, vicariously, the joys of insight. It was a cruel trick of time, that when he had the leisure he had lost the ability, but that is no bar to true obsession. Now, in the autumn of his life, it was as though spring had come again, bringing with it his old love.

> In this world, brought to its knees by hunger and thirst
> Love is not the only reality, there are other Truths…
> *Sahir Ludhianvi, Indian poet (1921–1980)*

There are times when Abdul Karim tires of his mathematical obsessions. After all, he is old. Sitting in the courtyard with his notebook, pencil and books of mathematics for so many hours at a stretch can take its toll. He gets up, aching all over, sees to his mother's needs and goes out to the graveyard where his wife is buried.

His wife, Zainab, had been a plump, fair-skinned woman, hardly able to read or write, who moved about the house with indolent grace, her good-natured laugh ringing out in the courtyard as she chattered with the washerwoman. She had loved to eat — he still remembered the delicate tips of her plump fingers, how they would curl around a piece of lamb, scooping up with it a few grains of saffron rice, the morsel conveyed reverently to her mouth. Her girth gave an impression of strength, but ultimately she had not been able to hold out against her mother-in-law. The laughter in her eyes faded gradually as her two boys grew out of babyhood, coddled and put to bed by the grandmother in her own corner of the women's quarters. Abdul Karim himself had been unaware of the silent war between his wife and mother — he had been young and obsessed with teaching mathematics to his recalcitrant students. He had noticed how the grandmother always seemed to be holding the younger son, crooning to him, and how the elder boy followed his mother around, but he did not see in this any connection to his wife's growing pallor. One night he had requested her to come to him and massage his feet — their euphemism for sex — and he had waited for her to come to him from the women's quarters, impatient for the comfort of her plump nakedness, her soft, silken breasts. When she came at last she had knelt at the foot of the bed, her chest heaving with muffled sobs, her hands covering her face. As he took her in his arms, wondering what could have ruffled her calm good nature, she had collapsed completely against him. No comfort he could offer would make her tell what it was that was breaking her heart. At last she begged him, between great, shuddering breaths, that all she wanted in the world was another baby.

Abdul Karim had been influenced by modern ideas — he considered two children, boys at that, to be quite sufficient for a family. As one of five children, he had known poverty and the pain of giving up his dream of a university career to help support his family. He wasn't going to have his children go through the same thing. But when his wife whispered to him that she wanted one more, he relented.

Now, when he looked back, he wished he had tried to understand the real reason for her distress. The pregnancy had been a troublesome one. His mother had taken charge of both boys almost entirely while Zainab lay in bed in the women's quarters, too sick to do anything but weep silently and call upon Allah to rescue her. "It's a girl," Abdul Karim's mother had said grimly. 'Only a girl would cause so much trouble.' She had looked away out of the window into the courtyard, where her own daughter, Abdul Karim's dead sister, Ayesha, had once played and helped hang the washing.

And finally it had been a girl, stillborn, who had taken her mother with her. They were buried together in the small, unkempt graveyard where Abdul Karim went whenever he was depressed. By now the gravestone was awry and grass had grown over the mound. His father was also buried here, and three of his siblings who had died before he was six. Only Ayesha, lost Ayesha, the one he remembered as a source of comfort to a small boy — strong, generous arms, hands delicate and fragrant with henna, a smooth cheek — she was not here.

In the graveyard, Abdul Karim pays his respects to his wife's memory while his heart quails at the way the graveyard itself is disintegrating. He is afraid that if it goes to rack and ruin, overcome by vegetation and time, he will forget Zainab and the child and his guilt. Sometimes he tries to clear the weeds and tall grasses, but his delicate scholar's hands become bruised and sore quite quickly, and he sighs and thinks about the Sufi poetess Jahanara, who had written, centuries earlier: "Let the green grass grow above my grave!"

I have often pondered over the roles of knowledge or experience, on the one hand, and imagination or intuition, on the other, in the process of discovery. I believe that there is a certain fundamental conflict between the two, and knowledge, by advocating caution, tends to inhibit the flight of imagination. Therefore, a certain naiveté, unbur-dened by conventional wisdom, can sometimes be a positive asset.
Harish-Chandra, Indian mathematician (1923–1983).

Gangadhar, his friend from school, was briefly a master of Hindi literature at the municipal school and is now an academician at the Amravati Heritage Library, and a poet in his spare time. He is the only person to whom Abdul Karim can confide his secret passion.

In time, he too becomes intrigued with the idea of infinity. While Abdul Karim pores over Cantor and Riemann, and tries to make meaning from the Prime Number theorem, Gangadhar raids the library and brings forth treasures. Every week, when Abdul Karim walks the two miles to Gangadhar's house, where he is led by the servant to the comfortable drawing room with its gracious, if aging, mahogany furniture, the two men share what they've learned over cups of cardamom tea and a chess game. Gangadhar cannot understand higher mathematics but he can sympathize with the frustrations of the knowledge-seeker, and he has known what it is like to chip away at the wall of ignorance and burst into the light of understanding. He digs out quotes from Aryabhata and Al-Khwarizmi, and tells his friend such things as: "Did you know, Abdul, that the Greeks and Romans did not like the idea of infinity? Aristotle argued against it, and proposed a finite universe. Of the yunaanis, only Archimedes dared to attempt to scale that peak. He came up with the notion that different infinite quantities could be compared, that one infinite could be greater or smaller than another infinite…"

And on another occasion: "The French mathematician, Jacques Hadamard… He was the one who proved the Prime Number theorem that has you in such ecstasies… he says there are four stages to mathematical discovery. Not very different from the experience of the artist or poet, if you think about it. The first is to study and be familiar with what is known. The next is to let these ideas turn in your mind, as the earth regenerates by lying fallow between plantings. Then — with luck — there is the flash of insight, the illuminating moment when you discover something new and feel in your bones that it must be true. The final stage is to verify — to subject that epiphany to the rigours of mathematical proof…"

Abdul Karim feels that if he can simply go through Hadamard's first two stages, perhaps Allah will reward him with a flash of insight. And perhaps not. If he had hopes of being another Ramanujan, those hopes are gone now. But no true Lover has ever turned from the threshold of the Beloved's house, even knowing he will not be admitted through the doors.

"What worries me," he confides to Gangadhar during one of these discussions, "what has always worried me, is Gödel's Incompleteness theorem. According to Gödel, there can be statements in mathematics that are not provable. He showed that the Continuum Hypothesis of Cantor was one of these statements. Poor Cantor, he lost his sanity trying to prove something that cannot be proved or disproved! What if all our unproven ideas on prime numbers, on infinity, are statements like that? If they can't be tested against the constraints of mathematical logic, how will we ever know if they are true?"

Vandana Singh

This bothers him very much. He pores over the proof of Gödel's theorem, seeking to understand it, to get around it. Gangadhar encourages him:

"You know, in the old tales, every great treasure is guarded by a proportionally great monster. Perhaps Gödel's theorem is the djinn that guards the truth you seek. Maybe instead of slaying it, you have to, you know, befriend it…"

Through his own studies, through discussions with Gangadhar, Abdul Karim begins to feel again that his true companions are Archimedes, Al-Khwarizmi. Khayyam, Aryabhata, Bhaskar. Riemann, Cantor, Gauss, Ramanujan, Hardy.

They are the masters, before whom he is as a humble student, an apprentice following their footprints up the mountainside. The going is rough. He is getting old, after all. He gives himself up to dreams of mathematics, rousing himself only to look after the needs of his mother, who is growing more and more frail.

After a while, even Gangadhar admonishes him.

"A man cannot live like this, so obsessed. Will you let yourself go the way of Cantor and Gödel? Guard your sanity, my friend. You have a duty to your mother, to society."

Abdul Karim cannot make Gangadhar understand. His mind sings with mathematics.

The limit of a function $f(N)$ as N goes to infinity….

So many questions he asks himself begin like this. The function $f(N)$ may be the prime counting function, or the number of nested dolls of matter, or the extent of the universe. It may be abstract, like a parameter in a mathematical space, or earthy, like the branching of wrinkles in the face of his mother, growing older and older in the paved courtyard of his house, under the litchi trees. Older and older, without quite dying, as though she were determined to live Zeno's paradox.

He loves his mother the way he loves the litchi tree; for being there, for making him what he is, for giving him shelter and succour.

The limit... as N goes to infinity...

So begin many theorems of calculus. Abdul Karim wonders what kind of calculus governs his mother's slow arc into dying. What if life did not require a minimum threshold of conditions — what if death were merely a limit of some function $f(N)$ as N goes to infinity?

A world in which human life is but a pawn
A world filled with death-worshippers,
Where death is cheaper than life...
That world is not my world...
Sahir Ludhianvi, Indian poet (1921–1980)

While Abdul Karim dabbles in the mathematics of the infinite, as so many deluded fools and geniuses have done, the world changes.

He is vaguely aware that there are things going on in the world — that people live and die, that there are political upheavals, that this is the hottest summer yet and already a thousand people have died of the heat wave in Northern India. He knows that Death also stands at his mother's shoulder, waiting, and he does what he can for her. Although he has not always observed the five daily prayers, he does the namaz now, with her. She has already started becoming the citizen of another country — she lives in little leaps and bends of time long gone, calling for Ayesha one moment, and for her long-dead husband the next. Conversations from her lost girlhood emerge from her trembling mouth. In her few moments of clarity she calls upon Allah to take her away.

Dutiful as he is to his mother, Abdul Karim is relieved to be able to get away once a week for a chess game and conversation with Gangadhar. He has a neighbour's aunt look in on his mother during that time. Heaving a sigh or two, he makes his way through the familiar lanes of his childhood, his shoes scuffing up dust under the ancient jamun trees that he once climbed as a child.

He greets his neighbours: old Ameen Khan Sahib sitting on his *charpai*, wheezing over his *hookah;* the Ali twins, madcap boys chasing a bicycle tyre with a stick; Imran at the *paan* shop. He crosses, with some trepidation, the increasingly congested market road, past the faded awnings of Munshilal and Sons, past a rickshaw stand into another quiet lane, this one shaded with jacaranda trees. Gangadhar's house is a modest white bungalow, stained an indeterminate gray from many monsoons. The creak of the wooden gate in the compound wall is as familiar a greeting as Gangadhar's welcome.

But the day comes when there is no chess game at Gangadhar's house.

The servant boy — not Gangadhar — ushers him into the familiar room. Sitting down in his usual chair, Abdul Karim notices that the chess board has not been laid out. Sounds come from the inner rooms of the house: women's voices, heavy objects being dragged across the floor.

An elderly man comes into the room and stops short as though surprised to see Abdul Karim. He looks vaguely familiar. Then Abdul remembers that he is some relative of Gangadhar's wife — an uncle, perhaps — and he lives on the other side of the city. They have met once or twice at some family celebration.

"What are you doing here?" the man says, without any of the usual courtesies. He is white-haired but of vigorous build.

Puzzled and a little affronted, Abdul Karim says:

"I am here for my chess game with Gangadhar. Is he not at home?"

"There will be no chess game today. Haven't you people done enough harm? Are you here to mock us in our sorrow? Well, let me tell you…"

"What happened?" Abdul Karim's indignation is dissolving in a wave of apprehension. "What are you talking about? Is Gangadhar all right?'

"Perhaps you don't know," says the man, his tone mocking. "Some of your people burned a bus on Paharia road yesterday evening. There were ten people on it, all Hindus, coming back from a family ceremony at a temple. They all perished horribly. Word has it that you people did it. Didn't even let the children get off the bus. Now the whole town is in turmoil. Who knows what might happen? Gangadhar and I are taking his family to a safer part of town."

Abdul Karim's eyes are wide with shock. He can find no words.

"All these hundreds of years we Hindus have tolerated you people. Even though you Muslims raided and pillaged us over the centuries, we let you build your mosques, worship your God. And this is how you pay us!"

In one instant Abdul Karim has become "you people." He wants to say that he did not lift an arm to hurt those who perished on the bus. His were not the hands that set the fire. But no words come out.

"Can you imagine it, Master Sahib? Can you see the flames? Hear their screams? Those people will never go home…"

"I can imagine it," Abdul Karim says, grimly now. He rises to his feet, but just then Gangadhar enters the room. He has surely heard part of the conversation because he puts his hands on Abdul Karim's shoulders, gently, recognizing him as the other man has not done. This is Abdul Karim, his friend, whose sister, all those years ago, never came home.

Gangadhar turns to his wife's uncle.

"Uncle, please. Abdul Karim is not like those miscreants. A kinder man I have never known! And as yet it is not known who the ruffians are, although the whole town is filled with rumours. Abdul, please sit down! This is a measure of the times we live in, that we can say such things to each other. Alas! Kalyug is indeed upon us."

Abdul Karim sits down, but he is shaking. All thoughts of mathematics have vanished from his mind. He is filled with disgust and revulsion for the barbarians who committed this atrocity, for human beings in general. What a degraded species we are! To take the name of Ram or Allah, or Jesus, and to burn and destroy under one aegis or another — that is what our history has been.

The uncle, shaking his head, has left the room. Gangadhar is talking history to Abdul, apologizing for his uncle.

"…a matter of political manipulation," he says. "The British colonialists looked for our weakness, exploited it, set us against each other. Opening the door to hell is easy enough — but closing it is hard. All those years, before British rule, we lived in relative peace. Why is it that we cannot close that door they opened? After all, what religion tells us to slay our neighbour?"

"Does it matter?" Abdul Karim says bitterly. "We humans are a depraved species, my friend. My fellow Muslims address every prayer to Allah, the Merciful and Compassionate. You Hindus, with your *Isha Vasyam Idam Sarvam* — the divine pervades all. The Christians talk on about turning the other cheek. And yet each of them has hands that are stained in blood. We pervert everything — we take the words of peace spoken by prophets and holy men and turn them into weapons with which to kill each other!"

He is shaking so hard that he can barely speak.

"It is in mathematics... only in mathematics that I see Allah..."

"Quiet now," Gangadhar says. He calls for the servant to bring some water for the master sahib. Abdul Karim drinks and wipes his mouth. The suitcases are being brought out from inside the house. There is a taxi in front.

"Listen, my friend," Gangadhar says, "you must look to your safety. Go home now and lock your doors, and look after your mother. I am sending my family away and I will join them in a day or so. When this madness has passed I will come and look for you!"

Abdul Karim goes home. So far everything looks normal — the wind is blowing litter along in the streets, the *paan* shop is open, people throng the bus-stop. Then he notices that there aren't any children, even though the summer holidays are going on.

The vegetable market is very busy. People are buying up everything like crazy. He buys a few potatoes, onions and a large gourd, and goes home. He locks the door. His mother, no longer up to cooking meals, watches as he cooks. After they eat and he has her tucked into bed, he goes to his study and opens a book on mathematics.

One day passes, perhaps two — he does not keep track. He remembers to take care of his mother but often forgets to eat. His mother lives,

Infinities

more and more, in that other world. His sisters and brother call from other towns, anxious about the reports of escalating violence; he tells them not to worry. When things are back to normal they will come and see him and their mother.

How marvelous, the Universal Mystery
That only a true Lover can comprehend!
Bulleh Shah, eighteenth century Punjabi Sufi poet

Logic merely sanctions the conquests of the intuition.
Jacques Hadamard, French mathematician (1865–1963)

One morning he emerges from the darkness of his study into the sunny courtyard. Around him the old city writhes and burns, but Abdul Karim sees and hears nothing but mathematics. He sits in his old cane chair, picks up a stick lying on the ground and begins to draw mathematical symbols in the dust.

There is a *farishta* standing at the edge of his vision.

He turns slowly. The dark shadow stays there, waits. This time Abdul Karim is quick on his feet, despite a sudden twinge of pain in one knee. He walks toward the door, the beckoning arm, and steps through.

For a moment he is violently disoriented — it occurs to him that he has spun through a different dimension into this hidden world. Then the darkness before his eyes dissipates, and he beholds wonders.

All is hushed. He is looking at a vast sweep of land and sky unlike anything he has ever seen. Dark, pyramidal shapes stud the landscape, great monuments to something beyond his understanding. There is a vast, polyhedral object suspended in a pale orange sky that has no sun. Only a diffuse luminescence pervades this sky. He looks at his feet, still in his familiar, worn sandals, and sees all around, in the sand, little fish-like creatures wriggling and spawning. Some of the sand has worked its way between his toes, and it feels warm and rubbery, not like sand at all. He takes a deep breath and smells something strange, like burnt rubber mixed with his own sweat. The shadow stands by his side, looking solid at last, almost human but for the absence of neck and the profusion of limbs — their number seems to vary with time — at the moment Abdul Karim counts five.

The dark orifice in the head opens and closes, but no sound comes out. Instead Abdul feels as though a thought has been placed in his mind, a package that he will open later.

He walks with the shadow across the sands to the edge of a quiet sea. The water, if that is what it is, is foaming and bubbling gently, and within its depths he sees ghostly shapes moving, and the hints of complex structure far below. Arabesques form in the depths, break up, and form again. He licks his dry lips, tastes metal and salt.

He looks at his companion, who bids him pause. A door opens. They step through into another universe.

It is different, this one. It is all air and light, the whole space hung with great, translucent webbing. Each strand in the web is a hollow tube within which liquid creatures flow. Smaller, solid beings float in the emptiness between the web strands.

Speechless, he stretches out his hand toward a web-strand. Its delicacy reminds him of the filigreed silver anklets his wife used to wear. To his complete surprise a tiny being floating within the strand stops. It is like a plump, watery comma, translucent and without any features he can recognize, and yet he has the notion that he is being looked at, examined, and that at the other end is also wonder.

The web-strand touches him, and he feels its cool, alien smoothness on a fingertip.

A door opens. They step through.

It is dizzying, this wild ride. Sometimes he gets flashes of his own world, scenes of trees and streets, and distant blue hills. There are indications that these flashes are at different points in time — at one point he sees a vast army of soldiers, their plumed helmets catching the sunlight, and thinks he must be in the time of the Roman Empire. Another time he thinks he is back home, because he sees before him his own courtyard. But there is an old man sitting in his cane chair, drawing patterns in the dust with a stick. A shadow falls across the ground. Someone he cannot see is stealing up behind the old man. Is that a knife agleam in the stranger's hand? What is this he is seeing? He tries to call out, but no sound emerges. The scene blurs — a door opens, and they step through.

Abdul Karim is trembling. Has he just witnessed his own death?

He remembers that Archimedes died that way — he had been drawing circles, engrossed with a problem in geometry, when a barbarian of a soldier came up behind him and killed him.

But there is no time to ponder. He is lost in a merry-go-round of universes, each different and strange. The shadow gives him a glimpse of so many, Abdul Karim has long lost count. He puts thoughts of Death away from him and loses himself in wonder.

His companion opens door after door. The face, featureless except for the orifice that opens and shuts, gives no hint of what the shadow is thinking. Abdul Karim wants to ask: who are you? Why are you doing this? He knows, of course, the old story of how the angel Gabriel came to the Prophet Mohammad one night and took him on a celestial journey, a grand tour of the heavens. But the shadow does not look like an angel; it has no face, no wings, its gender is indeterminate. And in any case, why should the angel Gabriel concern himself with a humble mathematics master in a provincial town, a person of no consequence in the world?

And yet, he is here. Perhaps Allah has a message for him; His ways are ineffable, after all. Exultation fills Abdul Karim as he beholds marvel after marvel.

At last they pause in a place where they are suspended in a yellow sky. As Abdul Karim experiences the giddy absence of gravity, accompanied by a sudden jolt of nausea that slowly recedes — as he turns in mid-air, he notices that the sky is not featureless but covered with delicate tessellations: geometric shapes intertwine, merge and new ones emerge. The colours change too, from yellow to green, lilac, mauve. All at once it seems as though numberless eyes are opening in the sky, one after the other, and as he turns he sees all the other universes flashing past him. A kaleidoscope, vast beyond his imaginings. He is at the centre of it all, in a space between all spaces, and he can feel in his bones a low, irregular throbbing, like the beating of a drum. Boom, boom, goes the drum. Boom boom boom. Slowly he realizes that what he is seeing and feeling is part of a vast pattern.

In that moment Abdul Karim has the flash of understanding he has been waiting for all his life.

For so long he has been playing with the transcendental numbers, trying to fathom Cantor's ideas; at the same time Riemann's notions of the prime numbers have fascinated him. In idle moments he has wondered if they are connected at a deeper level. Despite their apparent randomness the primes have their own regularity, as hinted by the unproven Riemann hypothesis; he sees at last that if you think of prime numbers as the terrain of a vast country, and if your view of reality is a two-dimensional plane that intersects this terrain at some height above the surface, perhaps at an angle, then of course what you see will appear to be random. Tops of hills. Bits of valleys. Only the parts of the terrain that cross your plane of reality will be apparent. Unless you can see the entire landscape in its multi-dimensional splendour, the topography will make no sense.

He sees it: the bare bones of creation, here, in this place where all the universes branch off, the thudding heart of the metacosmos. In the scaffolding, the skeletal structure of the multiverse is beautifully apparent. This is what Cantor had a glimpse of, then, this vast topography. Understanding opens in his mind as though the metacosmos has itself spoken to him. He sees that of all the transcendental numbers, only a few — infinite still, but not the whole set — are marked as doorways to other universes, and each is labelled by a prime number. Yes. Yes. Why this is so, what deeper symmetry it reflects, what law or regularity of Nature undreamed of by the physicists of his world, he does not know.

The space where primes live — the topology of the infinite universes — he sees it in that moment. No puny function as yet dreamed of by humans can encompass the vastness — the inexhaustible beauty of this place. He knows that he can never describe this in the familiar symbols of the mathematics that he knows, that while he experiences the truth of the Riemann hypothesis, as a corollary to this greater, more luminous reality, he cannot sit down and verify it through a conventional proof. No human language as yet exists, mathematical or otherwise, that can describe what he knows in his bones to be true. Perhaps he, Abdul Karim, will invent the beginnings of such a language. Hadn't the great poet Iqbal interpreted the Prophet's celestial journey to mean that the heavens are within our grasp?

A twist, and a door opens. He steps into the courtyard of his house. He turns around, but the courtyard is empty. The *farishta* is gone.

Abdul Karim raises his eyes to the heavens. Rain clouds, dark as the proverbial beloved's hair, sweep across the sky; the litchi tree over his head is dancing in the swift breeze. The wind has drowned out the sounds of a ravaged city. A red flower comes blowing over the courtyard wall and is deposited at his feet.

Abdul Karim's hair is blown back, a nameless ecstasy fills him; he feels Allah's breath on his face.

He says into the wind:

Dear Merciful and Compassionate God, I stand before your wondrous universe, filled with awe; help me, weak mortal that I am, to raise my gaze above the sordid pettiness of everyday life, the struggles and quarrels of mean humanity… Help me to see the beauty of your Works, from the full flower of the red silk cotton tree to the exquisite mathematical grace by which you have created numberless universes in the space of a man's step.

I know now that my true purpose in this sad world is to stand in humble awe before your magnificence, and to sing a paean of praise to you with every breath I take...

He feels weak with joy. Leaves whirl in the courtyard like mad dervishes; a drop or two of rain falls, obliterating the equation he had scratched in the dust with his stick. He has lost his chance at mathematical genius a long time ago; he is nobody, only a teacher of mathematics at a school, humbler than a clerk in a government office — yet Allah has favoured him with this great insight. Perhaps he is now worthy of speech with Ramanujan and Archimedes and all the ones in between. But all he wants to do is to run out into the lane and go shouting through the city: see, my friends, open your eyes and see what I see! But he knows they would think him mad; only Gangadhar would understand... if not the mathematics then the impulse, the importance of the whole discovery.

He leaps out of the house, into the lane.

This blemished radiance... this night-stung dawn
Is not the dawn we waited for...
Faiz Ahmed Faiz, Pakistani poet (1911–1984)

Where all is broken
Where each soul's athirst, each glance
Filled with confusion, each heart
Weighed with sorrow...
Is this a world, or chaos?
Sahir Ludhianvi, Indian poet (1921–1980)

But what is this?

The lane is empty. There are broken bottles everywhere. The windows and doors of his neighbours' houses are shuttered and barred, like closed eyes. Above the sound of the rain he hears shouting in the distance. Why is there a smell of burning?

He remembers then, what he had learned at Gangadhar's house. Securing the door behind him, he begins to run as fast as his old-man legs will carry him.

The market is burning.

Smoke pours out of smashed store fronts, even as the rain falls. There is broken glass on the pavement; a child's wooden doll in the middle of the road, decapitated. Soggy pages filled with neat columns of figures lie scattered everywhere, the remains of a ledger. Quickly he crosses the road.

Gangadhar's house is in ruins. Abdul Karim wanders through the open doors, stares blindly at the blackened walls. The furniture is mostly gone. Only the chess table stands untouched in the middle of the front room.

Frantically he searches through the house, entering the inner rooms for the first time. Even the curtains have been ripped from the windows.

There is nobody.

He runs out of the house. Gangadhar's wife's family — he does not know where they live. How to find out if Gangadhar is safe?

The neighbouring house belongs to a Muslim family that Abdul Karim knows only from visits to the mosque. He pounds on the door. He thinks he hears movement behind the door, sees the upstairs curtains twitch — but nobody answers his frantic entreaties. At last, defeated, his hands bleeding, he walks slowly home, looking about him in horror. Is this truly his city, his world?

Allah, Allah, why have you abandoned me?

He has beheld the glory of Allah's workmanship. Then why this? Were all those other universes, other realities a dream?

The rain pours down.

There is someone lying on his face in a ditch. The rain has wet the shirt on his back, made the blood run. As Abdul Karim starts toward him, wondering who it is, whether he is dead or alive — young, from the back it could be Ramdas or Imran — he sees behind him, at the entrance to the lane, a horde of young men. Some of them may be his students — they can help.

They are moving with a predatory sureness that frightens him. He sees that they have sticks and stones.

They are coming like a tsunami, a thunderclap, leaving death and ruin in their wake. He hears their shouts through the rain.

Abdul Karim's courage fails him. He runs to his house, enters, locks and bars the door and closes all the windows. He checks on his mother, who is sleeping. The telephone is dead. The *dal* for their meal has boiled away. He turns off the gas and goes back to the door, putting his ear against it. He does not want to risk looking out of the window.

Over the rain he hears the young men go past at a run. In the distance there is a fusillade of shots. More sounds of running feet, then, just the rain.

Are the police here? The army?

Something or someone is scratching at the door. Abdul Karim is transfixed with terror. He stands there, straining to hear over the pitter-patter of the rain. On the other side, somebody moans.

He opens the door. The lane is empty, roaring with rain. At his feet there is the body of a young woman.

She opens her eyes. She's dressed in a *salwaar kameez* that has been half-torn off her body — her long hair is wet with rain and blood, plastered over her neck and shoulders. There is blood on her *salwaar*, blood oozing from a hundred little cuts and welts on her skin.

Her gaze focuses.

"Master Sahib..."

He is taken aback. Is she someone he knows? Perhaps an old student, grown up?

Quickly he half-carries, half-pulls her into the house and secures the door. With some difficulty he lifts her carefully on to the divan in the drawing room, which is already staining with her blood. She coughs.

"My child, who did this to you? Let me find a doctor..."

Infinities

"No," she says. "It's too late." Her breath rasps and she coughs again. Tears well up in the dark eyes.

"Master Sahib, please, let me die! My husband... my son... They must not see me take my last breath. Not like this. They will suffer. They will want revenge... Please... cut my wrists..."

She's raising her wrists to his horrified face, but all he can do is to take them in his shaking hands.

"My daughter," he says, and doesn't know what to say. Where will he find a doctor in the mayhem? Can he bind her cuts? Even as he thinks these thoughts he knows that life is ebbing from her. Blood is pooling on his divan, dripping down to the floor. She does not need him to cut her wrists.

"Tell me, who are the ruffians who did this?"

She whispers: "I don't know who they were. I had just stepped out of the house for a moment. My family... don't tell them, Master Sahib! When I'm gone just tell them... tell them I died in a safe place..."

"Daughter, what is your husband's name?"

Her eyes are enormous. She is gazing at him without comprehension, as though she is already in another world.

He can't tell if she is Muslim or Hindu. If she wore a vermilion dot on her forehead, it has long since been washed off by the rain.

His mother is standing at the door of the drawing room. She wails suddenly and loudly, flings herself by the side of the dying woman.

"Ayesha! Ayesha, my life!"

Tears fall down Abdul Karim's face. He tries to disengage his mother. Tries to tell her: this is not Ayesha, just another woman whose body has become a battleground over which men make war. At last he has to lift his mother in his arms, her body so frail that he fears it might break — he takes her to her bed, where she crumples, sobbing and calling Ayesha's name.

Back in the drawing-room, the young woman's eyes flicker to him. Her voice is barely above a whisper.

"Master Sahib, cut my wrists... I beseech you, in the Almighty's name! Take me somewhere safe... Let me die..."

Then the veil falls over her eyes again and her body goes limp.

Time stands still for Abdul Karim.

Then he senses something familiar, and turns slowly. The *farishta* is waiting.

Abdul Karim picks up the woman in his arms, awkwardly arranging the bloody divan cover over her half-naked body. In the air, a door opens.

Staggering a little, his knees protesting, he steps through the door.

After three universes he finds the place.

It is peaceful. There is a rock rising from a great turquoise sea of sand. The blue sand laps against the rock, making lulling, sibilant sounds. In the high, clear air, winged creatures call to each other between endless rays of light. He squints in the sudden brightness.

He closes her eyes, buries her deep at the base of the rock, under the blue, flowing sand.

He stands there, breathing hard from the exertion, his hands bruised, thinking he should say something. But what? He does not even know if she's Muslim or Hindu. When she spoke to him earlier, what word had she used for God? Was it Allah or Ishwar, or something else?

He can't remember.

At last he says the Al-Fatihah, and, stumbling a little, recites whatever little he knows of the Hindu scriptures. He ends with the phrase *Isha Vasyamidam Sarvam*.

Tears run off his cheeks into the blue sand, and disappear without leaving a trace.

The *farishta* waits.

"Why didn't you do something!" Abdul Karim rails at the shadow. He falls to his knees in the blue sand, weeping. "Why, if you are truly a *farishta*, didn't you save my sister?"

He sees now that he has been a fool — this shadow creature is no angel, and he, Abdul Karim, no Prophet.

He weeps for Ayesha, for this nameless young woman, for the body he saw in the ditch, for his lost friend Gangadhar.

The shadow leans toward him. Abdul Karim gets up, looks around once, and steps through the door.

He steps out into his drawing-room. The first thing he discovers is that his mother is dead. She looks quite peaceful, lying in her bed, her white hair flowing over the pillow.

She might be asleep, her face is so calm.

He stands there for a long time, unable to weep. He picks up the phone — there is still no dial tone. After that he goes about methodically cleaning up the drawing-room, washing the floor, taking the bedding off the divan. Later, after the rain has stopped, he will burn it in the courtyard. Who will notice another fire in the burning city?

When everything is cleaned up, he lies down next to his mother's body like a small boy and goes to sleep.

When you left me, my brother, you took away the book
In which is writ the story of my life…
Faiz Ahmed Faiz, Pakistani poet (1911–1984)

The sun is out. An uneasy peace lies over the city. His mother's funeral is over. Relatives have come and gone — his younger son came, but did not stay. The older son sent a sympathy card from America.

Gangadhar's house is still empty, a blackened ruin. Whenever he has ventured out, Abdul Karim has asked about his friend's whereabouts. The last he heard was that Gangadhar was alone in the house when the mob came, and his Muslim neighbours sheltered him until he could join his wife and children at her parents' house. But it has been so long that he does not believe it any more. He has also heard that Gangadhar was dragged out, hacked to pieces and his body set on fire. The city has calmed down — the army had to be called in — but it is still rife with rumours. Hundreds of people are missing. Civil rights groups comb the town, interviewing people, revealing, in clipped, angry press statements, the negligence of the state government, the collusion of the police in some of the violence. Some of them came to his house, too, very clean, very young people, burning with an idealism that, however misplaced, is comforting to see. He has said nothing about the young woman who died in his arms, but he prays for that bereft family every day.

For days he has ignored the shadow at his shoulder. But now he knows that the sense of betrayal will fade. Whose fault is it, after all, that he ascribed to the creatures he once called *farishte* the attributes of angels? Could angels, even, save human beings from themselves?

The creatures watch us with a child's curiosity, he thinks, but they do not understand. Just as their own worlds are incomprehensible to me, so are our ways to them. They are not Allah's minions.

The space where the universes branch off — the heart of the metacosmos — now appears remote to him, like a dream. He is ashamed of his earlier arrogance. How can he possibly fathom Allah's creation in one glance? No finite mind can, in one meagre lifetime, truly comprehend the vastness, the grandeur of Allah's scheme. All we can do is to discover a bit of the truth here, a bit there, and thus to sing His praises.

But there is so much pain in Abdul Karim's soul that he cannot imagine writing down one syllable of the new language of the infinite. His dreams are haunted by the horrors he has seen, the images of his mother and the young woman who died in his arms. He cannot even say his prayers. It is as though Allah has abandoned him, after all.

The daily task of living — waking up, performing his ablutions, setting the little pot on the gas stove to boil water for one cup of tea, to drink that tea alone — unbearable thought! To go on, after so many have died —

to go on without his mother, his children, without Gangadhar… Everything appears strangely remote: his aging face in the mirror, the old house, even the litchi tree in his courtyard. The familiar lanes of his childhood hold memories that no longer seem to belong to him. Outside, the neighbours are in mourning; old Ameen Khan Sahib weeps for his grandson; Ramdas is gone, Imran is gone. The wind still carries the soot of the burnings. He finds little piles of ashes everywhere, in the cracks in the cement of his courtyard, between the roots of the trees in the lane. He breathes the dead. How can he regain his heart, living in a world so wracked with pain? In this world there is no place for the likes of him. No place for henna-scented hands rocking a child to sleep, for old-woman hands tending a garden. And no place at all for the austere beauty of mathematics.

He's thinking this when a shadow falls across the ground in front of him. He has been sitting in his courtyard, idly writing mathematical expressions with his stick on the dusty ground. He does not know whether the knife-bearer is his son, or an enraged Hindu, but he finds himself ready for his death. The creatures who have watched him for so long will witness it, and wonder. Their uncomprehending presence comforts him.

He turns and rises. It is Gangadhar, his friend, who holds out his empty arms in an embrace.

Abdul Karim lets his tears run over Gangadhar's shirt. As waves of relief wash over him he knows that he has held Death at bay this time, but it will come. It will come, he has seen it. Archimedes and Ramanujan, Khayyam and Cantor died with epiphanies on their lips before an indifferent world. But this moment is eternal.

"Allah be praised!" says Abdul Karim.

Thirst

IN THE DREAM THERE were snakes coiling about her, dark and glossy as the hairs on her head, and an altar, and the smell of sandalwood incense, her mother's favourite kind. When her eyes opened, she could not remember for a moment who she was. Even the familiar room, with the whitewash peeling off the walls and summer dust on the sill of the open window, the sag of the bed, the curve of the man's shoulders as he lay in sleep with his back to her — all that seemed imbued with remoteness, as though it had nothing whatever to do with *her*. Slowly her name came to her — Susheela — and with it the full weight of her misery returned. Her husband stirred in sleep, but he did not turn towards her.

Then she remembered (as she sat up very carefully so as not to wake her husband) that tomorrow was the day of Naag Panchami, the Snake Festival, and *that* was why the dream had come. The monsoons were late, and this was the hottest summer ever. Perhaps it would rain tomorrow. A festival day rain would be a good thing. She slipped out of bed, bathed quickly using an inadequate half a bucketful of water and dressed in a pink cotton sari. An early morning hush lay deep over the house; the ceiling fans had wound down during the night (another power failure) and even the birds in the bougainvillea outside the window seemed reluctant to break the silence. As Susheela entered the kitchen, she heard the creak of her mother-in-law's bed from the other end of the house and the old woman's plastic slippers slapping the bare floor as she shuffled to the bathroom. Susheela's son was very likely still asleep in his grandmother's bed; she could see him in her mind's eye, forehead beaded with sweat, plump hands closed into fists, cheeks flushed with heat, lips tremulous with the passage of some childish dream. For a moment she wanted desperately to see him and hold him, but she could not face the old lady just yet. Instead she put the tea water on to boil and turned on the taps so that when the water came (one precious hour in the morning and one in the evening) the buckets would begin to fill for the day's use. Now the tap only belched warm air; heat came in from the small window like the breath of a hungry animal.

She stood at the window, looking out into the courtyard and the untended garden behind it. The drought had reduced the back garden to a mass of dead, spiny shrubs dotting withered grass. Only the little harsingar tree stood proud, its young, leafy branches dotted with tiny orange and white flowers. It had survived on a daily cupful of water and her love.

Afterwards, as she rolled *paratha* dough for her husband's breakfast, hoping she would not (again) make him late for office, she heard the household stir; and the water came gurgling out of the taps. She felt the old hunger in her as though she was waiting for something. As the earth waits for rain, she thought, licking her dry lips.

She thought of the lake in the park, and — despite herself — the thin face of the gardener who worked there, and the way he said *namaste* so respectfully while his eyes looked at her in a way that dissolved all distance between them, all barriers of class and caste and propriety… She really shouldn't go there so often. But Kishore loves it, her mind said rebelliously, and she thought of how her little boy loved to walk under the trees and watch the parakeets eat the neem berries. She would make up stories for him about imaginary people who lived in the ruins around the lake and ate nothing but milk-sweets all day.

The park was on the way to the vegetable market that came up in the late afternoon like a miniature city on the sidewalks, complete with towers of jewel-toned purple eggplants and cascades of coriander leaves and citadels of fat, shiny little onions. The market was her excuse for surreptitious visits to the lake in the park, with her boy (poor, innocent boy!) as chaperone and protector. Sweat rolled off her temples; she dabbed at it with the free end of her sari and thought of the translucent coolness of the lake, the lips of the water against her bare toes. I am a cursed woman, she thought to herself with a shudder. My mother-in-law is right, the water draws me and draws me, to what other thing but death. Curses do run in families. She thought of her own mother, and her maternal grandmother, and she resolved that today she would not go to the lake, even though that would make Kishore cry.

In the end she broke her promise to herself, as she had done many times before. In the dry, breathless heat of the day, Susheela felt as though the air in her lungs had turned solid. She went blindly about her tasks, cooking and serving lunch, piling the steel dishes noisily in the sink for the servant boy to wash when he came in the evening. The grandmother took Kishore off for his afternoon nap. Susheela collected the kitchen leavings — potato peels, turnip ends and scraps from lunch — into a battered tin and went up the short driveway to the front gate. Dead leaves crunched under her feet. Piling the refuse by the side of the gate, she waited for Muniya, the milkman's ancient cow, to come meandering down the lane.

The lane shimmered in the heat. The three shisham trees in the garden stood very still, their small, round leaves drooping. Behind her the house crouched like a yellow cat. Plaster flaked off its front, revealing an underflesh of burnt red brick. Susheela leaned on the gate. A breeze, no more than a breath, stirred the dead leaves on the trees, smelling of dust. But Susheela smelled — or imagined she smelled — water.

Suddenly she made up her mind. She crept into the still, dark house and saw with relief that the grandmother had fallen asleep with Kishore.

The two lay together like exhausted children, damp with sweat, the old lady's arm protectively around the boy. I have not been a good mother, Susheela thought. Her eyes burned with tears. She went out into the bright and dusty afternoon.

In less than ten minutes she was at the iron fence, with the rusty, indecipherable Archeological Survey of India sign leaning over the entrance. She paused for a moment, looking around her a little apprehensively. A bicycle-repairman sat nodding under a tree with his paraphernalia around him, but there was no one else about. She let herself in through the gap in the fence where there had once been a gate; inside, tall neem trees made deep shadows. A clerk or two lay sleeping in the shade. Then she saw the gardener, sleeping, his turban spread out over his face. The bullock that had been pulling the lawn mower lay beside him like a white, humped mountain, chewing cud. Susheela crept soundlessly to the lake's edge.

The lake itself was small, more like a large pond. The edge was paved with stone, brown and weathered with age; at one end there was the old ruin with crumbling steps leading down into the quiet, green water. What ancients had built and frequented the place Susheela did not know, but it was tranquil here, under the neem trees. The water had receded with the heat of summer, but there was enough to allow a few fragile blue lotuses to bloom in the shade.

She leaned against a tree trunk, savouring the peace. Then she slipped a slender brown foot out of her embroidered shoe, over the sun-warmed stone paving and into the water. She felt the cool silk of the water on her foot, and a tremendous longing arose within her, a desire to feel the water lick the dry heat from her body, to envelop her in its fluid embrace…

Some small sound jolted her back into herself. She withdrew her foot hurriedly from the water, wiped it on the stone. What had she been about to do? A bead of sweat ran down her cheek to the corner of her mouth. Then she saw that there was something in the water, making ripples as it swam towards her. A turtle, perhaps — or a snake? She leaned forward, peering. In the emerald depths, apparitions of pale fish scattered as the thing came closer. It was a snake — a cobra.

Just as she identified it she saw a stone skimming over the water, falling a few feet short. The snake dived and disappeared.

Her skin prickled. The gardener was standing beside her.

"They say it is good to see a cobra the day before the Snake Festival," he said. He wiped the sweat off his face with his turban. 'It means rain. But better not to let the Naag Lords get too close, *behen*. Would you like some flowers? Amaltas blooms, yellow as sunlight, lovely tied in your hair, against your neck… or would you prefer… a delicate twig of harsingar?'

She edged away nervously. For a moment she imagined his fingers on the nape of her neck.

"No, I don't want anything," she said shortly. He was looking at her without any shame, as though she were a woman of his own class, not a respectably married housewife. But respectably married housewives didn't wander about parks alone.

"If ever there is anything you need… I will be happy to serve you. But tell me, where is your little boy?"

Oh, why hadn't she brought Kishore? She looked around her, terrified, and was reassured to see a young couple enter the park, holding hands surreptitiously. Some of her fear abated.

"I have to go," she said, drawing herself up. The gardener put his palms together, accepting her dismissal, his gaze licking at her face. "*Achha, behen-ji,*" he said. Yes, sister. He watched her leave. She was conscious of the movement of her hips, the slight swing of her arms, the dust she raised with every step. She did not draw breath until she was out in the lane.

She had grown up off-balance. All her life she had carried inside her an empty space that disturbed her centre of gravity, that drew her to the sheltering closeness of trees, walls, wilderness. Nothing she had done in her life — not her studentship, not marriage, not even the birth of her son — had assuaged that emptiness, that feeling of the earth waiting for rain. She was still waiting.

In her childhood the Snake Festival had been special. It was the one day she had always understood to be her own. Here in this small town where her husband had grown up, Naag Panchami would be marked only by a visit to the temple and prayers to the gods to prevent death by snakebite. But in her hometown of Ujjain, tomorrow, there would be special ceremonies and processions in the streets…

In her parents' house, every Festival day, the child Susheela had helped her mother arrange flowers and sweet offerings on the kitchen altar. Dressed in silks, Susheela had sat with her brother on the flower-strewn floor, watching as their mother lit the oil *diyas*. In the flickering light, her mother would become remote and solemn, chanting the ancient Sanskrit phrases: homage to the snakes of the earth. Homage to the snakes in the rays of sun, the tree-snakes. Homage to the snakes of the waters, homage to them all. The names of the Snake lords were then recited: Anantha, who supports the earth in his coils; Vasuki the king, who rules their fabulous, gem-studded underworld city; Takshaka; Muchilinda; all the greater and the lesser lords. They bring us life, her mother would say; they foster fertility and renewal. They bring also death. They are in the fire of Agni and in the primeval ocean.

Her mother would turn from the altar to her children and take the child Susheela onto her lap. Then the stories would come, wondrous tales, fierce or sad; about the Snake divinities speaking to gods and mingling secretly with humans; about their exquisite underwater palaces, where they kept the knowledge and wisdom they had accumulated, waiting until humankind was ready for the gift. As her mother spoke her hands would rise and fall in smooth and sudden gestures, and the stories, built thus of words and hands, would come to life in the fragrant air. Her mother's urbanized Hindi would give way to the sing-song village dialect she had spoken as a girl.

Even as a five-year-old, Susheela was aware that what was being passed on to them on these occasions was meant particularly for her; that her brother, sitting wistful-eyed across from them, was in some inexplicable way, excluded.

But the most wonderful thing about it all was that the three of them were sheltered for a while, in a cocoon of mystery and ceremony, from the mundane, silent bitterness between her parents. Her father kept away from them during Naag Panchami, leaving them to an unfamiliar peace. As she grew older, it became increasingly clear to Susheela that the undercurrents of ill-feeling in the house, the raised voices (mainly her father's) behind locked doors in the night, the misery, guilt and yearning in her mother's eyes — were all her fault. Her father treated her with a distant regard; his love he kept for his son, expressing it with his eyes whenever he looked at the boy, unaware that the boy feared him and longed to escape.

Coming home from school — she remembered how it felt to enter the dark, polished hallway, the high-arched ceilings — how the house diminished her. The respite of the garden and the parakeets in the guava trees, the three harsingar trees (her favourite kind) bright with tiny flowers... And then quite suddenly she was grown up and her marriage arranged with a stranger she had met only three times. He had come once for tea in the garden, and later they had walked together, chaperoned by her mother and aunts. She had lost her reserve, pointing out to him the trees and flowers and her favourite shady spot under the jamun tree, and he had impressed her with the way his hands touched the blossoms, the ripe fruit, so gently for such a big, quiet man. She had wanted him to touch her like that...

For the five years of her marriage, the Festival had brought her nothing but shadows from the past, and a small remembrance from her brother. Only this year — this year was different. The intensity of the old dream, the tightness in her chest, the feeling of breathless anticipation... Entering the dim stillness of the house, Susheela found herself longing for her son.

Thirst

But he was still asleep in his grandmother's bed. She wanted to hold him forever because she feared that she would not hesitate to leave him for the nameless hunger that was in her.

In the late afternoon, when the heat had abated a little, Susheela's husband came home from work. His name was Prakash, but she couldn't think of him by his name, only by the way he made her feel, a mixture of bewilderment and yearning. Kishore ran up to him at the doorway, calling "Baba!" in his high voice. The child had sulked all afternoon when she told him they were not going to the park. Finally she had made him a paper boat and told him he could play in the washing-up water. Now he held out the damp boat to his father. A brief smile broke the serious cast of her husband's face, accentuating the lines that made him look older than he was. He glanced at Susheela quickly, noncommittally, and went into the back to wash his hands, leaving in his wake a faint odour of musty offices and old ledgers. Standing in the silence and heat of the dining room, with the silver teapot and the array of delicacies arranged on the table, Susheela felt suddenly bereft of hope. How had she come to this?

Once she had almost loved him. Not at first — she remembered sitting terrified before the nuptial fire under a canopy of marigolds in the front lawn, with this man that she hardly knew. Her father had died the previous year. She had left the large suburban bungalow, the luxuriant garden that had been her refuge, and her mother, alone, serene now after years of unhappiness, but with a haunted, fragile air about her — all that, for the life of a senior accountant's wife in a strange town. Still, in the beginning, her husband's gentleness had won her over. He had been loving and attentive, filling her with a joyous, incredulous relief, allaying her fears that her married life would be as dreary and bereft of happiness as her mother's had been. She had started to fall in love with him, with his patience, his long, contemplative silences, and the inexplicable, endearing seriousness with which he took his work. But then, quite soon after the (nearly painless) birth of their son, everything had changed. Her husband suddenly began to avoid her as much as was possible, and sometimes she had caught him giving her peculiar, wary, sidelong glances that she could not fathom. It had disturbed the healthy, animal joyfulness of motherhood.

He had evaded her questions, meeting her pleas, tears and anger with a pained silence. Finally she had come to accept that things would stay this way between them. Four years later, he was still the kind, quiet man she'd known, but he had kept his distance; he no longer looked at her much, even when they (infrequently) made love.

The evening wore on — dark fell and mosquitoes came swarming in through cracks in the shutters. The power was still out so her husband lit candles in the rooms that cast large, tremulous shadows. The air was thick as a blanket.

There was a sudden loud crash in the house, and the sound of water splashing. Her mother-in-law screamed, "Susheela? *Arrey* Susheela! Look what your son just did! Don't cry, my darling..."

In the kitchen, which was lit dimly by a candle, Kishore stood soaked to the skin in the washing-up water. The bucket lay overturned on the floor. He was crying noisily, holding the soggy remains of the paper boat. As Susheela picked him up, her mother-in-law shook her head. "It's the curse on your family!" she said. "Drawn to water — and to death! He had climbed into the bucket with his boat. He would have drowned if I had not come in just then. My poor boy, what will become of him!"

"Let her be, Ma-ji," her husband said. He was standing in the doorway. He gave Susheela a quick, shy look. When she came towards the door with their son he laid his hand on the boy's dripping head.

"Susheela?"

He spoke her name tentatively, questioningly, but her eyes were already filling with tears. She stepped past him with her burden. In the bedroom she stood Kishore on the bed to dry him down and change his clothes. "I'll make you another boat tomorrow," she told him, glad that the semi-darkness hid her tears. Curses did run in families... She remembered her brother's escapades to the pond at the end of their street when they had been children, and how their father had scolded him as he stood dripping and half-naked on the polished floor of the hall. Nothing he said had made a difference to the boy; the next afternoon he would be gone again with the servant children, diving and splashing in the pond among gleaming green lily-pads, coming reluctantly home in the evenings through the dining room window, all aglow with his adventure, swearing her to secrecy...

The power came back suddenly. Susheela blinked in the light. The ceiling fans began their laborious circumlocutions, and the still air began to move. Her son laughed, jumped off the bed and went to find his father, holding out his little arms like airplane wings.

Late that evening, after the servant-boy had finished doing the dinner dishes and been dismissed, Susheela stood alone in the kitchen, finishing the day's chores. She could hear the low sound of the TV from the drawing room. In the small bedroom that her son shared with his grandmother, her mother-in-law was singing some old, half-remembered lullaby. In the storeroom, above the bins and sacks of grain, the gods gazed at Susheela from the altar — a brass statuette of Vishnu the Creator, reclining under the sheltering hood of the great serpent Ananth; Krishna with his flute, a meditative Buddha and a print of Lord Shiva. She cleaned the altar of dead flowers, lit an incense stick and watched the smoke curl up to the rough, white-washed ceiling.

One more task remained. She filled a steel bowl with cold milk, put the rest of the milk into the small fridge, and took the flashlight. She had watched her mother do this every night for years in their home in Ujjain. Now, with her mother gone, the ritual gave her comfort. She went into the silent, moonlit courtyard behind the house, staying close to the wall. She walked up to the harsingar tree, which stood green and proud amidst the detritus of dead bushes and thorny shrubs. It always bloomed out of season, as though it obeyed the laws of some other universe. Under the tree lay a great stone, upon which she set down the steel bowl of milk. She turned off the flashlight. Would the snakes come, as her mother had always said? Usually she'd leave the milk on the stone and go back into the house, but today she wanted to wait.

The fragrance of the harsingar flowers filled her nostrils. The little tree was doing well. It had appeared last winter, the day before the festival of Diwali. She had just got back from the market with her mother-in-law. The servant boy did not know who had come into the compound in the afternoon and planted the tree. Susheela's mother-in-law said it must be the gardener who worked in the park — he had been trying to hire himself out in the neighbourhood. Or maybe it was the lady from the Big House, the wife of Susheela's husband's supervisor, who had the huge ornamental garden that her mother-in-law had frequently admired. That is what Susheela wanted to believe.

The tree itself was innocent of its origins. She had loved it from the first moment she had seen it. Now it stood partly shading the great stone, beautiful in the moonlight. She shut her eyes and breathed in its scent. There was a sound — a soft, dry, sliding sound, scales against stone. When she opened her eyes the gleam of moonlight on the steel bowl vanished abruptly, and she thought she could see dark, coiled shapes against the stone. Let there be rain tomorrow, she said in her mind. She could not name the nebulous other thing she desired.

Very carefully, she gathered half a handful of flowers from the tree and walked back to the house without turning on the flashlight. Inside she put the flowers on the altar in the kitchen. I will put some in my hair tomorrow, she told herself, switching off the light.

That night Susheela fell asleep thinking of her mother's mother, the grandmother she had never known except from old family pictures. This grandmother had brought up six children in a huge, old-fashioned house in the ancestral village. One day the river had broken its banks and filled the emptiness of the big house. The family took refuge on the rooftop terrace. The eldest son was missing — he had been visiting a neighbours. Grandfather had injured his leg so Grandmother went in the little boat, steering with a long pole, in the muddy water full of debris, pots and pans and bewildered river fish. She found her son, delivered him, then went to the aid of her neighbors. She rescued a woman stuck in a tree, several other people clinging to hut-roofs, and a variety of animals, including dogs, goat-kids and muskrats. In the evening she cooked dinner on the rooftop over a coal fire, quite calmly, as though nothing unusual had happened. As dark fell, she told her eldest son, who was still awake, that she had to go do one more thing. She looked on the sleeping, exhausted family one more time, got into the boat, pushed off with the pole, and disappeared over the murky water. She was never seen again.

Stories gathered around the legendary grandmother like moths about a candle flame. She had given herself to the river, people said, so the floods would not come again. Susheela's mother, the youngest child, had been a teenager at the time of the disappearance; she remembered it well, years later, but she did not like to talk about it. Her face would fall slack with the memory. Then Susheela would gaze into her mother's eyes and think she saw what her mother saw: the flood, the dark water, the sole woman in the boat, steering herself away between the drowned houses, under a silent sky.

Her mother was a haunted woman, she knew. Soon after Susheela's marriage she had heard that her mother had gone to visit her ancestral home. At this, Susheela had felt a vague presentiment of disaster. But newly married, and pregnant, she had not been permitted to leave. A month later, Susheela had heard from her brother that their mother had walked to the river one morning, with flowers for worship, and that later that day, her clothes had been found floating some distance downriver from the house. Not long after that, Susheela had received a letter from her mother written a few days before the tragedy; the address on the envelope was nearly illegible and the ink was blurry and unreadable, as though the pages had been left out in the rain. Susheela had felt very clearly then that some intangible thing had passed from her mother's life into her own. For nearly five years it had been a heavy, mysterious presence within her.

She had seen that great river once, as a child. Now it came into her dreams, broad, serpentine, flowing between fragile cities, open fields and wilderness. She dreamed of floods, earthquakes, buildings tottering, the earth heaving, throwing off its old coverings, revealing roots, rocks, darkness. Twice she woke, and lay in the dark, trembling, her eyes wide open, listening to her husband breathe beside her. I must go, she thought, even if it is death that calls me.

Morning filled the house with a pale gray light; a cool breeze came in from the open windows, smelling of dust and anticipation. Susheela, breathless and light-headed, moved from room to room, distractedly applying the dust-cloth. In the kitchen she picked up a few of the harsingar flowers from the altar, hesitated, then put them down the front of her blouse for the fragrance. She did not have the patience to make a flower chain to weave in her hair. When her mother-in-law came into the kitchen Susheela was already rolling *paratha* dough for breakfast. She fed the family; she herself had no appetite. Her husband pushed away his empty plate with a sigh and unfolded the Sunday newspaper.

Susheela went to the front window in the drawing-room and perched on the cold sill. An army of storm-clouds was poised in the sky, and the breeze rattled the dry leaves on the trees. The raindrops fell, slowly at first, making pockmarks in the dust of the long summer; but in only a few minutes the dust became liquid mud, and the roadside ditches became torrents, and an aroma rose from the earth like a moist, cool breath of relief. All sounds were lost in the music of the rain. Neighbours gathered at their doorways, smiling, watching indulgently as children ran out of the houses and danced in the flooded, sparkling street. Then the clouds rumbled and lightning jagged across the sky. Parents called out to their children. Susheela, watching the rain, tried to decipher what message, if any, lay in its watery speech; what did it sing, as it drummed on the flat rooftops and gurgled in the ditches? She could not bear the thought that after all her waiting it would have nothing to say to her. Listening, she did not at first notice that Kishore was missing.

He'd been sulking; she had not let him go out with the neighbourhood children. He must have slipped away while she sat dreaming on the sill. She raised an alarm, feeling her knees beginning to shake. Her husband set down his cup, spilling tea, grabbed an umbrella and went into the storm.

But Susheela knew just where he would be: in the park that sloped down to the lake, their favourite walk. She gathered her sari about her ankles and went into the blinding rain. Her shoes were light and flimsy, they soon filled with muddy water, but she stumbled on. On this day of all days, to lose him like this!

The lake was a blur; the rain fell like thick needles. She looked fearfully around, shading her eyes from the rain. There he was — huddled by one of the neem trees that grew on the lake's edge. He was too heavy to pick up, he bent his head against the rain and sobbed wordlessly, but he let her set him on his feet. She thought she felt or heard something from the direction of the lake, but when she looked back, there was nothing.

She held Kishore to her in a tight grip, half-sobbing in her relief, babbling words of reassurance as she walked him back through the mud and rain to the house. She heard her husband call, saw him running up to them. Kishore looked up at her through a curtain of rain, and she thought she saw wonder in his face, then fear. He left her side and ran to his father, crying. Her mother-in-law was already at the front door with towels, scolding in her relief. Susheela stepped forward to follow her husband and son, anxious to reassure her little boy; what could make him look at her like that? But something made her hesitate on the top step. The rain streamed down her face, running in rivulets down her neck, between her breasts. Her bun had come undone and her hair lay wetly against her neck. Her sari was plastered to her skin. She itched all over. She saw now that there was a faint silvering all along her forearm, spreading rapidly over her skin. A tremor went through her.

She felt it now like a gravitational pull, as if whatever thread bound her to the lake was at last drawing her in. She turned, stumbled down the steps and began to run through the downpour. Behind her she heard her husband cry out her name, but her steps did not falter. Splashing through the water on the street and in the park, she stood at last, panting, on the lake's edge.

She had lost her shoes on the way and the stone paving felt slippery under her bare feet. There was only the sound of rain, sparkling on the lake's surface, drumming on the earth. Susheela put one foot into the water. A great shudder of desire went through her. She stepped into the lake, slipping a little on the stones. Mud squelched between her toes. The water rose to envelop her — it embraced her hips, her chest, her neck. As the water closed over her head she felt the change, like an electric current through her.

Her first feeling was that of sheer terror, as though something alien had invaded her mind and body. She thrashed about, rearing out of the water and falling back again with a splash, trying to see what or who was holding her arms to her sides, drowning her, but the rain fell in great curtains, obscuring everything. A spasm shook her from head to foot; as she lost consciousness she felt warm currents coursing painlessly through her, stretching and squeezing, shaping and molding, as though she were a lump of clay in a potter's wheel.

When she came to, she found herself afloat in the water, conscious only of a great need to fill her lungs with air. She struggled to free herself of her clothes, turning and twisting until she swam out from the limp, wet folds of her sari, raised her head into the rain, and breathed. She turned slowly, and saw that her new body was long, limbless and lithe. Her senses registered a thousand unfamiliar impressions: the agitation of water against her scales; the completely alien sensation of being able to feel, through her skin, tiny reverberations that hinted of life swarming all about her; and the presence, inside her mouth, of a strange tongue, forked and unbearably sensitive. An exultation rose inside her; she became aware of other presences around her, long, sinuous shapes, ancient, powerful, familiar. Their bodies were dark, their heads narrow, their eyes black, beckoning, alive. She turned smoothly in the water and saw that her underbelly was pale, like theirs. Now they were leading her, diving underwater. She took a breath of air and followed them into the depths of the lake, brushing against stone; she sensed she was swimming through the passageways of some underwater structure. Memories that were not her own, yet belonged to her in some mysterious way, came crowding into her mind: warm, narrow spaces in the earth, fluid darkness, the coilings of other bodies beside her. The earth, the womb, shutting out the wide emptiness of the world.

The snakes swam around her, guiding her with gentle nudges. In the dark water they were like slender, graceful ghosts. One touched his head with hers, wheeling around her in an intricate spiral. They went up to the surface together to breathe, and taste the rain. The water was sensuous against her skin, and when the cobra leaned his head close to hers, with bright, ardent, questioning eyes, she felt a small explosion in her chest, as though a dam had burst, letting out all the needs and desires of her barren other life. That life, which she could scarcely remember now, seemed a distant dream; what was real was the movement of scale against scale, coil against coil, the flaring of her partner's majestic hood as they danced, braided about each other in the ancient, intimate rite of procreation. When at last they moved gracefully apart, to lie companionably in the water, spent but not exhausted, a picture came rudely into her mind, an alien intrusion: a small, hot, dusty room, a man asleep, his back to her, unreachable as a distant mountain. It was incomprehensible and disturbing, and she dismissed it sharply. The other snakes were coming up below her, swimming to the surface for air, and she joined them, moving playfully among them, dodging the raindrops. A feeling came to her then that she must have done this before, that this was all familiar, the snakes, the rain, the coupling in the water. That couldn't be — but the seed of a realization took root in her mind, and slowly flowered into certainty: that her mother had once done this. That this was how Susheela had been conceived... It was too enormous a discovery to comprehend all at once. When the snakes dived again, calling to her in their wordless tongue, she followed them into the submerged ruins. She understood it was a place of pilgrimage, sacred to her companions, and that they remembered its history in fragments that had been passed on from generation to generation. The pictures that arose in her mind hinted of calamitous events, heroic battles and long, golden periods of peace and prosperity. They were making her a gift of their story, she realized. She had no stories of her own but the memory of her mother and grandmother, which they accepted, she thought, with generosity.

But now the rain was slowing. She swam up to the surface and saw the sun emerge from behind the clouds. The other snakes swam sedately away from her, their farewells echoing in her mind. Until next time, she thought they said, whenever that was, and she had so many questions, so much to ask. But they were already gone, gliding over the ancient paving at the edge of the lake, disappearing into cracks and crevices in the old ruin, and into bushes, tree-holes, and other secret places. All that remained of their presence were wide ripples spreading and crisscrossing on the lake's sunlit surface. Why had they left her alone? Rainwater dripped off the neem trees; in their shade a small emerald-green frog perched on a lotus leaf. She drifted in the middle of the lake, feeling bewildered, abandoned. Then she remembered as if from long ago, the small, heavy weight of her son on her lap, the way he tilted his chin up to her to ask for a story, his upper lip rimmed with milk. She turned and began to swim back to the lake's edge, feeling herself grow heavier and heavier, until she could feel her arms again, and her naked, muddy skin, from which the scales were already fading. Her body felt strange, awkward; at last she stood in knee-deep water, looking at her brown arms glowing in the sunshine, her mud-streaked breasts, the shiny stretchmarks on the slight, taut curve of her belly. The world swam into focus; she felt her head clear a little. She passed her tongue over her lips, and felt the slight notch on its tip that had not been there before. Behind her, under the shimmering green surface of the lake, lay the promise of that other world. She looked around and saw that her sari, blouse and undergarments were floating near her, amidst a sprinkling of harsingar flowers.

For a while she stood quietly in the water, feeling dazed and new, thinking, but not in words, or words she had known before. She knew her mother had stood thus once, filled with excitement and confusion, feeling the new life she had made stir inside her. At last she could stand inside her mother's skin and sense what she had gone through — the dilemma of choosing between two worlds, the prison she had made for herself, of love and guilt. Her brother's wistfulness; like her own son, he had been fathered by a man; he would always hear the call of his mother's kind, but could never transform, never know what it was like to turn underwater in an exquisite dance, to taste the world through his skin, to be life-giver, rain-bringer, death-lord. This new child she carried would be like her, an entity capable of existing in two worlds.

Two worlds... Pictures rose in her mind: the warm yellow house, the harsingar tree. She remembered the rhythms of the day, the slow course of the white cow Muniya's morning journey from house to house, the taste of fresh milk. And Kishore... No, she was not quite ready to leave it all behind. It was not yet time for that. She would come back to the lake again tomorrow, to begin to learn how to parcel her life between water and earth, fire and shadow, until it was time for the final leave-taking. Slowly, dazedly, she gathered her clothes and emerged from the lake. She went behind a bush and began to squeeze the water from her sari.

Her skin prickled; she sensed the gardener's presence a moment before he came around the bush. His eyes were filled with wonder and desire — he came slowly towards her as though she were a dream that would dissolve with the first stumble. She watched him curiously, without fear, still in the twilight state between her two worlds. He put trembling hands on her bare shoulders. She let him draw her close so that her breasts flattened against his wet shirt; she felt the angular roughness of his chin against her cheek. "Lady," he said, and she tasted his skin, his smell with her tongue, and remembered, with the suddenness of a thunderclap, the old fear and confusion. A bitter taste filled her mouth; as he pulled her down into the wet grass she reached up blindly and bit the side of his neck.

She watched him thrashing about on the ground. After he had stopped she spat and rubbed her face with her hands to try to clear her head. Then she gathered her clothes, squeezed and shook the water from them and dressed. Her hair was wet and tangled, but she managed to comb it back with her fingers and tie it into a bun. She looked once more at the gardener's still body, feeling the beginnings of a vague uneasiness.

She began to walk slowly home, looking about her like a child, letting the sights, sounds and smells wash over her: men on bicycles, ringing their bells, children splashing into rainwater puddles, shouting in their clear, shrill voices, cars all shiny and wet, honking, lurching as they negotiated potholes, the smell of wet earth and the vapours already rising from the moist ground, the drip of rainwater from the tree branches above her. Slowly it came back to her. The way home. It was familiar and strange all at once.

And there, meandering down the street was Muniya the cow. She caught up with the great white bovine matriarch and stretched her arm toward her, but the cow shied away from her as though stung, and began to edge away, fear in her dark eyes. Dismayed, Susheela stood there helplessly, tears welling up in her eyes. She made a small, experimental, cajoling sound, thinking of the way Kishore had looked at her last. The cow let out a breath redolent with the odour of grass and carrot ends, and let Susheela come up to her. She shuddered as Susheela stroked her back, but did not move away.

Susheela felt an urgent need now to see her son. Taking leave of Muniya she began to walk rapidly, knowing that passersby were staring at her, with her dishevelled hair and sodden clothes. She had to win back her little boy, to take that look from his eyes. She would do it, she thought in the wordless tongue, with patience, with stories, but — it came back to her now with horrifying clarity: the body of the gardener in the wet grass — how to protect her family from what she had become? What would she tell them? She couldn't even begin to articulate it, she realized in terror. People on the street were talking, laughing, and they might as well have been speaking some incomprehensible foreign language, because their speech had no meaning for her.

Then, slowly, she remembered the words, and understood them. It was Naag Panchami, the Festival of Snakes, and the monsoons had arrived at last. A car went by, fast, and two glittering arcs of water rose in its wake. There was the house; the shisham trees, their round leaves glistening, the trunks dark with moisture. Through the open front window she could see her husband's profile as he waited, reading his paper, one brown hand on the sunlit sill. A picture came into her mind's eye: that brown hand scooping up earth, making a hollow like a womb for the roots of the harsingar tree, patting the soil in place. She trembled, as though a string had been plucked deep inside her. The door was open. She walked into the house as if for the first time.

Conservation Laws

I MET GYANENDRA SAHAI for the first time in the bowels of the Lunar Geological Institute, in front of a display case containing an old-fashioned, heavy-built moonsuit. There was a large crack along one side of the suit and a rust-coloured discolouration along the opening. I was thinking about the pre-colonization days of moon exploration and the dangers that had beset the early explorers, and wondering what the story was behind this particular specimen (there was no label) when a mournful cough interrupted my musings. The man standing near me was gaunt, not tall, but with a presence that suggested height. His bald head was a baked brown dome, fringed with hair of a startling silvery grey; his eyebrows were of the same colour above heavy-lidded, lugubrious dark eyes.

"Ah yes, the ill-fated expedition of 2031," he said, shaking his head. I was delighted to recognize in his heavily accented English the speech mannerisms of Bihar, the state in India where I am from. Biharis are not very common on the moon. But before I could say anything about my origins, he launched into the story behind the space-suit.

He had been there. He had been part of the 2031 expedition, along with an international crew of explorers. They had been mapping water resources on the moon, an essential requirement for the future settlement.

While investigating the half-caved-in edge of a crater, they had found the entrance to a large cavern, such as had never been seen on the moon, and within it a body, possibly from some earlier mission, although the moon-suit was strangely constructed. The story involved the ultimate, mysterious disappearance of the corpse and the subsequent unravelling of the friendship between two of the team members, one of whom eventually took a hatchet to the other. What was perhaps worse, the databots containing the map of the water resources (and therefore of the location of the cavern) were destroyed in the melée. The expedition was called off, and only this tragic reminder remained.

My new friend peered at the suit in the cabinet.

"Poor Harrison!" he whispered. "Well, goodbye, old friend."

He looked at me as though seeing me for the first time.

"You're from India, yes?"

His joy in finding a fellow Indian and Bihari was touching. He confided to me that having retired from exploration work, he had become a part-time consultant, and that he was weary of his present life.

"Where I stay, it is too busy. People keep on coming to me, wanting things — information about this and that. I am looking for a quieter place to live…"

That is how Gyanendra Sahai came to live in Sinha Auntie's boardinghouse, one of the oldest structures in Luna City. It is in the area known informally as the Ghetto of Selene, where, among the quaintly derelict remains of what was once the first human habitation outside Earth, the unfortunates, ne'er-do-wells and poor university students of Luna City live. It is not really a ghetto, but the modern city, which rises just south of us, is such a dream of tall towers and gleaming polyhedral buildings that we look grimy and provincial in comparison. Sinha Auntie's boarding house is a small place, with only five of us, including Sahai-ji — and not including our august landlady, who occupies (in a manner of speaking) the entire lower floor. The house is one of those dome-shaped prefab constructions from the early days of Luna City's history, tough and durable; we have supplementary power via the giant solar panels on the roof, which stand atop the dome like a bad hair-do. We like the warren-like feel of the domehouse — the tiny rooms, rounded corridors, and most of all, Sinha Auntie's incredible authentic Bihari cooking. She used to be a medical researcher in her younger days but is now content do that part-time. She rules over our little establishment, bullying us to study, making us do our chores. But she makes up for her totalitarian ways with her cooking — jackfruit curry, and pickled boiled potatoes, and *pakoras* that burn off your taste buds and leave you begging for more. We don't yet know where she gets all the rare and expensive vegetables. All she says (with a giggle that shakes her vast and genial frame like a miniature earthquake) is this: Biharis may be few here on the moon, and we may spend most of our time arguing, but we do look out for each other.

The addition of Sahai-ji brings the total Bihari contingent of the boardinghouse to three.

The other boarders include Meena Sreenivasan, the mathematician and artist, who lives downstairs in a room off our landlady's apartment because the latter has old-fashioned views; Kunaal Kapoor, a student of planetary geology, whose eyes are on Mars; Dave Pratchett, the sole non-Indian (he is American), studying sociology. We keep busy with our separate lives, but Saturday afternoons Sinha Auntie does a huge old-fashioned Bihari-style tea, complete with *suji halwa*, *litti*, *pakoras*, *matar-ki-gugni*, crisp-fried *chura* with *sev* and roasted peanuts, and the best tamarind chutney on the moon. Saturday afternoon is an occasion for the sharing of stories about the week, vehement arguments, and the occasional cushion-fight. I find it very pleasant, watching the graceful arc of the cushions in low gravity, listening to the animated, expressive Meena Sreenivasan talk about art or mathematics, while Kunaal tries his best to be as unpleasant as possible. Dave puts in a word or two, uncoiling his lanky frame to reach the *matar-ki-gugni*, his eyes swimming with happy tears as he chokes on a chilli pepper. He's earned the sobriquet of Spy, partly because we Indians are compulsive nicknamers, but also because nobody understands what he's doing in this low-tech boarding house with a gaggle of Indian students. He claims it is the food that draws him, but we wonder.

I was somewhat nervous about Sahai-ji's reaction to our Saturday afternoon free-for-all; and indeed the first time he kept quiet, his large eyes mournful as he wrapped his fingers around a *pakora*. The others were polite, in deference to his age and stature, but after some time they forgot the niceties and broke into heated debate. I had to intercept the cushions a few times so that they did not strike our new tenant's elderly pate, for which he gave me a grateful smile. Sometimes it seemed as though he was on the verge of saying something, that words of great import were trembling on his lips — but he would change his mind and remain quiet.

I found Sahai-ji fascinating, and tried to draw him out in private, but he seemed reticent about his past, despite his earlier volubility. I was supposed to be studying for my finals (I am studying lunar botany, a fascinating field), but instead I would find myself thinking about Sahai-ji, wondering what he had endured; why, in his eyes, there was always a look of perpetual melancholy. Somehow I would have to draw him out, see what other stories he had to tell.

I only had to wait until the next Saturday tea.

"My new exhibit," Meena Sreenivasan said, her delicate fingers hovering over the plate of *pakoras*, "my new exhibit is going to have to do with Dr Delgerbayar's new theories. You know? Mirror universes, symmetries, all that."

Kunaal snorted. He has the practical scientist's scorn for theorists and pure mathematicians, especially mathematicians who indulge in art.

"I'm sick of hearing about Delgerbayar's theories," he said, beating Dave to the last samosa. "There's been nothing else on the news screens. The discovery of the Ares aquifer has taken second place! Can you imagine?"

"The Ares aquifer has been the top news story for a month," said Meena indignantly. "Besides, Delgerbayar's ideas are important. He's made a fundamental discovery about the universe, and you're excited about a few ice crystals on Mars!"

The first cushion flew. Dave caught it neatly.

"Perhaps," he said diplomatically, but with a twinkle in his eye, "Kunaal can explain why he hates Delgerbayar's theories, and Meena can tell us why she likes them."

This was a clever move, since Kunaal and Meena are the physics and mathematics experts, and both love to talk. I glanced at Sahai-ji and was disappointed to see that he was apparently asleep, lying back in the room's most comfortable chair with a printout of the daily news feed covering his face. The pages rose and fell with his breathing. The ruins of a vast tea lay on his plate.

We listened to Meena and Kunaal expound. Briefly, Delgerbayar, the brilliant Mongolian theorist who was the latest glamourous addition to Lunar U's physics department, had come up with a new theory. His Universal Field equations exhibited interesting symmetries that had ultimately led to the theoretical possibility of a hyperspace (and hence faster-than-light travel) and the existence of a multiverse — that is, a succession of universes that branched off the base hyperspace as bananas branch off their central stem. According to the theory, some of these universes were startlingly like our own, with a few properties reversed. Delgerbayar had dubbed these 'mirror universes', and since the symmetries of the equations were not perfect, he had speculated that mirror universe space-time occasionally leaked into our own, causing the anomalies that physicists had recently observed.

"You're not explaining the role that symmetry plays," Kunaal said to Meena. "Let's take, for instance, your face as an example. If you didn't have that pimple on your face it would not only be passable but would possess bilateral symmetry—"

"I don't have a pimple!" Meena said fiercely, touching her cheek with one hand.

"It's all right, Meena, it's probably a bit of chutney," said Dave soothingly. Meena glared at him. He covered his face with his hands.

"Hey, don't open your third eye at me!"

"I'll show you jokers what I mean," said Kunaal, taking down a picture from the wall. It was a rather boring abstract still of an unmoving geometric landscape.

"This picture, hideous as it is, will explain an important point," he said. "Look, if I rotate it by ninety degrees, it looks the same. That is because it has a certain symmetry. You see? Symmetry implies that some attribute of the whole remains the same. Hence conservation laws."

"First discovered in the early 1900's by Emmy Noether, a *woman* mathematician in Germany," said Meena, her eyes flashing, "not that she got much for her pains. Her area was abstract algebra but on the side she discovered that there was a connection between symmetries and conservation laws — one of the deepest results in theoretical physics. Certain kinds of symmetries always imply that some physical quantity remains the same, before and after the transformation. So, if your equations have a symmetry with respect to a time transformation, energy is conserved. Translational symmetry means momentum conservation."

"Rotational symmetry," Kunaal said, spinning the picture violently on the table, "means that the angular momentum before and after the process remains the same."

There was a rending sound. The picture frame had cracked.

"Or, in this case," said Kunaal with fake contriteness, as he put the picture back on the wall, "the End of Art."

Meena looked daggers at him. "You'll have to replace that or Sinha Auntie will go nuclear. Well, anyway, about my project," she said, with undiminished enthusiasm, flinging a cushion at Kunaal for good measure, "I was thinking of a mainly visual display — symmetries, subtly broken, mirror shards reflecting unfamiliar realities — and some sound piped in — music and speech. Palindromes, I think, would make the point."

"Sounds like garbage," Kunaal said. I sometimes think he was born scowling. He drew breath in to make his speech, when he was interrupted by a gale.

The pages on Sahai-ji's face blew off and on to the table. It took me a moment to realize that the breeze was an exhalation, a long sigh that no human pair of lungs should have the capacity to execute. Sahai-ji coughed, sat up and looked at us out of his tragic eyes.

"Conservation laws," he said, and sighed again.

We stared at him in stunned silence.

"All these theories are interesting," he said. "Delgerbayar is right about the mirror universe idea, and it is good that he is now so famous. But will we ever get to hyperspace? Not through the normal means. Will we ever get to the mirror universes? Let us hope not! In the meantime let us not scoff at the humble conservation laws of classical physics. In fact, one of them saved not only my life but…"

We waited. Almost on cue, Sinha Auntie came in with fresh *pakoras* and a vat of her killer mint chutney. Sensing a story, she settled her ample form into the second-largest chair and made herself comfortable.

"It has to do with wheels," began Sahai-ji, "but let me start from the beginning."

I was born Gyanendra Sahai in a small village in Eastern Bihar (he said). All my life, my ambition was to explore the unknown territories. When I finally got sent to the moon, I was happy. But that expedition ended in tragedy, as Vikram here knows. (The others gave me startled glances).

I had the chance to return home after that, as there was much sympathy for us. But I was infected with the space bug, and volunteered to go on a mission to Mars. My conduct during the Lunar expedition of 2031 had impressed my superiors so there was no problem. At that time there was no large settlement on Mars: small habitation domes were being built for the scientists and explorers. I was sent to one such place near the Vallis Marineris.

Now as you know, if you think of Mars as a hard-boiled egg, the Vallis Marineris is a big crack across it, a very deep canyon. (At this point Kunaal, our Martian expert, looked as though he was about to interject, but Sahai-ji silenced him with a look.)

This is not a story about Mars, although it begins there. Nor is it about the Moon or Earth. Makes you wonder, doesn't it, since these three are the only inhabited worlds? Well, then, listen carefully, because this story is known only to a few.

You may have heard, if you have studied Martian history, that many of the early explorers died. There are reasons enough — Mars is a hostile place for Earthlings. But there was also a persistent rumour that some of these old explorers had not died but simply… disappeared. When the International Space Council took over operations in Mars and said that you cannot do this or that but you must obey our rules, some of the old timers simply faded into the famous Martian dust haze. They call them Ghosties. There are all kinds of stories about the Ghosties — that they retreated into secret habitats, found ways to survive that allowed them their freedom. Now most of these stories are probably fabrications, but it had been reported that a lone person had been seen in the area near my camp. So as part of my exploration duties I was told to keep watch and see if there was really someone out there, a ghost from the past.

This was also around the time that anomalies were first being reported — aha, you think Delgerbayar's anomalies are a recent phenomenon? Nonsense! They were first reported around that region of Mars. Peculiar things were happening. Sudden flashes of light in the air. Strange temporary illusions, such as the time my friend Jack Moray's eyes got switched —

he had one blue and one brown eye, and one day, I swear, they had apparently swapped places. There were optical distortions, such as the kind you get in a heat haze, except there was no heat haze. You looked at the pale sunlight hitting a rockface, and you'd see a shadow where there should be none. These anomalies shifted, appeared and disappeared. One time the ground shook, and there was a rockfall. Mars, as our young friend here will tell you, is not exactly seismically active.

The people in my team were, as the Americans say, spooked. Perhaps it was no wonder that they imagined the silhouettes of long-dead Martian explorers on distant cliff-tops. In fact the first time I saw such a figure, I thought I was going crazy too.

I was camped in a high, dry valley, between two towering cliffs. I was making some geological measurements on behalf of a team member who was sick and had returned to Base. It was comfortable enough in my little mobile habitat, which was fully sealed from the harsh Martian environment. I had completed the measurements, which had taken three sols, and was within site of the habitat when I saw him.

He wasn't far away. He was up on a ridge, against the cliff face, attired in a bulky, old-fashioned environment suit, capering about like a madman. I would not have noticed him had not the setting sun glinted on his visor.

For a moment I staggered, thinking I must be hallucinating. But soon I realized that what I was seeing was real. I shouted out to him, forgetting that he would not hear me. Then I began climbing up the cliff-face.

I think he saw me then. When I looked up in mid-climb, he was gone.

That night I set out some food from my rations on a rock near my habitat. The next morning it was gone.

Now I was in radio contact with Base, but I did not want to tell anyone as yet about my discovery. I was sure that the others would rush up here and want to investigate, and my quarry might be scared off. I imagined that it would be much better to befriend him and bring him triumphantly back to camp.

Conservation Laws

So for the next two sols, that is what I did. I left food out, and all of it was taken. I wondered how the poor fellow lived, without an assured supply of food, water and breathable air. I wondered how he recharged his environment suit. It seemed to me more and more likely that there must be a hidden camp of survivors like him, deep in the maze of this part of the Vallis Marineris. Perhaps they made their own oxygen, grew food in hydroponic tanks? I was determined to find this hideout, if it existed.

(At this point Sahai-ji paused and looked around at us to make sure we were paying attention. Apparently satisfied, he sighed and brought out of his pocket a knotted white cotton handkerchief. Opening the knot he produced some roasted black gram, that flavourful smaller cousin of the chickpea, and a few balls of sweet *suttoo*, which is made from the gram flour. It had been years since I had seen Bihari peasant food. Both Sinha Auntie and I looked startled. Sahai-ji apologized for not having enough to share, and proceeded to munch while we waited with ill-concealed impatience for the rest of the story.)

Ah yes, there is nothing like roasted gram and *suttoo* sweetened with *gur* (he said). When I was a child growing up in Bihar, I would run off the whole day, playing with the buffalos in the rice fields, or looking for ber fruit in the forests. My mother would tell me every morning that even if I went to the stars, I should take some *suttoo* or roasted gram with me. You never know when you need the extra energy, she would say, not dreaming that one day her wayward son would actually go off to the stars. Anyway I've followed her advice ever since. I even brought some roasted gram and *suttoo* to Mars.

Now back to my story. Finally the day came when I was able to entice the fellow into my habitat. There I encouraged him to take off his helmet, which he did, revealing a face so burned and scarred (presumably from radiation) and so obscured by a full beard, that I could hardly make out his features. Only his eyes were visible, small, round and glinting. The poor fellow was completely mad, spouting gibberish and executing his peculiar dances. I could not place his nationality, except that he was definitely not

Bihari, for when I offered him some of my precious roasted gram he peered at it as though unsure it was edible. Nor was his speech of any mortal tongue. He seemed to want to tell me something, and kept wheeling his arms at me and pointing out at the cliffs. I imagined then that he wanted me to follow him, to show me his secret hideout. Much excited, I left a cryptic radio message for my team at Base, saying that I was going to be gone for a while but that I was on the verge of a great discovery. Then I set out with him.

He took me over a tortuous path between the cliff faces and mesas. I was certain I would not remember the way back, which was why I was glad I had brought my little geobot. This bot communicated with the then new Martian satellite network so that I always knew where I was (unless I was in a particularly deep and narrow canyon). The geobot was autonomous, moving on little robotic legs like a round-bodied millipede. My companion kept giving it looks that I could not fathom — once he bent down and patted it like a dog. I imagined then that it brought back memories of some long-lost pet.

Suddenly his face, behind his visor, widened into a grin. In a swift movement he grabbed the little bot, gave me a mischievous look and darted behind a jutting rock-face. Alarmed, I cried out and ran after him, but he was always a few steps ahead of me, darting up and down the rocks like a mountain goat, grinning and leering at me, and pretending to drop the bot off the two-mile-high cliff edge. Finally I saw him run into a crack in the opposite rock face. I followed him, my breath coming in frantic gasps. As darkness closed around me, my suit lights came on automatically and I saw that we were in a warren-like passageway. The walls were smooth and rounded, and the ceiling high. I was struck with wonder. It would have been nearly impossible for a tribe of derelict old explorers to cut such a wall, yet it was clear that the passage was artificially made.

This brought to my mind half-remembered tales I had read in childhood, of an intelligent Martian race. Was I being taken to some vast underground city, where aliens dwelt? As it turned out, I was wrong — but not quite.

Our race ended in a round chamber. Still holding the bot as though it were a baby, my quarry stopped, and hit a spot on the wall. Immediately and soundlessly, a great slab of stone moved across the passageway entrance, closing it off.

"Hey!" I shouted, quite frightened now. "What are you doing, open that…"

The words died in my throat. I saw that there was a soft glow coming from the walls, which were covered with strange symbols carved into the rock. In the middle of the floor was a round pedestal made of some kind of silvery metal.

As I gazed about me in wonder, I noticed that the madman was taking off his suit. There he was, naked and ugly as the day he was born. He indicated to me that I should also divest myself of my suit.

I was about to refuse when I saw that the fellow seemed to be quite comfortable. He was breathing just fine. My suit registered an outside pressure of 1 atmosphere. I opened my airlock cautiously. The air smelled slightly pungent, but I could breathe.

Curiously I stepped out of my suit. For the first time I stood outside a habitat on Mars in my normal clothes.

A sense of adventure was beginning to replace panic. My companion now indicated to me that I stand on the pedestal. I did so, hoping to wrest my bot from him. But before I could do anything, thick, membranous rope-like curtains — I can think of no better term — shot out from the walls and enveloped us. I screamed and struggled, but the sheaths wrapped themselves around my body completely from head to toe. I must have blacked out after a while, because when I came to, I was being dragged, not ungently, toward an opening in the wall of the chamber.

I realized suddenly that I was still breathing, and that I could see through the translucent sheath. My skin tingled wherever it was bare — the membranes appeared to be putting out little roots that tickled the skin. I struggled to my feet, tearing at the sheath with my hands, which, being also covered by the same material, could not get a good hold. In my terror I heard voices inside my head, speaking languages I had never heard before, but I could almost understand. There were pictures in my head of giant spinning wheels. The madman pulled me toward a great metallic structure that took up most of the room in the other chamber.

How can I describe my first glimpse of that artifact? I stood there, struck dumb. It was a vast wheel-shaped object, perhaps twenty metres in diameter, with a silvery lustre. The wheel had no rim, only eight motionless spokes. Inside the hub was an open, hollow space.

What manner of life had come up with such a device? What was its purpose? Again, fear ebbed, to be replaced by curiosity and awe. I reasoned that whatever this device did, it could not be harmful, for my companion had survived it. I imagined bringing news of this great discovery to all humanity. So I did not protest when my companion led me to the space inside the hub.

We stood there like two mummies. I saw that the fellow still carried my bot, which was not covered by the membranous sheath. So the mechanism in the first cave was intelligent, knowing the difference between life and non-life. It was also able to discern the needs of human beings, such as the kind of air we needed to breathe. Did this mean that the aliens who had devised this were like us? Or just that they had kept the needs of other species in mind? My mind swam with strange images as we waited, for God knows what.

Then, slowly, the chamber began to grow dark before us. I could now see more clearly the images that had been clamouring for attention in my mind. I saw vast fields of stars and all manner of strange beings. I saw strange and wonderful worlds, and pathways in utter darkness, that led to distant universes. I was reminded of the story where Krishna's earthly mother, Yashoda, happens to look into the child's mouth. There she sees the entire cosmos, and at that moment she knows who her son really is. That is how I felt, beholding the vistas that no other human being but my companion had ever seen.

Conservation Laws

At that moment I only half-understood what I was seeing, and only later was I able to form a hypothesis or two about my experiences, because what happened next was so fantastic I thought it was a continuation of the images projected in my brain. Only when the image persisted did I realize that we had been transported to an entirely different place.

We were not on Mars any more. We were still in the hub of a vast wheel, but this wheel was suspended in space, with the rimless spokes turning slowly. Before us, in every direction, was an enormous array of such wheels, stretching into space as far as I could see. The darkness between them was not speckled with stars, but was a true darkness, as would be found, perhaps, in the gulf between the galaxies. Yet the giant wheels seemed to be glowing faintly, and from the ends of each spoke I could discern a pulse of some sort emerging at fixed intervals. The wheels hummed and sang; although I could not hear them in the vacuum, I heard their song in my mind.

We were afloat in the middle of the hub. I touched the wall carefully, and found protuberances that served as handholds. Very slowly I brought myself to the edge of the chamber, in order to better observe this great vista. I was aware of my companion beside me, his mouth opening and closing behind the translucent sheath as he babbled soundlessly. Although there was no gravity to make me fall up or down, I momentarily felt sick with vertigo. I clutched the edge of the hub, rotating gently with the wheel, making no sudden moves. Newton's Third Law could have fatal consequences.

Now I could hear what the alien voices were telling me inside my mind. The music of the wheels swelled to a crescendo and back again to a soft murmur, in a regular rhythm like the heartbeat of a great beast. As the wheels turned, an energy field of some kind was generated — I could sense the invisible hills and valleys. The light beams from the ends of each spoke of each wheel crisscrossed, forming areas of light and shadow. I realized that in order for me to see the beams at all, the space around me must be filled with something that could reflect light. Interstellar dust? Or was it the strange emanation itself, that I called, in my ignorance, the energy field?

I also saw, to my utter surprise, that there were light beams that appeared to have different properties. Some simply intersected each other and continued, the way that two flashlight beams in a dark room intersect. Others, when they intersected, appeared to stop at the point of intersection, which created a dark spot. This great, undulating display of ordinary and extraordinary light (or whatever the radiation was—there could have been frequencies beyond the visible) somehow was responsible for the energy field.

My mind was flooded with images and symbols that I later pieced together. Although there is much I can never understand, it became clear to me that this whole spectacle had one purpose: to prevent two distinct universes from crossing each other.

Apparently this place was a potential crossing point. The other universe was similar to our own, but for some attributes. I believe it was a universe dominated by anti-matter, as ours is by matter. But it was also dominated by this other form of light, which I dubbed anti-light.

Think about it, my young friends — what is the opposite of light? Not darkness. Darkness is the *absence* of light. No, strange as it might seem, its opposite is anti-light. An anti-photon can form a bound state with a photon, like an atom — an atom of light! — or the two can annihilate each other, releasing an exotic form of energy.

The great wheels, spinning in concert as they did, must have been designed by some wise alien race. I doubt they were Martians. They had been to Mars and built the portal to this place, but their dwelling place was elsewhere, I was sure of it. Where they were now, I could not say, but they spoke directly to my mind through the sheath that I was wearing. They had built this vast array to save our universe from destruction.

It became clear to me at that moment that the anomalies we had observed on Mars must be the result of some kind of malfunction of this protective array, because the strange optical effects we had seen could only be explained by anti-light leaking in from a mirror universe. What could have caused the malfunction?

The answer came to me almost as I thought the question, because at that moment my mad companion, whom I had quite forgotten in my contemplation of the marvels before me, suddenly launched himself off the edge of the hub. He shot into space even as I cried out in consternation, for the entire wheel shuddered. I could sense that the regularity of the emanations was disturbed; the array as a whole appeared to tremble, and the scene distorted before my eyes. Then the whole thing adjusted, like a rubber band that has been pulled and released. As my vision cleared I saw the fool sitting inside the hub of the wheel across, gesturing and grinning at me, still holding the bot.

He did it again, launching himself from hub to hub, each time causing a perturbation of the array. Each time it adjusted, but every such occasion allowed (I hypothesized) some leakage between the universes. The madman seemed to be possessed of vast reserves of strength, and it came to me that perhaps he fed off the energy field in some way, thus needing neither food nor drink. At last he settled in the hub of the wheel next to mine — I had to peer over the edge to see him. He released my bot so it floated by his side, and waved something small and white at me — it was my knotted handkerchief, with my roasted gram and sweet *suttoo*! He opened the handkerchief and began to eat, pushing the food through the membrane in front of his mouth, at the same time making the most insane —even lewd— gestures at me. This so infuriated me that I began to yell and scream — uselessly across the void — and to wave my arms about in a fury. He seemed to enjoy the display, and after he had finished his repast, grabbed the bot as though to toss it to me. I held my hands out, but he flung it—not quite toward me, but toward one of the spokes of my wheel. I saw him launched into space in the opposite direction by the action. He flew between the great wheels, getting smaller and smaller — indeed, that was the last I ever saw of him. I had more immediate problems to worry about.

Vandana Singh

For the bot hit the edge of the spoke and careened away, breaking up as it went, causing my wheel to shudder and spin faster. Immediately I sensed the delicate energy field being distorted, tearing like a rubber sheet that has been pulled in a weak spot with excessive force. Voices screamed in my mind, and I saw a gulf of the other universe opening up before me like a giant mouth. The scene before me began to undergo fantastic optical distortions — my own wheel seemed to have gone liquid, like a new painting that gets runny if you spill water on it. But when I touched the wheel, it was still smooth and hard. Then it came to me that restoring my wheel's normal spin rate was quite a simple matter. I remembered how I used to spin in my father's swivel chair as a child, stretching out my arms when I wanted to slow down.

I began to crawl up one of the spokes of my wheel, being careful to do so slowly. I had to move just the right distance along the spoke so that the increase in rotational inertia would cause the angular velocity to decrease. I did not even know whether my mass was large enough to affect the rotational inertia of the wheel. But as I moved, I felt the wheel slowing down, until suddenly everything seemed to lock into place. The energy field was restored, the distortions ceased. The great dark mouth of the other universe closed. I stopped where I was, sweaty with relief, thanking all my physics teachers that I had remembered the conservation of angular momentum. I knew, of course, that I would have to stay here for all time, but at first I felt little regret. The energy field would keep me alive, perhaps for eons, and my mind would, in time, learn to communicate with the sheath that protected me from my surroundings.

Still, I felt a pang, because I would no longer be able to tell my fellow human beings about my great discovery. I would never see the blue skies of Earth, or eat roasted gram and sweet *suttoo* again. I admit that I felt tears well up in my eyes. Time passed without impressing itself on me — what need had I of time? I must have fallen into a stupor, then, that perhaps lasted weeks or months. I dreamed of strange beings, other worlds. In one dream I was lying on my spoke, gazing at the apparently infinite array of wheels, when I saw an injured moth flying from wheel to wheel, coming toward me. As it approached I saw that it was a very strange moth indeed, with enormous, delicate, gauzy wings, one of which was held only half opened. Its two foreshortened arms waved at me, as the long, thin, frog-like hind-limbs crouched for the next leap. It seemed to skim the surface of the energy field like a water-skating insect. And then it was floating before me, its smooth, triangular head bending close. Around this time the realization slowly dawned on me that this was no dream. Upon the creature's head was an array of small, bulbous organs that lit up in complex patterns, conveying some message to my fevered mind that I could not yet understand. The creature had evidently sustained some damage from the disturbance in the field, because one of its wings, I saw now, was tattered at the edges, explaining its lopsided flight.

The creature's message must have ultimately soothed me, because I fell into a deep sleep. I remember half-waking at various points, and seeing before me the rounded cave, deep within the cliffs of Mars. I remember fumbling with my environment suit and picking up something white off the ground. I must have staggered through an infinity of dark passageways, led by a persistent voice in my mind, until at last I saw light ahead of me, and fell to the ground in a faint. When I opened my eyes again, I was lying outside the cliff face in the middle of a dust storm, clutching my empty handkerchief. How it came back into my possession I cannot say. In fact it is this very handkerchief you see now.

I must have staggered around, light-headed for a while. As the dust storm ebbed, my senses seemed to clear as well; I found myself hopelessly lost, with no sign of the opening in the cliff. Then I remembered my suit's radio. The sound of a friendly human voice lifted my spirits beyond imagining. A team from Base rescued me and took me to camp, where I told them my fantastic story.

Vandana Singh

Of course they did not believe me, but they did go back to where they had found me. They could not find the place where I had emerged from the cliff, nor did they find any evidence of the madman. Finally they put my story down to hallucinations brought about by lack of food, water and human company. What could I do? There was no proof that anything strange had happened to me, except for one thing.

I believe that the moth-like creatures, whatever they were — caretakers or simply beings who fed and lived their lives in the great energy field — somehow restored the correct functioning of the wheels. Because after I returned, the anomalies stopped occurring. So much so that scientists who had observed them began to doubt that anything unusual had ever happened. The anomalies were not observed again until all these years later.

Now they have been seen on Mars, on the Moon, and even on a spaceship en route to Mars from Earth. The return of the anomalies must mean that parts of the mirror universe are pushing through into ours — that the great field of wheels has suffered a serious disturbance. What could be the cause? Perhaps the madman is on another rampage. Perhaps... who knows?

That is more or less the end of my story. I was sent back to Earth for a rest, but since the stars kept calling, I didn't stay there long. I tried, sometimes, to forget what I had gone through, but there was a constant reminder, the souvenir I carried with me. What? I haven't told you what it was? Here, I will show you. Let me roll up my sleeve. See this little white patch? Feels like smooth plastic, doesn't it? It's all that is left of the sheath. When I returned to the cave-room where I had left my environment suit, the sheath fell off my body, except for a large patch on my forearm. I think this is what guided me through the passageway in the cliff, at the end. Over the years it has kept shrinking, but even now, if I concentrate, I can hear bits and tatters of the music of those great wheels as they spin endlessly in space.

Sahai-ji's story was greeted with stunned silence. There was a collective letting out of breaths as the tension eased, then Sinha Auntie said:

"Well, I've never heard such a marvellous tale!"

She surged to her feet and poured a fresh cup of tea for Sahai-ji, all the while looking at him in wonder.

"What a great thing for Bihar!" she said cryptically, and went out of the room to see to dinner.

Meena shook her head, as though to clear it of a spell.

"Anti-photons!" she said ecstatically "Aliens! Great wheels of space and time! Oh, how wonderful!" She seemed incapable of saying any more. I looked at Dave. His eyebrows had nearly disappeared into his brown thatch of hair.

"Sahai-ji, why didn't you tell your story to the news screens? Somebody would have believed you. Perhaps some private individuals could have launched a search for the passageway entrance — isn't all this too big a thing to keep to yourself?"

Sahai-ji popped a ball of *suttoo* into his mouth.

"Ah, you Americans, such an impatient people," he said indulgently. 'I told my tale until I was sick of it, and nobody believed me. It is true that the news screens would have carried the story, but I didn't want to start a cult following of crackpots. Only now that the anomalies have reappeared have I tried to do something. But the fools at the top don't believe my story! Especially since the crack in the cliff – the entrance to the chamber on Mars — has never been found. My own feeling is that it is not a crack so much as a door that can be opened and shut."

"I don't believe it," Kunaal burst out. "Sorry, Sahai-ji, but I think your team-mates were right. You had an amazingly coherent hallucination."

"What about the patch on his arm, then?" I said.

Kunaal shrugged, as though my question did not even deserve a reply. He got up. I could see from the light in his eyes that he was determined to get to the bottom of this story. Then Dave said:

"Hey, Meena, you've lost your pimple."

Meena touched her cheek. "I tell you I never had one," she said indignantly. "Kunaal just likes making things up."

"It probably was a bit of tamarind chutney," I said.

Kunaal turned from the doorway. He seemed surprised that Meena's pimple was gone. But we were even more surprised when we saw his face.

"It's on your face now," Dave said, in a tone of gentle wonder.

The world turned surreal.

"Nonsense," said Kunaal, wildly, feeling his chin. "I don't feel anything."

Sahai-ji shook his head sorrowfully.

"Look in the mirror," he said.

Three Tales from Sky River: Myths for a Starfaring Age

"Listen!" said the Tipi-Bird
A Myth of the Saras People of Planet Jehana
Star system Kumboja.

IN THE LONG-AGO, WHEN people had just begun to settle in the fertile river valleys of the Saras plains, there lived a tipi-bird. In those days, tipi-birds were not only curious, as they are today, but they could talk. They would sit on the riverbanks near the human settlements, gossiping and munching river shrimp and algae all day long. By evening their little balloon wings would fill up with gas and they would float away, still gossiping, blowing out gas from their three ends to change direction. Well, this particular tipi-bird was so curious that she could hardly bear to go to sleep, in case she missed something interesting.

One night she saw a vast darkness come down from the sky. At first she was afraid, but then she realized that it was the Great Shaper himself, and her curiosity got the better of her. She floated up toward him, and saw that his arms were full of enormous, bulbous creatures with many limbs.

"What are these monsters, Great Shaper? What are you going to do with them?" piped the tipi-bird excitedly. The Great Shaper saw her and was annoyed, so he didn't answer. He squatted down on the edge of the marsh near the fertile river valley where the humans lived, and began to release the monsters into the slushy soil. Each of the creatures burrowed into the wet ground at great speed, leaving only a ripple or a bubble to mark their passage. Meanwhile the tipi-bird kept plying the Great Shaper with questions until he was quite put out.

"I will tell you what I am doing, if you promise not to breathe a word of it to the humans. I am tired of them changing and reshaping my river valleys, building dams and blowing up hillsides, and I don't want them to get too arrogant. Therefore I have made a plan to destroy their civilization every three hundred years."

The Great Shaper pointed up into the starlit night.

"See the bright point that burns with such a steady light? That is Eenah the Wanderer. Every three hundred years Eenah will become brighter and brighter. Terrible floods and earthquakes will then visit you all. The river valleys will become watery graves. The only place that will be a little safer than the rest is the high plateau beyond the mountains. But to get to the mountains the humans will have to cross these marshes, in which I have planted the monsters. When the first floods come, these monsters will awake and devour all who attempt to cross the marsh. After Eenah has dimmed to its normal brightness, the few humans who are left will have to begin again. Humans will therefore never have a chance to dominate this world."

The tipi-bird listened, horrified and fascinated. Then the Great Shaper leaned down toward her and said:

"But breathe a word of this to anyone, tipi-bird, and I will exact a terrible revenge on all your kind."

The tipi-bird trembled and promised that she would be silent. Then the Great Shaper, having fulfilled his purpose, sprang once more into the sky and was lost from sight.

The next morning the tipi-bird went to the human settlement, where the other tipi-birds were gathered as usual, watching everything that was going on and chattering away. She longed to tell them what she had seen and heard, but with a great effort of will she managed to keep the secret. But at the end of the day, when dark was falling and the humans were taking to their beds, she thought she would go quite crazy if she didn't tell someone. So she floated over the houses until she came to a window. Inside the room, an old woman called Rema was fast asleep. The tipi-bird perched on the bedside and whispered "Listen!" And she told the sleeping woman everything the Great Shaper had said.

But as she floated up into the night like a little balloon, she felt a great hand snatch her up until she was level with the burning eyes of the Great Shaper himself.

"You broke your promise," he said in a deep, angry voice.

"Oh, but I didn't, Great Shaper. Listen! I spoke only to an old woman, who was fast asleep. Your secret is still safe!"

The Great Shaper looked relieved. Then he shook his head.

"Nevertheless, you broke your word," he said. "I now curse you and all your kind. You will lose your ability to talk, except for one word. I leave you the word 'listen'."

"Listen!" said the tipi-bird in great agitation.

The tipi-bird felt herself falling toward the river valley like a flake of ash. The other tipi-birds were just rising from the riverbanks, calling to each other. And the only word they could say was "listen!" Which is all they have said ever since.

But it was not long after that when the bright point in the sky known to the humans as Eenah began to shine a little more fiercely than before. And the tipi-bird went back to the human settlement and went from house to house, frantically calling, "Listen!" The humans laughed at her and said: "Listen to what?"

Then at last she came to the house of the old woman, Rema. When she said "listen!" Rema didn't laugh at her. Instead she remembered a dream that had come to her not long ago, and she saw in the three eyes of the tipi-bird a great urgency. So Rema summoned the settlers and told them that floods and earthquakes would besiege them if they did not at this instant set out for the mountains. She also warned them of the marsh monsters that would waken with the first floods. Some humans sneered at her and refused to leave their homes, but since Rema commanded no little respect, the rest followed her over the marshes and mountains to the comparative safety of the high plateau, where they lived bleak and difficult lives, but they lived.

And old Rema gave this warning to all the children and they in turn passed on the story to their own children. So to this day the tipi-bird is venerated as a friend of humankind, and every three hundred years the humans leave their settlements and go to the plateau, where they need only fear earthquakes, and not floods or monsters. Here they bide their time until Eenah's anger has passed and the great river is peaceful again. Then they leave the old and the dead behind and return once more to rebuild their homes.

Haiho's Knife
A Myth of the Sonahli People
Great Archipelago of Planet Kutch, Star System Alamir

ONCE THERE WERE NO PEOPLE in this land. The islands were empty of them and they did not swim in the warm seas of this Earth. All the people then were sky-people, and they moved in silver boats in the sky. They took with them only a few living things, the most intimate of which was a creature that lived on their bodies, that was as yet peaceful and dormant. It consisted of thousands of fine filamentous appendages that attached themselves to the skin on the head and in the region of pleasure.

After uncountable years in the sky, the sky-people wearied of their travels and began to look with longing at the Earth below, with its warm seas and lush islands. So some of them came down in their silver boats and swam naked in the strange seas of their new home. As the waters closed over them, the creature that lived on their bodies came alive. It withdrew its ten thousand tentacles from their heads and bodies and swam away into the sea. When the people left the water and waded up to the bright beaches of the islands, they found that their bodies were smooth and bare, and their bald heads shone in the light of the new sun. And they looked at each other and thought: we are beautiful.

They lived peacefully on the islands for two generations. Then one night, when the fires had been lit and there was feasting and dancing, a young woman called Amaila, who was inordinately fond of swimming, waded up from the sea.

Her scalp was no longer bare, but covered with tentacles, each as thick as her little finger. They writhed and looped about her face, and gave her otherwise pleasing appearance a terrible aspect. People ran from her in fright, but she reassured them, saying:

"Do not be afraid. This is the medusa, the creature that once lived on the bodies of the sky-people. The sea changed it, but it has not forgotten us. It will do us no harm."

People were then calmed, and the evening festivities continued. Only one man, an elderly hunter called Haiho, kept a wary eye on the young woman. It seemed to him that she was not as she had been before: her voice was low and strained, and she looked pale as death. After watching her for a while he went to his hut and took his double-bladed hunting knife. He carefully made notches along one side of the blade. This took him a long time, so when he emerged from his hut he found that people were already retiring for the night.

"Where is my son?" Haiho asked them. For he meant his son to help him keep watch on the young woman during the night.

"Why, he has gone with Amaila to her hut," said the people.

At this Haiho was filled with fear for his son. He ran to Amaila's hut, where a dim light burned. He clutched his knife strongly in his hand.

Inside he saw a terrible sight. Amaila lay lifeless and naked on the floor, her body bleached of all colour. Her head was bare again, and marked by tiny red pocks. Haiho's son lay next to her, asleep, and upon his scalp crawled the medusa, inserting first one, then another tentacle into his skin.

Haiho let out a bellow that raised the whole village. As people came crowding in, he had them lay burning branches on the body of the medusa, which writhed and twisted in a most terrifying manner. He then took the serrated edge of his knife and began to scrape away at his son's scalp. His son woke in great fright and confusion and tried to lash out at his father, but the village folk held his arms fast to his sides. Haiho had made the notches on his knife to fit the tentacles, so they were caught in the serrations and came away from the skin, leaving red blotches on the young man's skull that made him cry out in pain. At last the medusa was loosed from Haiho's son, and taken to the beach and burnt. And Haiho's son came back to his senses and wept, and thanked his father and the other villagers. He told them that Amaila, no doubt under the influence of the beast, had enticed him to her hut for a night of pleasure, and that after a most memorable copulation he had known nothing else.

When the villagers took Amaila's body in a boat for the customary sea burial, they noticed that small boils were erupting all over her skin, and tiny filaments were emerging from the boils. They took fright and would have tipped her body into the sea, had not Haiho stopped them. 'It will not do to increase the numbers of the beast,' said he, and had them row back swiftly to the beach, where they burned the body and the boat.

After that the people of the islands armed themselves with the double-bladed knives that were serrated on one side. The medusa had infested their waters in great numbers, and many died before help could be given to them. The people began to use boats to move from island to island, and it was forbidden to swim more than a few strokes from the beaches.

One day a new thing happened. A sky-woman fell from the sky in a burning silver boat. The boat was wrecked but the woman was still alive, although barely so. Her head and groin were covered with the fine tentacles of the quiescent medusa. As she lay in Haiho's hut, moaning, Haiho himself took charge of removing the medusa. It came limply off as he scoured her scalp and pubis, and he was pleased. The woman began slowly to recover. A few days later, however, he found that fine filaments were springing up again through her skin. "It must have gotten into her body," he said in sorrow. There was only one thing to be done.

The villagers helped drag the woman to the beach. Haiho took the knife in his hand, raised it so that it flashed in the sun. He turned the knife over so that the serrations were along the outer edge, and brought it gently down on the woman's neck. Then they built a bonfire and disposed of the body. Thus did Haiho the Wise again save his people from the medusa.

Ever since then, every hunter on every island in the archipelago has made sure that his knife has one serrated edge and one edge that is smooth, sharpened and deadly.

The Marriage of Tree and Stone
A Myth of the Angudka Tribe
Continent of Zakrug, Planet Omasa, Star System Proxima

IN TIME'S CHILDHOOD THE trees could move and talk. They would pull their short, thick roots out of the ground and walk to the river every morning. They would dip their roots in the water and drink.

In those days the stones could also move and talk. They would roll from one place to another and mingle with trees and with the other stones.

The world sounded with the creaky, whispery voices of the trees, and the low, grating language of the stones, and all was well.

Often a tree would fall in love with a stone, and the stone with the tree, and they would marry. Their offspring were green in colour, smooth-skinned, with four limbs and no roots. Their bodies had the pliancy of young, green shoots but within them was a hard framework, like stone.

These children, being rootless and light of limb, could move quickly, and they soon began to explore their world. They bathed in the watery channels the stones made for them and they ate the fruits from the trees.

Among the first children there was a boy called Angud, who always played apart from the others. He had been lamed as an infant when one of his older brothers had dropped him, so he could keep up only with the slow gait of the stones and trees. He limped along with the stones and trees all day and heard their stories, and played tunes for them on his whistle. In return they found him hiding places and protected him from the teasing of the other children. As he grew, he mated with both stone and tree, and awaited the time when his own children would be born.

The other children were also by this time grown to adulthood, and they saw that they were quicker than the trees and stones, and were able to use their limbs to build or to take apart. Soon they grew proud; all except Angud.

So they scoffed when a tree father walked unsteadily by on his roots and they frowned when a stone mother rolled too close. They knocked Angud down when he tried to defend his parents, and they took from him his whistle and threw it away. Then they asked the trees and stones to stand forever still.

At first the trees and stones were angry and scolded their children, but the children turned their backs on them and walked away. Only Angud stayed behind. He did what he could to soothe the trees and stones, but the weight of their sorrow was such that they stood still.

At first, Angud limped among them, wailing his grief in the two languages he knew, and trying in vain to rouse his kin. But when he saw that there was nothing he could do, he found himself shelter and lived as he had done before, but in great loneliness.

Soon, dust and debris covered the stones. The roots of the trees became long and thin and reached deep into the ground, blindly seeking the stone underneath.

Three Tales from Sky River

Then one day Angud heard the wailings of many voices, and emerged from his shelter to find his infant children crawling out of stony caves and the hollows of trees. Then a great joy filled him. He brought them up to love the trees and stones, and taught them all the old stories.

One day, when he was very old, one of his grandchildren brought to him a long piece of wood with holes. "My whistle!" said Angud joyfully, and blew on it a single quavering note. He thought he heard a faint rumble, deep in the forest, but he was too weak to blow another note, and died not long after. Then his weeping children buried both him and the whistle in the ground. After that the Angudka lived as their father had taught them, and the forest protected them from harm.

As for the ungrateful children who had walked away, Angud's brothers and sisters, they soon forgot their parents. They lived and mated among themselves and they made their own language. They cut tree and stone and built houses and lost the green tint of their skin, and in time they forgot their origins.

But the trees and stones still remember, even in their sleep. Their memory is not as clear as before, and the old sorrow has dulled. Only, when the descendants of the ungrateful children come to the forest with axe and rope, they sometimes hear the sound of a whistle among the trees, sweet and low. They see no one, not even their fabled Angudka cousins, and they tremble with wonder and fear. As the whistle plays its melancholy tune, the trees and stones are roused from the sleep of ages and memories come thick and fast, as clear as yesterday. Then the stones shudder in the ground and shake and crack the earth, and the trees uproot themselves. But neither can move at will any more, so the stones split and the trees crash. The ground thunders in the old tongue of tree and stone, and they say to the ungrateful children: You are our offspring. We made you, they say, but the ungrateful ones don't understand. They turn in fear and run. They do not remember their mother tongue.

The Tetrahedron

THE STORY OF THE Tetrahedron — its mysterious appearance in the middle of a busy street in New Delhi, India — is known in the remotest corners of the globe. There are pictures of it everywhere, towering over the trees and buildings while an anonymous crowd stands outside the fenced area, staring up at it in awe. But few know the story of one of the witnesses of this extraordinary event — an apparently ordinary young woman by the name of Maya, who stood waiting at a bus-stop near the intersection known as Patel Chowk on the fateful morning when the Tetrahedron first appeared. To understand her story we must look upon her with the gaze of someone who cares, so she becomes more than a face in the crowd. The way her brother Manoj considers her, perhaps, when he imagines her standing at the bus-stop at the start of it all — the thin, heart-shaped face, the wistful curiosity in her brown eyes, like a child in a china shop that has been told not to touch things...

She was dressed in a somewhat gaudy, red patchwork tunic over narrow black trousers; a cloth bag hung over her shoulder, declaring her unequivocally a student of Delhi University. She was late for Accounting class, had long since given up hope of arriving in time, and was therefore letting buses bound for the university pass her by. It was this philosophical resignation, and her preoccupation with her thoughts, centred at that moment on her fiancé, Mr Perfect Kartik, that resulted in her witnessing the manifestation (for lack of a better word) of the Tetrahedron.

She stood a little apart from the crowds at the bus-stop: young, sleek-headed men with cellphones, steely-eyed women in saris carrying briefcases, students in a colourful knot discussing politics. It was a cool morning in February and the crows were hunched on the neem trees over her head, watching the peanut-seller with beady eyes. The air smelled of traffic fumes and roasting peanuts, and somebody's flowery perfume.

What she was thinking about at this moment was how Kartik was beginning to irritate her. Maya's engagement to Kartik represented her final surrender to the demands of respectability. Every foray she had made into the out-of-the-ordinary — playing cricket with the boys, climbing trees, buying an entire tray of bangles from a beggar girl in the market, making friends with the girl in the next apartment block who rode a motorbike and was reputed to be "wild" — had been met with parental consternation, lectures on family honour and marital prospects, and had left her with busloads of guilt. So she felt like a traitor even *thinking* about how Kartik was starting to annoy her...

Lately, whenever she met Kartik (under the watchful eyes of some elderly relative or other) he would lecture her on her failings. The *halwa* she had made for tea was a little too sweet, that sari was a little flashy — and by the way, could she bring him the newspaper? But the worst was the way her mother and father acted around Kartik, as though he were some minor deity that must be kept in a constant state of appeasement. If only her brother Manoj, two years her senior, had been there — he would understand, but he had escaped many years ago. He was in the Merchant Navy, stationed now in Vishakhapatnam. Her three elder married sisters were harried mothers and quite useless. As for her friends in college, Maya no longer found their obsession with the latest fashions, jewellery and eligible young men diverting. These days she had been feeling very much alone.

At precisely 10.23 a.m. IST, her musings were interrupted by the appearance of an enormous tetrahedron in the middle of the street before her. It came suddenly and incongruously into existence — a monstrous black thing, about two stories high, broad enough on its triangular base to span all four lanes of the road. There was a chorus of screeches as cars and scooters and auto-rickshaws braked in desperation, and then a series of prolonged metallic crashes as vehicles behind them made contact. A woman near Maya dropped her bag and began screaming.

Curses, exclamations, invocations to various gods, the sounds of running feet as a stampede began — then a fearful, wondering silence fell upon the crowds that remained on the sidewalk and the people emerging slowly from the vehicles. Even those who had started to run slowed down and turned back to stare. Faces peered out of windows in the buildings on both sides of the street. The crows themselves stood silent on the branches of the old trees.

Astonishingly, nothing had crashed into the Tetrahedron itself, which stood quietly in the street. To Maya's amazement, it seemed as though the two buses, the cars and bicycles that had been in the place now occupied by the Tetrahedron had simply ceased to be.

Moments later, Maya found herself walking towards the Tetrahedron with a straggle of other bold onlookers. They stood gazing at its opaque sleekness, its geometrical perfection, wondering, but too afraid to touch. Until a small street urchin held out a dirty hand and touched the thing; then everyone followed suit, patting and feeling the smooth, unyielding surface. Behind them the crowd grew as people emerged from cars and buses to gaze open-mouthed at this unexpected sight and proffer theories. Depending on which religion the theorist professed, it was a signal from the gods that the end of the era of *kalyug* was come, and destruction was imminent, or that the one true God was about to emerge and pass judgement on the sinners... It was a government ploy (from a disgruntled clerk who refused to speculate as to how or why). It was a bomb from a neighbouring country that would explode any minute now and why were they standing there anyway. It was a new secret weapon the government had developed. It was an invasion by Martians (from a boy in school uniform) or by Egyptians (from his friend, who was contradicted by another schoolboy: "It's a tetrahedron, not a pyramid, stupid!"). Arguments broke out regarding the possible validity of each theory. Some bemoaned the fate of the people who had been in the space now occupied by the Tetrahedron. They must lie crushed flat under this monstrous thing, they said, shaking their heads ghoulishly. Well, well, who knew where you'd end up when you left your doorstep of a morning?

Then the press came, eager-eyed TV cameramen, the All India Radio people, and, following at their heels, the police. The latter were rather at a loss — there was nothing in the Indian Penal Code about this. The police officer fell back on old ground and began waving his baton at the crowd, "Move on, You're obstructing traffic!" while some responded, "What about that thing? It's obstructing traffic. Are you going to arrest it?" But finally, in the anarchistic, reluctant way of a large beast, the crowd was pushed back and railings set up around the Tetrahedron. Sirens wailed discordantly while stalled traffic was diverted, and finally army trucks rolled in. Soldiers leaped out and took their places with clockwork precision, rifles agleam, but the Tetrahedron answered no questions or challenges. On the sidewalks a large crowd still stood and stared, and pickpockets and vendors of spicy and sticky concoctions did a roaring trade. Maya was interviewed by a reporter from *The Statesman* ("Did you really touch it? What do you think it might be?").

When she went home (who could sit in a class after this?) her parents were watching the whole thing on TV. The TV was blaring because her mother had the sewing machine going, trying to finish an order from the tailoring shop where she worked. The youngest of her married older sisters, who was here for a visit, was cooking something in the tiny kitchen of the flat, while her firstborn, little Chanchal, babbled in her grandfather's lap. Maya's parents were horrified when she told them she had been there and had touched the thing, but when she mentioned that *The Statesman* had actually interviewed her, their horror knew no bounds. What would Kartik say?

Fortunately Kartik did not subscribe to *The Statesman*. When he came for tea on the following weekend, he talked at length about the Tetrahedron, unaware that Maya had actually been there when it appeared. Kartik's theory was that it was a Pakistani secret weapon. Gratified by the attention of his hosts (his future father-in-law had nodded several times) he grew expansive, dandled little Chanchal on his knee (ignoring her outraged cries) and gave Maya a significant look. Maya, lost in thoughts of her own, stared blankly back at him, although her sister gave her a dig in the ribs and blushed and simpered. Maya had cause to be distracted.

The day after the Appearance, she had gone back to the Tetrahedron as though pulled by an invisible string. There were officious looking policemen guarding it from the public and a small army contingent occupying an entire block. Within the cordon, a group of people had been busy with instruments, in the important, oblivious manner of scientists. Among them she recognized Samir, a Ph.D student of astrophysics, who sometimes used the same university bus Maya did. He had once been introduced to her by an acquaintance on the bus, and she remembered his intense, intelligent gaze sweeping over her then with no more than a polite interest.

She had gone over to the cordon and called impulsively out to him, to his considerable surprise — but he was just finished and it had been only natural to go to the university together and to talk about the whole thing at the tea-shack. Nursing her tea in the chipped glass, Maya had told Samir about her witnessing of the Tetrahedron's arrival. "It didn't arrive," she'd said, "I didn't see it come down from the sky, or through the trees. One moment it wasn't there, and the next moment it was." Samir had listened with great interest.

Now, as she poured Kartik more tea (the best Darjeeling her parents could buy), she thought about the past two days of drinking strong, cheap *masala chai* with Samir on the old wooden benches in front of the tea-shack. She imagined her parents' shock and horror. What would Kartik say to that?

Samir had told her that the night before the arrival of the Tetrahedron there had been an unusual event — a series of radio pulses from the vicinity of an ordinary yellow star that was not known for such activity. He hypothesized that the Tetrahedron was an alien device, travelling at near-light-speed through space via some unknown mechanism. He was disarmingly frank about his bias towards an astronomical origin for the Tetrahedron — he was a student of astrophysics after all — but next to the Pakistani-American-secret-weapon-theory, the astronomical one was the most popular. The people whose relatives had been in the buses and cars that had disappeared were demanding a complete investigation of every possibility. Foreign scientists had flocked to Delhi in droves, as had New Age groupies, end-of-the-world cults, members of the international press, and ordinary gawking tourists. The President of the United States had been restrained with difficulty from declaring war on India for possessing secret weapons of mass destruction, and had only been placated with promises of a substantial American presence among the investigators. Other suspicious governments from the West had also sent their representatives. Suddenly, New Delhi had become one of the most popular travel destinations in the world. Maya and Samir had laughed over newspaper headlines — the government was building more hotels! The Western press was floundering, unused as they were to reporting anything but disasters and political unrest from the Third World! A tabloid reported that India had been chosen for a special reason by a wise alien race, and would shortly receive a message of epic importance concerning the next elections!

But what Maya relived most often in her mind was the feeling when she had touched the Tetrahedron — the feeling of how useless and insignificant her life was against the unending mystery of the universe. Now, with Samir talking eloquently about aliens traversing the distances between stars, she had felt it again, the pointlessness of a life lived small. In a few years she would be like her sisters, plump and resigned, children running at her feet while Kartik gazed benignly at her from the sofa over the evening paper. "Maya, you know that sari does not suit you…" Maya this and Maya that. Could she take a lifetime of it?

Of course, she had only herself to blame, choosing Kartik. Her parents had left the final choice up to her, from an army of eligible bachelors of the appropriate class and caste. Dressed in her best, serving tea to a succession of potential in-laws and their self-conscious offspring, she had been dazzled by Kartik's assurance. Her parents had approved whole-heartedly — Kartik had a good future in a small company that manufactured shoes, and his parents' flat was huge — large enough to accommodate a young, married couple. But now she was no longer sure of her feelings.

She stopped going to class. Every day she went dutifully to the university, where she hung around the tea-shop, waiting for Samir, listening to old film songs that the proprietor, Ramu, insisted on playing loudly on the radio. They drank strong tea in ancient glasses that had seen better days, and speculated about the Tetrahedron. The scientists had found nothing. The object was made out of an unbelievably hard substance that could not be chipped off for testing. X-rays bounced merrily off it. It was much too heavy to be moved (this to the disappointment of an American software billionaire who wanted to transport it to his mansion in the US). Neither controlled explosives nor corrosive chemicals had the slightest effect on it. Digging under it for the remains of the unfortunate bus and car passengers, the authorities found nothing — no bodies, no crushed bones or flesh, no evidence of charred remains, just dirt and the impenetrable substance of the Tetrahedron standing over it. It stood implacable, a question with no answer.

When she was not at the tea-shop, Maya began to spend her time gawking at the Tetrahedron with the large crowd that was always there. Like others in the crowd she felt as though she, too, was waiting for something. The road where the Tetrahedron stood was now blocked to traffic, of course, and its immediate vicinity was patrolled by a now international team of soldiers on permanent alert. Meanwhile a series of shops had sprung up as if overnight in the parking lot of an adjacent building. Soft drinks, tea, hot *samosas*, cameras, film, knick-knacks such as plastic replicas of the Tetrahedron were being sold at exorbitant prices. Foreign languages from all over the world mingled with radio music from the shops and live commentary from TV station crewmen. Rich businessmen rubbed shoulders with hippies and street urchins; Americans and Middle-Easterners, Japanese, Koreans, Kenyans all stood gawking and chattering in little groups. People-watching became Maya's hobby. Her favourite pastime was to eavesdrop on the conversations that sprang up in her vicinity — fragments of arguments, discussions, both academic and untutored — it was a feast for the ears.

"… the heat, the dust… Why here?"

"…the weapons theory has been more or less defused by now, no pun intended… except for the politicians, paranoid as usual…"

"Beats me… Place wasn't even what I expected. No elephants, or dancing girls, or any of that shit… Got my camcorder along and for what… All that thing does is to sit there while we sweat our butts off."

"Reason… there's a reason it's special, if you read the paper by MacArthur…"

"…and they don't even eat monkey heads, man, so much for Indiana Jones… bunch of vegetarians…"

"Don't grumble, dear, it was your idea…"

"…what do you expect Hollywood to do, make documentaries…"

"Well, the Johnsons, they went all over this country… couldn't stand their boasting…"

"…the term 'synchronicity'? Meaningful coincidence…"

"…got some shots of the cows on the roads, weird enough for me…"

"… yes, like when you're thinking of a song and the DJ starts playing it — what's that got to do with…"

"…even the fast food joints aren't the same…"

"…only in a place like this, look at the traffic. By Western standards, with conditions like this, most people ought to be dead or dying. What keeps them going, eh? How anything functions here is a small miracle. A modification of the Jungian concept of synchronicity…"

"…did you hear what happened to the Gustafsons? The hotel didn't have any record of their reservations, poor things. They ended up you'll never guess where…"

"…Never in Japan, no. Far more disciplined people. There's something in the air over here, as though the chaos is intrinsic to the place…"

"… in the home of the student they'd hosted ten years ago, back when they were in Tucson.."

"…dimensional anomalies… fellow called Bhaskar, native — I mean Indian mathematician, cosmologist… yes, in *The Times*… no, no, *The London Times*… theorizes that dimensional anomalies must exist in this region, hence the Tetrahedron…"

"…intrinsic anarchy, I like that, no wonder we couldn't hold on to the Empire…"

Maya would listen, fascinated. Sometimes a tourist would come up to her and ask if she'd agree to be photographed in front of the Tetrahedron. She was always discomfited by these requests and would back away with a muttered "sorry". Mostly she kept a low profile, watching, listening, sipping a drink or two, letting her thoughts drift, wondering at the silence, the serenity of the Tetrahedron in the midst of all the noise and bustle.

At home, nobody guessed what was going on in Maya's head as she pounded spices in the little kitchen, or hung wet laundry on the nylon clothesline on the balcony. In the evenings the tiny flat was full of the sound of the sewing machine. Her mother's scissors went snip-snip as iridescent piles of cloth accumulated on the drawing-room floor. She would put some of the bright cloth aside to make a dress for Chanchal or a patchwork *salwaar kameez* for Maya. Her customers never found out. "Your mother is a marvel," her father said one day, when the dress was ready. "She can add two and two and get five!" "Dimensional anomalies!" Maya said with a small smile, and went into the kitchen to wash dishes. She gazed moodily out of the window at a view of rooftops and TV antennas, crowded streets, music and conversations blaring from tiers of lit open windows — over all this, in a hazy, dark sky, glimmered a faint star or two. Maya wondered what she was going to do with her life.

Tea with Kartik. Endless teas and breakfasts and dinners with Kartik. When he came the next evening he looked tired and a little vulnerable, and she felt a small pang. But seeing her parents bustling about him, deferring to his every wish, she felt her old irritation arise again. To make matters worse, Kartik started talking about the Tetrahedron. This time he was convinced China had something to do with it too. After all, why stop at Pakistan? Maya set the teapot on the table down so loudly that everyone stopped talking and stared at her in amazement.

"What do you know about it?" she snapped at Kartik. Her heart was hammering in her chest. She was conscious for a moment that she was opening a door she would not be able to shut again. But her anger and confusion, held back as long as it had been, surged over what was left of common sense.

"China! Pakistan! Has it occurred to you that nobody — not anybody — can understand what that thing is? None of the foreign scientists, none of ours. Can't you see anything outside your own damned backyard?"

She turned on her heel and went into the kitchen, shaking violently, leaving a dead silence behind her.

Then a clink as her mother set down her cup, and her apologetic voice saying desperately to Kartik,

"Please understand, she is just... you know, sometimes young women... that time of the month... she doesn't mean it..."

And her father now beside her, looking at her in shock and hurt, saying, "What have you done, child?"

What had she done? Insulted the man who was going to be her husband, damaged the fragile alliance between Kartik's parents and her own, lowered the family honour by behaving like a squabbling fish-wife instead of a girl from a respectable family. She looked at her father's upset face, at his shoulders stooping from disappointment, and burst into tears. She went blindly into the room she shared with her visiting sister and the child. Her sister patted her head.

"Listen, you donkey, that is no way to behave before marriage. You can quarrel all you want afterwards; look at Ashish and me — I shout at him all the time…"

"I don't want to marry Kartik," she said between sobs. It was a relief to have said it at last. But she could hear her parents in the drawing room, anxiously trying to placate Kartik. She heard his chair scrape on the floor as he rose, heard him say,

"I hope I have not been mistaken in her. If she comes to her senses…"

Then the front door shut.

After that, for some days, she really tried. She hadn't understood before how vulnerable her parents were, how frightened at the thought that their youngest daughter might never get married. Three daughters had slowly depleted them of their meagre savings, and Kartik's family had not even asked for "gifts" (the euphemism for the illegal dowry). They'd never find anyone like him. So the very next day, she went to the phone booth at the corner of her street, called Kartik and apologized rather stiffly. He did not say anything except to tell her that he was going out of town on business for two weeks, and he would think about this when he returned.

Three days of attending classes and bearing with the questions of her friends put her in such a black depression that she returned to Patel Chowk. One day, when the square seemed particularly crowded, she fought her way to the edge near the parking area, clutching her soft drink in her hand, to stand beneath the generous shade of an ancient tree. It was then that she noticed a white van marked with the words "Ravindra Refrigeration Systems" parked near her. It looked familiar — she must have seen it there before without really noticing it. The side door of the van was open and a motley group of people were gathered around it, talking.

They were all so different from each other that it took her a moment to realize they were a group — three elderly men, two young women who looked Japanese, a lean young man who could have been from the Middle-East, and most incongruous of them all, an old lady in a beige *salwaar-kameez* perched in the open doorway of the van, knitting away. There was something indefinably different about them compared to the rest of the crowd — they seemed relaxed, they hardly glanced at the Tetrahedron, they spoke to each other in low, easy tones.

Maya wondered why she had never really noticed them before. But the Tetrahedron attracted so many kinds of people that perhaps it was no wonder. Now someone with a loudspeaker was shouting; policemen were pushing the crowds aside with batons. Another politician? No, it was a movie star, said a plump woman in a purple sari excitedly to Maya. Look, Malini Mehra herself in a glittering pink sari with a daring backless blouse, at the souvenir booth, waving flirtatiously at the gawking, camera-clicking onlookers. Maya turned away in exasperation. There, behind the trees, was the Tetrahedron, the cause of all the excitement. As she glanced at its pinnacle rising into the sky above the treetops, she thought she saw one of the ubiquitous crows flying directly towards it. What was the bird doing? She squinted up at it but the sun was in her eyes. She thought she saw the bird reach one edge of the Tetrahedron; then it disappeared.

She rubbed her eyes and blinked. The plump woman was still beside her, chattering away about Malini Mehra. "Did you see that?" Maya said. "Of course," said the woman, "Malini Mehra likes reds, they suit her skin, don't you think?" Maya looked away again, but the Tetrahedron was just as before. Turning back she met the eyes of the old woman knitting in the doorway of the white van. The old lady smiled at her. Maya wondered if the woman had seen the crow vanish into the Tetrahedron...

Later she met Samir at the tea-shop. He did not ask her where she had been the past three days. It was a relief to sit with him and watch old Ramu boil tea in a battered saucepan over a kerosene stove. He added a thick pinch of powdered tea and cardamom to the simmering mixture of water and milk. The aroma filled her nostrils. Ramu's radio, tuned to a station that played only classic Hindi film songs, sat perched on the stained wooden counter.

She told Samir about what she had seen.

"I know, I wasn't quite close enough to see clearly if the crow did disappear. But so many strange things have happened, no?"

Samir was looking at her thoughtfully. As he started to answer, a sleek gray car stopped in the road across from them. A bright, confident, charming face leaned out of the back window, radiating ethnic chic — from the casually scooped up hair to the embroidered collar of what was probably a very expensive designer *salwaar-kameez*.

"Bhaiya, don't forget to be on time tonight!"

Bhaiya — Elder brother. Samir waved and looked faintly embarrassed. "My sister," he said apologetically as the car drove off in a puff of dust. "It's her birthday today."

It occurred to Maya suddenly that Samir was from a quite different stratum of society than herself. She had known this all along — he lived in Greater Kailash, after all, probably in one of those obscenely big houses — but it had never mattered, never seemed important, until now. His English was polished, hers just fluent enough to get by. She remembered meeting a friend of Samir's on their way to the tea-shack some days ago, and the way the friend had looked at her and then again at Samir with astonished surprise. Samir hadn't introduced her. The friend had smiled at Samir and dug him in the ribs and muttered something to him before sauntering off. Something about fraternizing with the vulgar proles? Words she only half caught and did not understand. After that Samir had kept talking to her as though nothing had happened, but just for a fleeting moment he had looked discomfited... Abruptly Maya was aware of herself as hopelessly lower-middle-class, belonging to the petty-tradesmen-uncultured *bhainji* sub-culture with all its implications. She didn't know anything about Samir's life, nor he about hers — what was she doing here with him?

But he was talking on, oblivious.

"...and maybe it was nothing, but maybe, just maybe, you've hit on something here. There's been a lot of speculation about this. Look," he drew out his notebook and tore off two pages. He tore one into a rough disk and put it against the edge of the other sheet, at right angles.

"Suppose you were a two-dimensional creature living on the surface of this rectangular sheet of paper. Would you know that this disk existed? No, because it is in the third dimension, right, which is not accessible to you. You would only see the straight line that is the intersection between the disk and the sheet where you exist."

She concentrated, pushing back her other thoughts.

"*Achha*, so if I put the edge of my hand against my face," she said, doing so, "my face feels only the edge. It has no idea of the extent or shape of my hand."

"Yes, something like that. You see, it may be that the Tetrahedron is only a projection of a more complicated object in our three-dimensional world. This object extends in a dimension that is inaccessible to us — all we perceive is the Tetrahedron. To us it appears closed. But in another dimension, there may be doors..."

He stopped, lost in thought. Maya was fascinated.

"You mean that somehow the crow I saw got through into another dimension, got into the Tetrahedron? But..."

He took a sip of his tea and set the glass down on the edge of the bench.

"Do you know what topology is?"

She shook her head.

"Simply put, it's a branch of mathematics that concerns itself with very general, basic properties of objects or spaces. Topologists look at what happens if you continuously deform the space or the object without breaking or tearing it… Here, let me give you an example."

He held the page he had torn from his book in one hand, and the paper disk in the other.

"This rectangular page and this disk of paper are topologically identical, because you can shrink or stretch one to become the other. And your *chai* glass is identical to them both because I can theoretically deform the sides until it's flat. But —"

He tore a small hole in the middle of the page.

"Now this is no longer topologically equivalent to the disk, because by the rules of topology, however much you deform this page, you can't get rid of the hole. So the page without the hole is a simply connected two-dimensional surface, and the page with the hole is what we call multiply-connected…"

"Oh… like a tea-cup… I mean one with a handle, not Ramu's *chai* glasses."

"Yes, yes," he smiled delightedly at her, immensely pleased. 'Topologically you and I are identical to a teacup, or a *vada*, if you like South Indian food — the human alimentary canal is the analog of the hole in the *vada*!'

She was staring at him, wide-eyed.

"*Achha*, but what has all this to do with —"

"The Tetrahedron? Plenty. Topology is relevant in two ways. One, if the topological structure of the universe is non-trivial, multiply connected in several dimensions, then it might provide shortcuts for faster-than-light travel. Like the wormholes in space that the newspapers keep talking about. Two, the true shape or structure of the Tetrahedron itself. If we could see it completely in all the dimensions that it inhabits, we might see something topologically very complicated. It would be incomprehensible to us — our notions of in and out, edge and surface would be lost, or at least very confused. Ever seen a Möbius strip?"

She shook her head, feeling awed and small before the vastness of his knowledge. Now what was he doing? His hands, brown and slender, she'd never noticed before how nice his hands were — tore a strip of paper from the long edge of the page. His eyes were alight with enthusiasm.

"Look at this strip of paper — see how I can put the ends together to form a ring?" He suited the action to the word. "Now suppose, before I do that, I twist the paper once, like this. Now I put the ends together. A ring with a twist! This is a Möbius strip."

She put a tentative finger out to touch it. He smiled.

"Go on, move your finger along the outer surface, along the length of it... yes, just so!" He grinned at her surprise. "You start at the outer surface and before you know it, you are inside! Except that inside and outside have lost their meaning in this case, because a Möbius strip has only one surface, not two like the ring." He was talking fast in his excitement. "People think that spacetime may be a generalization of a Möbius strip or some similar non-trivial topological object, in several dimensions... So also an object like the Tetrahedron could be very complex, very interesting, if we could see it in its entirety..."

Words failed her. She imagined a complicated structure with smoothly contoured edges and sculptured pathways curving dizzily, leading to hidden doors. She stared at him in wonder and envy.

"*Hanh*, I understand the idea... I think."

He nodded approvingly.

"If the Tetrahedron is a projection in our space of a more complicated, multi-dimensional object, it might also explain the disappearance of the people who were on the road at the time the Tetrahedron appeared. Who knows?"

"You mean they might be *inside* the Tetrahedron?" she said incredulously. The thought had never occurred to her. Instead she had imagined that perhaps some kind of exchange had taken place, the Tetrahedron for the people. That the bus riders, the car passengers and the bicyclists were at this very moment on some other world, walking about under alien skies with their mouths open. Another world! Her mind had conjured up bizarre vistas. Yet the thought of what the inside of the Tetrahedron might be like was equally mind-boggling.

Maya sat talking to Samir for another hour. He told her about current theories of the birth of the universe, the mysteries that arose with each new discovery. She liked the way he gesticulated in his excitement, the way his eyes seemed to see the wonders his words described. Now he was expounding on the eventual death of the universe.

"The solar system, of course, will die long before that," he said. "The sun will swell and swallow the earth, the moon, all the nearer planets, before collapsing into a white dwarf star."

He stopped to take a sip of his tea, and suddenly the radio started playing an old Hemant Kumar favourite: *"Na yeh chand hoga, na taare rahenge..."* The moon will be no more, nor will the stars remain...

They both laughed at the same time.

"I always wondered how in Bollywood films they contrive to have a song with the right words come on at the appropriate moment," he said, smiling. "Just the other day a similar coincidence happened. There I was, wondering about what kind of star the aliens are from, if they are aliens, that is, and Ramu's radio started playing *'chand ke paas jo sitaara hai'.*" That star by the moon...

"Oh yes, Lata Mangeshkar and Kishore Kumar," Maya said. "I love old film songs. I think Ramu's radio is tuned to the aliens' favourite station!"

It was very pleasant to be able to laugh companionably with somebody. (Maya wondered with a pang whether she and Kartik would ever have anything to laugh about.) Then she remembered fragments of a conversation she had overheard.

The Tetrahedron

"It is syn… synchronicity," she said carefully. He looked amused.

"That's a big word. Not a scientifically valid concept, of course, but… wasn't it in one of the papers? Where did you come across it?"

"I heard it somewhere." She felt a slight indignation. What did he think — that she was hopelessly ignorant? Then she thought, depressingly, that it was true.

But Samir was getting up, setting his glass down on Ramu's counter with a rather awkward air.

"Got to go," he muttered. He looked shyly at her, as though seeing her for the first time. "See you tomorrow!"

She didn't understand until the radio sang the refrain again: *"Na yeh chand hoga, na taare rahenge, magar ham hamesha tumhaare rahenge…"* The moon will be no more, nor will the stars remain, yet I will always be yours…

She stood staring after him, her face hot with embarrassment. She hoped he didn't think — surely he didn't?

When Maya came home one evening, her sister and mother were talking about a story on the afternoon news about a mental sickness that the tabloid press had nicknamed Tetra-fever.

"Isn't it terrible, Maya, there are these people who are obsessed with the Tetrahedron, they can't eat or sleep or function normally — they dream about it all the time," her sister said, setting a plate of hot onion *pakoras* before Maya. "Some of them starve themselves almost to death, there is this fellow being kept alive in a hospital, fed through a tube…" Maya nearly choked over her tea, then took an extra-large helping of the *pakoras*. Her mother nodded.

"Yes, yes, they talked on TV about a man who stopped going to work, lost his job. He spends all his time staring at the Tetrahedron. He has three children! Poor things, such a terrible thing to happen. At least your father is a sensible man. And there's this housewife, can you imagine, goes shopping at the plaza every day, has the largest collection of plastic tetrahedrons in the city, chee chee!"

Maya nodded, mouth full, and took another *pakora*.

"Still," said her mother, pouring herself more tea and liberally adding sugar, "it is all in God's hands." She sighed, and Maya knew what she was going to say. "Nothing to do with us."

Her father came in at the door, stooping, tired from a long day of work and the hot, sweaty bus ride. Maya felt guilty. Maybe I am one of the crazies, she thought to herself, thinking of all the time she spent away from class, with Samir or at the Tetrahedron. Thank goodness Kartik was out of town… If only her brother, Manoj, was here! She had written to him some time ago but he was on a ship, and his reply would take time. Besides, letters were no substitute for seeing him face to face.

But at least she was able to talk to Samir about the Tetrahedron. Their mutual embarrassment had been short-lived; at their next meeting, they were comfortable with each other again. There was so much to talk about that she no longer paid any attention to Ramu's radio. However Samir had not been very interested in the occupants of the white van. On a visit to Patel Chowk he had looked them over rather dismissively – they were not a fascinating astronomical phenomenon after all. He did remark on the old woman knitting away — she was like Madam Defarge, he said, a character from some famous book she'd never heard of. She found this evidence of his class and education annoying, but at least he did not think she was crazy.

They talked about the latest development in the saga of the Tetrahedron. A man had been found wandering in the Thar desert a few hundred miles west of New Delhi. He had been pushing a bicycle over the sand dunes, a strange sight indeed for the villagers who found him. They related that the man did not seem to know where he was going. Upon being questioned he had replied in what seemed to be gibberish, or another language. He seemed happy enough to be led to a villager's hut, where he had been fed and housed for several days. A social worker had come across him and, based on the contents of a bag strapped to his bicycle, had gathered that he was from Delhi and contacted the police there. It had finally been established that he was one of the people missing when the Tetrahedron had first appeared.

As could be expected, this caused a sensation. Search teams were sent to comb the Thar desert, and there an astounding discovery had been made. The missing bus had been found in a sandy valley, with fifteen people in it — eleven of the original bus passengers, and four people who had been in cars when the Tetrahedron appeared. All fifteen were alive and well, physically that is. But two of them were in the same state as the bicyclist, and the rest kept eerily silent, reacting to nothing and nobody, confounding doctors and family members alike. Meanwhile the bicyclist's family — he was a postal clerk — appeared on TV expressing relief that he had been found, and hope that he and the others would be cured of their strange malady. The tabloid press had a field day. Headlines across the world proclaimed, "16 People Kidnapped by Aliens Free — But What Happened to Them?"

Maya and Samir could only speculate. As they sat drinking tea, a thought struck Maya.

"The world is like a cracked egg," she said. "Our world, I mean, where we live. Everything we know and see and understand is in this egg. But the cracks tell us that there are things outside — a world outside our understanding…"

Samir gave her a startled look.

"You sound quite poetic," he said, smiling. He cleared his throat, as though to say something. Maya shook her head. An idea had been nagging her for some time, and she had suddenly found the words for it.

"What if the Tetrahedron isn't a spaceship? What if it is something we can't even imagine, something totally unknown? You know, what bothers me about all this is that there is so much talk. Just talk. You scientists seem so sure about one theory or another theory — but how can you be really know something without any experience of it?"

Vandana Singh

"That's where experiments come in," Samir said patiently, ready to expound.

"No, that's not what I mean," she said. She grinned. "The other day when you were holding your cup of tea and you told me about what the tea was made of, atoms and molecules, remember? You said if we could understand the smallest constituents of matter we would be able to know everything there is to know about tea."

"Well?"

"You forgot to drink it. Your theories can tell you a lot about tea, but not about the experience of drinking it. That is what I mean. I don't have the words to explain it, but... do you know what I mean?"

She was conscious of his gaze suddenly, and it seemed that there was something faintly wistful about it. He hadn't been listening to her. Embarrassed, she began to talk at once about something else that had occurred to her.

"You know, if the idea about the Tetrahedron being — what was it — a projection — of a larger object in another dimension — if that is true, then maybe this object is huge — so huge that it extends all the way to the Thar desert..."

He raised his eyebrows.

"*Hanh*, that is possible. Yes, perhaps there is another door somewhere in the Thar where they let them off. But what about the rest of the people who vanished?"

"Maybe they don't want to come back, who knows. Maybe the aliens are nicer to them than humans are to each other. Maybe this and maybe that. Samir, what I'm trying to say is, how can we know anything about the Tetrahedron without ever having been in it?"

"It isn't as though we haven't tried," he said a little defensively. "We've gone over every square centimetre..."

"Would you, if you could?" she interrupted. "If you found a way, would you go in? Go off on a journey through space?"

"Of course I would!"

He fell silent, rubbing his chin. He gave her an unexpectedly awkward look, then looked away.

"Listen, Maya… I'd like to go inside the Tetrahedron, of course, to study it. But I would have to be sure I could come back. You know," now he looked at her directly again, but it was a very different kind of look. "I am very attached to my family… They've been wondering why I've been spending so much time here. My friends, too. They don't always understand me, but still… family is family, don't you think?"

He was looking at her meaningfully, his brown eyes sorrowful, and still she did not understand. Then suddenly she realized what he was saying, what he must think of her and the direction their relationship might be going. Young men and women didn't fraternize one-on-one for weeks on end unless there was some intention, some basis for a very different kind of relationship. Through the host of confused thoughts in her mind, her pride rose like a sword unsheathed.

"I am close to my family too," she said a little too hurriedly. "In fact I am engaged to this really nice fellow, Kartik, you must meet him some day…"

He was staring at her, open-mouthed. She couldn't be sure whether he was angry or upset or both. Her face burned. How dare he presume? Their friendship had been strictly in the context of the Tetrahedron — she had expected no more from him than that… well, yes, she liked him, the way he thought about things, his generosity, the kindness in his eyes, the fact that he didn't automatically assume she was stupid, oh and his hands, how they moved when he was describing something — and yet he had assumed. How could he think her so callow, so simple, like a heroine from a third-rate movie? She wanted to tell him: Yes, my father is a clerk and my mother works in a tailoring shop, but I have a sense of dignity. And, she wanted to say, if we *were* really interested in each other in that way, so what? Coward, getting cold feet before anything had begun! She couldn't trust herself to speak. Angry tears pricked at the corners of her eyes. To hell with you and your expensively dressed-up sister and those snobbish friends you never introduce me to, she told him silently. He was getting up, looking at his watch, making some excuse. He had a class very soon. And some exams coming up... he was going to be very busy from now on. He gave her an uncertain, apologetic smile and walked away through the trees and down the street.

On Ramu's radio, Geeta Dutt began to sing *"Na jao saiiyan, chura ke baiiyan..."* Don't leave, beloved, stealing my heart away. She looked at the old man suspiciously. He winked, shrugged his shoulders and went back to scrubbing the counter, a pointless task, she thought inconsequentially, since it always seemed to be dirty.

The next day she did not go to the university. She went straight to Patel Chowk and stood watching the crowd. A crow watched Maya from the roof of souvenir stall. "What do you see," she asked it in her mind. "What do you see when you look at the Tetrahedron?" The bird cocked its head and stared at her with beady eyes. It gave a caw that sounded like raucous laughter, then took to the air, flapping its wings heavily. Maya sipped her drink and sighed. She saw the old lady in the white van, watching her in a benign sort of way. On an impulse she went up to her.

"What are you knitting?" she said in Hindi. The old woman looked puzzled. Maya asked the question again in English.

"Ah! Only a sweater for my grandson." She spoke with a peculiar accent. "I'm from Mexico," she said, smiling.

"Here to see the Tetrahedron?" Maya asked, feeling stupid. What else?

"*Si...* yes. Three times I make the trip to your country. Much like Mexico, here. Hot desert, mountain, seaside, we have them all." She smiled enigmatically. "Also old buildings. Yesterday I see the tall Minar, many tombs."

"Are you with a tourist group?" Maya asked, wondering what Ravindra Refrigeration had to do with sightseeing.

"Tourist? Tourist, yes. Like to come?"

Maya shook her head, smiling distractedly. "I have to go..."

"Come see us if you like to come. We here until weekend — Saturday. What's your name? Maya? We have that name too!" She smiled with great pleasure.

Maya waved goodbye and wondered rather miserably what she should do. Go back home? Kartik had written to say he would be back next week. It had been a cold sort of letter — clearly he was expecting her to make amends for her behaviour. She could go to class, for a change. Samir could go jump in a well. With that comforting thought, she took the bus to the university. Once there she could not bear the thought of dealing with the inane chatter of her friends. It was a hot day — she walked to Ramu's *chai*-shack, thinking maybe she'd have some *nimbu-pani* instead of tea. The small open space in front of the shack was deserted. She watched the traffic on the road as she sipped her drink, trying not to think about whether Ramu ever washed the glasses. She tried to push away bitter thoughts of Samir. She would miss his friendship — and, she had to admit, the possibilities their relationship had contained. Lata Mangeshkar began singing on the radio: *"Aaj koi naheen apna, kise gham ye sunaayen…"* Today I have no one to call my own, to whom shall I tell my sorrow…

Irritably she looked at Ramu but he had his back to her, doing something industrious with a rag. You go jump in a well too, she told him silently. Moisture beaded her glass of *nimbu-pani*. She wiped sweat off her forehead with a handkerchief her mother had embroidered, and found a sudden lump in her throat. It's not just space and time, she thought bitterly, that are multiply connected. If she could talk to Samir now, she'd tell him: outer space, inner space, both have unknown topologies. You couldn't overlook one at the expense of the other. But he wouldn't talk to her anymore, curse him…

On Friday night she was unable to sleep. A pale wash of streetlight lit the room — on the other bed her sister lay sleeping, her arm about Chanchal, who stirred fitfully in a dream. Maya went up to the window and sat on the sill, leaning against the grillwork. Down on the street a watchman banged his stick on the sidewalk as he passed. There was a light on here and there among tiers of darkened windows — she wondered what was keeping those people awake. She thought about the Tetrahedron, dimensional anomalies, synchronicity. The man walking his bicycle in the middle of the Thar desert, the old woman knitting for her grandson, smiling, saying she'd be here till Saturday. Which was tomorrow. In a few days Kartik would be back in Delhi.

Abruptly, everything fell into place. She got up with sudden determination, got the flashlight from her drawer and went softly into the dark drawing-room. Carefully she found a sheet of paper, sat in a chair and began to write to Kartik in the dim light of the flashlight, hoping and praying that her parents, in the next room, would not wake up. After she was done she put the letter in an envelope and put a stamp on it. She would mail it tomorrow. She felt a great relief.

Next, she wrote a long, affectionate letter to Manoj. "Try to explain it to them, Bhaiya," she wrote. "I don't think I can..."

She went back to the bedroom. Chanchal was awake, crying to go to the bathroom.

"I'll take her," Maya told her sister, who lay back in sleepy gratitude. Chanchal did her duty and was amiable again. She climbed into bed with Maya. Maya sang to her the old children's song about Uncle Moon, about the child going up in a flying ship to play hide-and-seek among the stars. It was Chanchal's favourite song, and she always asked the same question at the end, "Will I come back?" Only this time she said, sleepily, "Will you come back, Maya Mausi?" And Maya said, through her tears, "Of course I will."

In the morning she rose early, cooked breakfast for everyone and washed the dishes so her mother could rest a while before going to work. She saw off her father at the bus-stop and went to the postbox where she mailed the two letters. Then she took the bus to Patel Chowk, where the white van was parked.

The Tetrahedron

"I will come," she told the old lady. The woman smiled as though she had always known Maya would.

Maya's disappearance on the day the Tetrahedron left New Delhi earned only a small item in the newspapers. What was a missing girl — one of those crazies, to judge from what she had written to her family — what was her absence, compared to the most significant event of the century, the appearance and disappearance of the Tetrahedron? Her family mourned, all except Chanchal, who assured the puzzled grown-ups that Maya would be back. Kartik wrote to say he had always been afraid Maya was a little unstable, and her running away (not to mention the lack of respect in the letter she had written to him) proved it — he considered he had had a narrow escape. If she were found, he hoped the family would punish her suitably for dragging their name in mud. Although they didn't deserve it, he was sending back the little gifts her family had given him. Maya's parents wept over the small package he sent — the final end to their dreams for their youngest daughter. Meanwhile, Manoj took leave and came home, torn between grief and hope.

It was one of the hottest days of the season — the square near the Tetrahedron was nearly empty. Even the man selling cold spiced cucumber slices gathered his things and wandered off into the shade, where he sat dozing. A group of bored soldiers watched Maya, the old woman and the others as they walked up to the Tetrahedron. They just wanted to touch it, and they were unarmed, the soldiers said later. They must have wandered off after that, the soldiers said. We weren't really looking. But what really happened was that Maya and her companions went all the way up to the Tetrahedron and turned in a place where she had not known it was possible to turn. It was a kind of narrow corridor and she could still see the soldiers, the white van with Ravindra Refrigeration on it, the driver getting ready to leave — she could still see the hot, dusty square under the neem trees. But also she found herself in a large room which seemed to be made up of walls arranged at impossible angles, like an Escher picture — and the outside world, if it still made sense to talk of outside and inside — the outside world was projected on a plane slanting up from her feet, making her feel giddy. She looked up and she could see the dark of space amid spiral stairways going towards some distant destination; she saw with a shock that there were creatures going up on it, great beings made up of planes and angles and curves that didn't quite fit. Some of them had human-like faces. She turned in wonder to the old woman beside her and stopped with her mouth hanging open.

For the old woman too, had changed. Her face was still the same, but her eyes had grown large and dark, and a succession of crests and ridges rose from her body in great arcs. There were growths dangling from her arms like the appendages of sea-creatures. She smiled at Maya.

Maya drew back. "You are an alien," she said.

"No, my dear," the woman said in chaste Hindi. "I am who I am. Remember what I told you? Do not expect to understand everything all at once. I will be your guide. But first, take a look at yourself."

And the old woman took Maya gently by the shoulders and turned her to a silver wall that was opaque and reflective. Maya saw herself. Saw her face, mouth open in shock, her hair streaming around it, the great crenellations and sweeping ridges that rose from her body as gracefully as the plates on a stegosaur's back. She looked at her two hands, the familiar river-valley of lines and tributaries, and she saw that they were the same as before, and not the same. Other hands branched off her hands, fading off into an infinity of hands, young hands, old hands, smooth and wrinkled. She took a deep, sobbing breath.

"What has happened to me?"

"Nothing. You see yourself as you are in more than three dimensions. Now don't think about it too much. I want you to look around and tell me where you want to go first."

Around — whatever that meant — was the darkness of space, and stars caught in a thin, delicate mesh. She saw the great rings of Saturn, the shadows

The Tetrahedron

of three of its moons like black pimples on its bright face. She saw other planets, dead stars, worlds that drifted in space without suns. And the spiral stairways moved up and up like escalators, vanishing into the fine intricacy of the web.

"Shall we start with something close to home, like the moon?"

"I thought you said this wasn't a spaceship!"

"It is and it isn't. You will get used to not thinking in the old ways, my dear. The categories we are accustomed to on Earth have little meaning here. A square does not have the same meaning for a flat-land person as it does for a three-dimensional one. You'll see."

Maya took a deep breath. Around her the Universe beckoned. She thought she heard Lata Mangeshkar and Mohammad Rafi on Ramu's radio, singing, "Chalo Dildaar, chalo, chand ke paar chalo…" Come, beloved, let us fly beyond the moon.

"Let's go further," she said.

Was that what really happened to Maya? How can we know? All she left behind was a very detailed letter to her brother, and some ideas and theories. Her story came alive from those scribbled pages, but it necessarily came to a stop when she left home. Perhaps in some dimension orthogonal to time and space, it is possible to see what came after, to follow her world-line, to see the post-script to her letter. But caught in the stream of time as we are, all her brother could do was to wait. He thought of all kinds of other scenarios, of spaceships that swept silently through space like owls through night, of aliens and alien languages, and Maya among impossible worlds, her face filled with a softness and yearning, a kind of tender curiosity. He remembered the child she had been, always straining at the barriers, being scolded and cajoled into doing whatever she was supposed to do. She had learned to replace outward defiance with a quiet raging within herself. He thought of her waiting at the bus-stop on that fateful morning before it all began, unaware of the person she would become, the person who would write so passionately in her last letter: 'What if the Tetrahedron is something that is completely beyond our understanding? How can we know it without experiencing it?'

One day, some weeks after the disappearance, Samir climbed the three flights of stairs to the little flat and talked to Manoj rather incoherently about his conversations with Maya. He never doubted that she was out there somewhere in the distance between the stars. He was about to finish his Ph.D, he was going to an observatory in Chile later in the year, he would keep an eye out for her. At this, Manoj laughed a little bitterly. He guessed something from the dazed look in the young man's eyes.

"I'll be watching too," he said. "I think if she comes back it will be in the Thar desert."

"The Thar... why there?"

"She told me about the white van. It said Ravindra Refrigeration, Udaipur, Rajasthan. No such company, by the way, I checked. But my guess is that was where the Tetrahedron used to appear, in the middle of the desert. This time they made a mistake — or something — who knows? Although there was, I think, at least an exit door still over the Thar..."

Samir ran his fingers through his hair.

"But what does it all mean?" he cried.

He took his leave and returned to campus. He had an appointment with his professor in twenty minutes, and a class to attend after that. It was a hot, still, dusty sort of day, and the grit in the air burned in his throat. He stopped in front of the Physics building, then, abruptly, turned around and made his way to the tea-shack. It was deserted, except for Ramu stirring a potful of aromatic brew. Samir sat down on the bench. Ramu poured out some tea and handed him his glass wordlessly. In the background, the radio was playing an old Kishore Kumar favourite...

"Chalte, chalte, mere yeh geet yaad rakhana, kabhi alvida na kehena, kabhi alvida na kehena..." As you go through life, remember my songs, never say goodbye forever, never say goodbye...

Samir's eyes filled with tears. In the tree overhead, a crow cawed.

The Wife

IN OCTOBER PADMA BEGAN to dream of the woods behind her house. In the dreams, the woods came all the way up the slope of the backyard; there were branches poking through the bathroom window and leaves falling in the living room. She dreamed she was nibbling on unfamiliar fruits, swallowing the seeds whole, letting the wood take root inside her. And surely there was something — an animal, small, perhaps furry or feathery, and possibly lost — making a nest somewhere in the jungle of her mind…

Once she dreamed that she was following the creature — refugee or interloper — through caverns where there were only the roots of trees overhead, tangled and interwoven like neurons. She caught glimpses of it in the twilight of the passageways, among the withered, dendritic limbs of ancient roots; at times it looked like a rat or a mole, with a long, prehensile tail, but sometimes it was a bird with pale, delicate wings like banners. After a breathless chase, she caught up with the animal; she threw the free, trailing end of her sari over it and grabbed it swiftly through the cloth. On her knees she gathered the thing to her and it stopped struggling. It began to dissolve into the folds of her sari, leaving behind the hint of a shape, the outline of a face she knew or had known — and she woke. She lay in the big bed in the pre-dawn gloom, trying to bring the moment back, but she could not remember whose face it was that she had recognized.

After Keshav left — it had only been five weeks, although it seemed considerably longer than that — after he left her, she took to walking in the woods. In the woods was the silence that precedes the first snow of a New England winter — a silence of waiting, broken only by sudden gusts of chill wind that made the skeletal tree-limbs rattle. She had the feeling that the dream-creature she was seeking was here, somewhere, roaming among the pines and elms and birches, rooting in the undergrowth. But all she found were old birds' nests caught in the branches of bare trees. And once a pair of battered boots covered with mud, by the side of a small stream, which made her wonder whether somebody had once tried to drown himself in one foot of water. But then, what had become of the body? The clothes? The ring he wore, if he wore a ring? It occurred to her that the wood held many stories and mysteries, not just her own, and that perhaps there were other people wandering about in it, following threads of dream or the trails of booted feet. Sometimes she would be filled with a breathtaking certainty that around the next corner, among the foreign trees, she would find the ruins of her grandmother's house, the shell of the mango tree that overshadowed it, cocooned in the heat of an Indian summer. Or that a silhouette in the distance would turn out to be the idiot uncle who babbled and made animal noises, who had died of a fall when she had been eight. But the paths she found through the wood never led to any places she had known before, nor did she meet anybody, except, once, an athletic young woman in sweatpants and parka out for a hike. Once she came upon a clearing where she startled a stag that stood frozen in surprise for a brief moment. Then it flung its antlered head back, flaring its nostrils at her, and crashed out of sight. Another time she found the remains of a barbed wire fence and a sign half-buried in the mud that must have hung from it once; it said "Private Property". There was nobody there but a squirrel on the tree above, looking at her and scolding.

There were twenty-seven cardboard boxes in the living room. Some were empty and some were already packed and labelled. She had a roll of labelling paper on which she had written their names separately for the first time: Keshav, then Padma, and so on; these labels she would affix to the boxes that were packed. Under the boxes labelled 'Padma' she would add "Salvation Army donation" or "Send to Sarita, L.A." Once a week Keshav would drive down from his apartment on campus to pick up his boxes. During his visits she would take her car and drive aimlessly up and down the empty country roads for an hour, to give him enough time to leave before she returned.

Next week he would come for the last time. After that she would no longer be what she had been for twenty-three years: a wife. All the fuss and bother of the wedding negotiations, the smoke of the sacred fire, the smell of *ghee* and flowers, the leave-taking when she left India to join Keshav in America, the weeks and months and years in a country of strangers, learning to adjust and adapt, the visits home, brief and increasingly infrequent, the deaths of her parents, the two children now grown and living away from them — all that was over. What was left felt like a sinkful of unwashed dishes the morning after a half-remembered party: the old house, the inevitability of solitude — and her face growing increasingly alien to her day by day.

Everything in the bedroom had been sorted already. The children's things she could keep, Keshav had said. She need only put aside some of the furniture for him, pack his books, his clothes, his memorabilia, the golf-clubs, the cocktail glasses. He would take care of the things he kept in the basement and his tools in the shed. Some days she sat on the sofa or the kitchen chair in a kind of trance or daze, letting memories jostle about in the attic of her mind — the faint, milky, talcum smell of her babies, the way Keshav's breathing used to fill their room at night, the texture of his skin, his beard, the musky odour of his sweat after he came home from the gym… The way he had of probing at things, people or phenomena that he found interesting, like a dog worrying a bone, until he could capture their essence in words.

That reminded her of their first fight, after those rumours reached her about Keshav and his famous new colleague, Professor Marya Somebody, the one who had travelled through war zones and written a monumental novel based on her experiences. When she'd confronted Keshav he had been rather annoyed. "How conventional can you get," he'd said to her, his tone slightly mocking. "I could have slept with her, you know, but I did not. What I want from her is an intimacy beyond the merely physical… Don't you see, I am not interested in this woman as a woman. What I want to do is find the words — make a box from metaphor and symbol, meaning and simile, and put her in it…"

She had wept a lot, wanting to believe him although she did not understand him, and he had held her and soothed her and sighed. Then he had lifted her chin with one hand and looked into her face.

"I do this with everyone, you know," he'd said. "Including you. I ask the question, who is she? How do I find the words that mean Padma? Who are you, Padma?"

"Your wife," she had said with tremulous dignity, and he had shaken his head and smiled.

No, it hadn't started then, the rift between them. But why couldn't she remember that precise moment when he had first begun to close the door to her in his mind? She had come to know only gradually that she had disappointed him, like that time — the time she could never remember without a prick of anger, even after all these years. One night she had come home from the bookstore where she used to work, to find the house silent, with only the hall light burning. Her older son had been six then; his tennis shoes lay at the bottom of the stairs, soaked with blood. There were bloody footprints all over the floor and the stairs. Padma's bag had fallen from her grasp; she had flown up the stairs, calling for Keshav, for her sons, but the boys were peacefully asleep in their room. When she turned around, Keshav was standing in the doorway, watching her with an amused, rather satisfied expression on his face.

"An experiment," he explained as she stared at him in disbelief. "One I am going to conduct tomorrow in class, to demonstrate to my verbose young first-year students the importance of *brevity*. Isn't it amazing how much the human mind can make of a pair of tennis shoes, half a bottle of ketchup and a suitable setting?"

He had drawn her into his arms, apologizing, smiling.

"Do you realize how all our conclusions about the world are based on purely circumstantial evidence? What is real, and what is not real — all the universe gives us is raw *data*. We make realities out of *words*, Padma, words in our minds and on the page. Do you see?"

He was talking like he did at faculty parties. He had not understood her anger — he had thought that after the first shock she would laugh with him. But despite a Bachelor's degree in sociology — now gone to waste, like everything else — she was not sophisticated enough, she could not appreciate his cleverness. All the time she had been bringing up the boys, supplementing the family income with a series of small jobs, cooking and cleaning, reading her mystery novels, she had been unaware that she was, in a subtle way, a failure. At university functions she stood self-consciously in her silk sari, feeling overdressed and out of place, while talk and champagne flowed around her in torrents. Faculty wives sent her glances full of curiosity and pity; professors talked around her as though she were a museum exhibit, the exotic bride of that brilliant, if unpredictable Keshav Malik.

Over the years he had stopped teasing her; he had periods of black depression, weeks at a time when he left her to the children and the house to brood in his study or the basement, alone. Slowly he had uprooted himself from her. She could have forgiven him for his flirtations, for the way he turned everything into a game, but she could not understand or forgive his retreat from her. The thin fissure that had opened between them slowly widened over the years, bridged occasionally by shared moments like the serious illness of the older son or the death of Keshav's mother, a woman they had both loved.

When her boys were young, she had no idea of the fragility of the world; it all seemed written in stone: her marriage, homework with the boys in the evenings, the rituals of cooking, sewing, making love. Now the past came to her in disconnected pieces. Fragments without context or meaning, like the time Keshav and the boys had caught butterflies in their nets and released them into the living room… Her elder son, eleven at the time, had dragged her from the kitchen, breathless with laughter, saying "Ma, come, look!" The butterflies fluttered in and out of sunbeams like miniature magic carpets. They alighted on the stereo. They flew into reproductions of landscape paintings on the walls. Keshav, opening a book, began to identify them. "That one's a cabbage white. Look, a swallowtail, a sulphur…" Suddenly she couldn't bear it. She tugged open the window, knocked out the insect screen. Keshav gave her a long, speculative look, then laughed. They joined her in chivvying the crazy butterflies out of the room and into the brightness outside. When the window was closed again Padma saw a couple of corpses on the speaker and on the coffee table. One was yellow and the other was orange and black. There was a dusting like pollen on the shelves and the furniture.

"There's one trapped," she said wildly. "In the picture. Behind the glass."

It was an orange butterfly. She thought she saw its wings tremble against the glass.

"It's painted on, silly," Keshav was behind her, pointing with an indulgent finger, stroking her hair with his other hand. And she saw it was so.

As she sat brooding over the recent past — trying to find without success some hint, some foreshadowing of how she had ended up like this — a thread of remembrance would take her inevitably into the deeper antiquity of her childhood in India. The big, untidy house with four generations living in the warren-like rooms: bright flocks of aunts chattering like mynahs, the milkman's cow at the gate every morning, the swish of milk in the pail. The mango tree, her favourite haunt and refuge — an old tree, a dark, multi-armed goddess with its labyrinthian trunks branching off into the sky, its long green, waxy leaves murmuring like priestesses. A sparrow's nestful of naked fledglings, their yellow mouths open, crying. Lying on a broad branch, the bark rough against her cheek, she had looked down on to the flat roof of the house, with the flower pots on the low wall that ran around it, and the clothes flapping on the line like little coloured flags. A view of her grandmother picking wild jasmine in the tangled garden at the back, looking up at Padma, smiling and shaking her head and calling her a monkey. But always, like a pariah kite circling, her mind came back to that one afternoon when time had stopped.

From her tree that bright, cloudless summer day, she had seen the idiot uncle come up on to the roof. She had watched him with interest, wondering what a grown-up with the mind of a three-year-old — a reliable source of entertainment for her small tribe of siblings and cousins — would do on the rooftop, a place that was strictly out of bounds for him. He had a way of assuming the identity of things other than himself. Once he had sat for hours in the floor of the drawing-room, pretending to be — or thinking himself — a chair. Another time he had decided he was a muskrat — he'd run along the walls of the house, out into the back, where he had dug and snuffled among the bushes. He was not supposed to be on the roof, Padma knew — her grandmother lived with the fear that one day her youngest son would take on the identity of a bird. But that afternoon was golden, so filled with light and air and ease, that she had no presentiment of disaster. At first her uncle had simply wandered in circles, moving with the disjointed, disproportionate grace of a giraffe, patting the flowerpots, the clothes on the line, with his kindly, octopus-like hands. It had occurred to the eight-year-old Padma that she should perhaps call to somebody to tell them that Chotey-Mamu was up here alone, but watching him was too interesting.

She had been debating whether or not to throw twigs or leaves down at him to see what he would do, when he began to climb up to the roof over the stairwell.

The stairwell roof was about fifteen feet above the rest of the rooftop. Her uncle hauled himself up using the spaces between the bricks as footholds. The child watching him began at last to comprehend that he was in danger, that she should tell someone. But her voice seemed to have died in her throat. Her uncle stood up on the stairwell roof, spreading his arms wide, a breeze filling his white cotton shirt and pajamas. Below him was a sheer drop to the paved floor of the courtyard. He leaped.

After all these years, when she shut her eyes she could still see him. He was aloft in the hot blue sky, his arms flapping, suspended a few feet above the stairwell roof. A wordless shout of ecstasy burst from his lips. He was flying, he was lighter than a cottonseed. For an eternity he swam in the air, his wild, unruly hair blowing behind him.

Then there was just the empty sky. She heard the sound of a fall, but did not immediately connect it with his absence.

The child Padma had stayed in the tree, watching as the house filled with neighbours; the doctor's car drove up, and a curious throng gathered about the front gate of the compound. As dark fell she saw lights spring up in the house and in neighbouring houses. She could hear the wailing of women and other voices in the rooms below and in the courtyard, but nobody came calling for her. Not her mother or grandmother. She lay on the branch of the mango tree, getting sleepier and hungrier, but nothing would make her come down by herself. She would stay there forever…

Then she heard someone calling to her from the darkness below, and she had climbed down at last, slowly and sleepily, following the voice as it led her through the undergrowth, deeper and deeper into the wilderness at the back of the garden. She could not remember whose voice it had been, whether it was Chotey-mamu himself or her grandmother, or a koel-bird calling in deep, flute-like tones from some hidden arboreal grotto. But

The Wife

there was clearly a path through the jungle, a narrow thread of moonlight woven through the darkness of trees and shrubs. Stumbling, scratching herself on thorny bushes, she had come at last to a warm, soft place and curled herself up to sleep, feeling comforted, forgiven, thinking how good it was to be home, to be safe.

The next thing she remembered was bright daylight. She was standing by herself under the mango tree. There was blood on her lips and some of it had stained her cotton frock. She felt neither hungry nor thirsty, only as though she had just emerged from deep sleep. In the house a woman was crying loudly. Abruptly the door in the wall of the courtyard opened. It was her father, standing looking about. He hadn't combed his hair and his shirt was all crumpled. He saw her, stared, then ran to her, calling her name, gathering her in his arms. Inside there was a smell of death and disinfectant. The strange woman with dishevelled hair and reddened eyes who enveloped her in the folds of her tear-stained sari was her mother. Her fingers had combed through the tangle of Padma's hair, brushing the leaves from it. "Where were you, you wicked child? We looked for you all night… in the garden and the park and everywhere…"

She wanted to tell them that she had seen Chotey-Mamu fly, but the words would not come. All day they had asked her the same unanswerable question: where had you been?

Thirty-seven years later, sitting alone in a house full of boxes, she still did not have the answer.

As she mused, the room would fill with evening shadows, a still-life in shades of gray, and she would get the feeling that the wood was waiting for her just outside the window of the room, that the trees were pressing on the walls of the house, whispering. In the ornamental mirror hanging from the dining-room wall, her reflection would look back at her like a wild animal from its lair: unruly hair framing a face gouged with shadows, the nose like a bird's beak, the eyes huge, nocturnal, like lemurs' eyes. She would shudder and shake her head to clear it of fancies and get up with a little sigh.

Turning on the lights, she would fix herself a chutney sandwich or a roti wrap, and eat it absent-mindedly in the kitchen. Then she would get to work.

For days she drifted through the house like a moth blinded by the light, sorting, packing, labelling, until the rooms lost their dreadful familiarity. She took breaks in the afternoons to walk aimlessly in the woods. She tried to think of practical things, like what she should do next. Her elder son, who was working in California, wanted her to sell the house and move closer to him. Her friend Usha in India kept writing, asking her to come home, to start a new life.

Home. Her parents were dead. Her brother and two sisters had their own families. Her grandmother's house had fallen into ruin. Where was she to go?

Sometimes she got lost walking in the woods. There were no trails, no landmarks, and if she were not paying attention the trees in their wintry nakedness would begin to look the same, and the only sounds to guide her would be her own footfalls crunching on dead leaves. She would walk for miles until something in the landscape began to look familiar, and then quite abruptly she would come across her house sitting atop the slope. She never took the same paths through the wood, or so she believed.

Finally the day came when the boxes were all done — everything separated, sorted and labelled. Tomorrow he would come for the last time. Only the wedding pictures defeated her — at last she decided to put them in a box in the basement until she could make up her mind. Keshav would not want them, of this she was certain.

At first she couldn't find the basement key. She had not been down there for so long, it had not occurred to her to wonder until now why Keshav had kept the basement locked. There were boxes there that were university stuff, he had told her, some records from the English department. She looked for the key in all the usual places: the cupboard in his study, the little embroidered bag hanging on a nail in the kitchen where she kept her own keys. Finally she found it at the back of a drawer in his desk. It looked shiny and unused, probably a spare. The door did not yield at first, although she put her whole weight against it; then she saw in the half-light (it was evening) that there was a bolt also. She had forgotten about that. She drew the bolt and the door opened, creaking. The air below came slowly up into her lungs: still, and faintly musty. She had a sudden feeling of dread. But there was no going back. She took a deep breath, stretched out her hand and turned on the light.

The stairs creaked a little as she went down, holding the banister. At last she stood on the cold cement floor, gazing about her a little fearfully. There was nothing there but the old oil furnace with its pipes and dials, and dusty boxes stacked on the shelves. She realized she had left the wedding pictures upstairs after all. She began to walk around the basement, turning on the lights as she went. All was in order. It was just that the air smelled a bit stale. No wonder she had never felt like coming down here into the depths. No need for Keshav to have told her not to. But in the middle of the basement, suddenly, she smelled the wood. A tendril of fresh air that smelled of cold earth, bark, moisture, animal droppings. She looked around her apprehensively, but there was no place for anything to hide — no rats, not even a cockroach. The windows were high in the wall, narrow little slits opaque with age; they had been shut for years. Nothing could have got in. But the forest scent — how to explain that?

One end of the basement had been finished — it had a linoleum floor, bookshelves, a desk, and a wooden partition separating it from the rest of the basement. Keshav kept odds and ends here, old theses of various students, yellowing articles, obscure travel records. She remembered this vaguely from the last time she had been down here — was it two years ago, or three? She went into the partitioned area. The forest smell was much stronger now, but it was dark in this corner. She remembered the light turned on with the pull of a string — she searched the air before her until she felt the cold chain touch her hand. When the light came on, she saw a wooden cage on the desk, its door broken open, and tiny droppings and urine stains over pages of notes in Keshav's tiny, fastidious hand. On the shelves there were jars containing a variety of unidentifiable substances, a pile of delicate pencil drawings of a half-dozen impossible creatures, and a number of old books with peeling spines. But what finally held her gaze was the open window above the shelf: something had clawed at the catch, leaving dark stains on the wooden frame, until the window had tilted open just enough to let out whatever had been trapped here.

At first she simply stood there, breathing hard in her anger, reminded of ketchup-stained tennis shoes long ago. This was Keshav's parting gift to her, another set-up, a trick to remind her of the old days. But why? What did he mean by it? Leaning forward she saw that some of the stains on the pages were still moist. Keshav had last been here a week ago. She didn't know what to think.

She stood very still. Suddenly everything became clear to her. She felt as though she had, at last, wandered off-stage; she was the stranger looking into the lit windows of her own house. All these years she had thought it was her home, her refuge from the world, but after all it was only a *sarai*, a temporary stop on the way to the other place. The path lay before her like that silver thread of moonlight all those years ago, leading her to sanctuary: a single current of cool air, the forest's breath, the lifeline of dreams.

The Room on the Roof

THE OLD WOMEN, the grandmothers and widows in white saris, say that the monsoons awaken longings in all beings. The rain calls, they say, to hidden things, to seeds sleeping in the earth, to desire in the desiccated branches of trees and in the hearts of the young. As they tend the stove in the houses of their grown sons or daughters, as they sit on the balcony to sort rice or shell peas, as they look unseeingly at the grimy skyline of the city of their exile, they recount these myths and village lore, embroidered by their own imaginings and unfulfilled longings. Nobody listens but the young ones; the grown-ups, busy with jobs, chores and bank-balances, have no time to draw from wells of wonder. News of a story-telling grandmother goes from house to house, and soon the audience swells to accommodate the children of neighbours.

The girl who watched from the window was one of these; not having grandparents of her own living with her (the two surviving ones lived in a remote village in Bengal), she had grown up with stories told by the grandmother of a friend on the next street. So her mind was open to the notion that behind the dreary ordinariness of the world were wonderfully strange impossibilities. Her name was Urmila and she had just turned thirteen.

It was the first rain of the monsoons. It had started with dark falling in the middle of the afternoon; then a mad wind had come down from the sky, banging doors and windows, making the washing flap crazily on clotheslines, driving before it the litter on the streets, blowing summer dust in clouds everywhere. When the rain came down in great, roaring, shining columns, there was a dash for shelter amid laughter and rejoicing, and dusty umbrellas blossomed. The children pulled free of scolding mothers and ran into the street to dance and shout. Only the girl Urmila and her nine-year-old brother, Somnath, stayed indoors, in the upstairs room they shared.

In past years Urmila, too, had celebrated the advent of the monsoons by dancing on the street with her friends; this year she felt a reluctance to do so. She waved at the yelling, gesticulating, laughing children below, and she smiled and shook her head, although there was a wistfulness about the way she perched on the damp sill, the way she cupped her chin in her dark, slender hand. Leaning on the metal grillwork of the window, she looked back at her brother, who was sprawled on his stomach on the other bed, his crutches flung carelessly on the floor. He was absorbed in a game of chess. The girl shivered suddenly and looked out again at the sky, the rain.

Over the steady, friendly sound of the rain Urmila was aware of other sounds: the movements of chess players over the board, her brother muttering, negotiating with an enemy knight, taking an enemy pawn by surprise. There was a beetle clattering about on the cold, bare floor of the room. Urmila's mathematics homework lay neglected and slightly damp on the desk near the window: a page full of carefully drawn Venn diagrams, circles intersecting circles, like so many overlapping universes. She had recently come to the conclusion that the world she lived in was not a separate, self-contained thing, but actually an intersection of many worlds. There was the world of the beetle, the world of her mother pounding spices in the kitchen downstairs, the chess world, where her brother battled the evil enemy king, and who knows how many hidden worlds outside her awareness?

She was given to fanciful thoughts such as these, most of which she kept to herself out of embarrassment or shyness; but as she sat musing,

The Room on the Roof

looking out at the slowly drowning world, something extraordinary appeared at the end of the street.

It was a woman. She was walking down the street without an umbrella or a sense of urgency, looking about her, shading her eyes from the rain with one hand. Her bright green *salwaar kameez* clung wetly to her skin as she splashed slowly through the water-logged street. The girl saw all this and a thought came into her mind: this is the woman who will change everything.

The woman paused at the girl's front gate, opened it and walked the few steps to the front door. The next moment a bell jangled in the house.

Later, when Urmila remembered the events of that rainy season, she wondered why she hadn't felt more surprised that the woman upon whom she had laid such a great responsibility — that of changing everything, or at least that one thing that had been worrying her — should have chosen, of all streets in Delhi, her particular street, and of all houses, this one house. Of course they had the room on the roof to rent, and an advertisement in the local paper, and they weren't more than a twenty-minute bus-ride from the Vishwakarma Institute of Fine Arts, so you could explain the whole thing quite logically. But it was still quite extraordinary how it turned out...

At first, nothing much changed after the woman moved into the room on the roof. Her name was Aparna Bhuvan, and she was a sculptress; she brought with her just one suitcase, several lumps of clay and a faint fragrance of wet earth. She went every morning to the institute and returned in the evening with clockwork regularity. Urmila's mother approved of her because she was polite and decent, ate all her meals out and never brought anyone home. She was only a small ripple in the melancholy orderliness, the dull routine of the household, but to Urmila, she was a presence redolent with significance. The room on the roof was another world that had nothing to do with the rest of the house: the drawing-room with its decades-old furniture, its display shelves crowded with bric-a-brac, the mute sitar propped in the corner; the neat parental bedroom with the mauve and brown sheets, the venerable sewing machine and gargantuan steel cupboards that smelled of mothballs and old dreams when they were opened. No, Aparna Bhuvan lived in a different world, Urmila imagined, one with earth-smells and rain-smells, colours and carefree untidiness. The woman herself was quiet and unobtrusive, but her brown eyes were alight with laughter and secrets, and her hair was always loose, resting on her shoulders like a cloud on a mountaintop. Her clothes were coloured like rainbows, in swirls of red and ochre, or green and mustard-yellow. Every evening she would pass the children's room as she went light-footed up the stairs, and when she saw one of them looking out at her she would smile.

It rained without respite on most days, and dark fell early. In the evenings Urmila stayed in her room, reading and watching over her brother as he played his interminable games of chess with an invisible enemy. It had long ceased to be merely a game; last year, Som had cut a giant chessboard out of a piece of cardboard, marked the squares and then proceeded to put in the other features: the fort walls, the river, secret passages. The board was alive with mysterious symbols in black ink. The rules, too, had changed: the movements of the chessmen (each of whom had a name) were governed as much by intrigues, secret loyalties and betrayals, past histories, future aspirations — as by the traditional rules of chess. Urmila remembered how voluble and eager he had been last year, describing it all to her, building his world brick by brick. In this world the boy who could not play cricket or even walk without his crutches became a tall, turbaned warrior, fearless and compassionate. In her mind's eye she had seen him walk the passageways of the fort, inspecting the defenses, encouraging the men at the narrow slit-windows on the ramparts. His short brown fingers had lingered over a knight or pawn, his eyes seeing not the chessboard but the hills and valleys and townships of his embattled country.

But now he had shut her out with his silence. For months he had been reticent about his made-world, responding to Urmila's questions with a mulish sticking-out of his lower lip, or a shrug or a grunt, not meeting her eye, turning away from her as he had not done in all the years of his life. He had always been quiet, wary with strangers, set apart from his schoolmates by disability and temperament, but he had never been distant from her before. She was haunted by the growing certainty that one day he would disappear completely into the chess world, leaving nothing behind but a pair of crutches — and that this silence between them was the first phase of his retreat. There was nobody she could confide in; her one close friend was out of town for the holidays. Her parents constantly fretted about Som's future prospects — who would marry a cripple? How would he manage after they were gone? But now, as long as he did well in school and was healthy, they saw no reason to worry about him. Once Urmila had talked to her mother about Som, and her mother had said,

"He will be a chess champion one day, like Kartik Krishnan." And she had wiped her eye with the corner of her sari and sighed.

When the sculptress had wrought no magic in her first week of tenantship, Urmila began to lose hope. One evening, after the dinner dishes had been cleared away, and her father had established himself on the sofa with the newspaper, Urmila went up to him.

"Papa?"

She had rehearsed it all in her head: Som's retreat into the chess-world, his silence, his turning away from her. But her father said, in his soft, deep voice:

"Turn on the TV, child, it's time for the news."

The words died on her tongue. She did as she was told and stood leaning against the doorway. The TV man's prophet-of-doom voice filled the room: the gross national product had fallen again and the North-East crisis had taken a turn for the worse. Urmila's mother came in and sat down on the sofa, stirring isabgol into a glass of water with a spoon, a nightly ritual to ward off constipation. The sofa dipped and creaked with her weight. Her husband glanced at her in irritation and she stopped stirring and began to drink, talking between gulps in her tentative, Bengali-accented Hindi about her day, the rise in the price of flour, the servant-maid's tardiness. "Quiet!" snapped Urmila's father, leaning forward into the TV's glare. "This is important…"

If Aparna Bhuvan had truly possessed magic, Urmila thought, the TV would have blinked out with a wave of the hand. And then the sitar in the corner, the sitar her father had studied and given up when his father died, would have spoken; the strings would stir, softly at first, and then the music would fill the room. As her parents looked around in wonder (she imagined) the souvenirs on the shelves (gifted by globetrotting friends and relatives) would come alive: the little dancing girl from the mountains of Assam would begin to smile and sway, the windmill from the Netherlands would start turning its great wheel… Urmila let out a deep breath and left the room.

Now even her room, which had been a refuge of sorts from the rest of the house, began to oppress her, with the moist patch on the ceiling and the square window framing incessantly falling rain. "This terrible rain," Urmila's mother would say, oiling Urmila's hair, combing it out in long, slow strokes. "Your red kurta took three days to dry on the veranda — three days! I told Dhanu to iron it for you but she has left early again, the lazy girl…"

Every week Urmila braved the murky weather to go to Charu's house on the next street, where Charu's grandmother held court. From the open windows came the endless pattering of rain and odorous gusts of wind from the swollen river. The children waited restlessly for the stories, munching crisp, spicy hot *pakoras*, wiping oily hands unconsciously on their clothes. The grandmother's stories matched the mood of the season: they were delightfully scary tales of ghosts in banyan trees and things that came out of wells. "Dead things," the grandmother would say, "rocks and dust and bones, all desire life. Their hunger is so great that it brings the monsoons to us, so that they may, at least for a while, know what it is to be alive. And the fire-fiend comes out of the marshes, and disturbs the village girls…"

The Room on the Roof

But nothing ever happens here, thought Urmila.

One evening after dinner, after her brother had retreated upstairs, Urmila went to help in the kitchen — the maidservant had been unable to come. When her parents were huddled together before the TV, listening to the news with the blind innocence of grown-ups, she made her way slowly up the dark stairway. Light spilled from the open door of her room, and the bass cackle of the TV retreated with every step. Her eyes suddenly filled with tears.

But her room was empty. She looked up the stairs to the light from another doorway, from which she heard the soft murmur of conversation punctuated with laughter. She stood on the landing for a long time, caught between the two worlds, above and below. Then she went into her room, found a book and gazed unseeingly at it until her brother returned. She did not look at him. When he turned out the light a little later, she heard the familiar creak of his bed and a small sigh against the wall.

After that Som went up to see the sculptress nearly every evening. Once Urmila crept up the stairs and crouched on the fifth step from the top. Her brother was standing leaning against the part-open door, silhouetted against the light from within, his crutch held idly under one arm. She could just see Aparna Bhuvan's brown, skilled hands shaping a moist lump of clay on the table with sinuous, graceful movements. Every once in a while her face would come into view, with the humorous, mobile mouth, the eyes agleam in the light, a strand of black hair falling across her clay-streaked cheek. The window in the room must have been open because the air smelled cool and moist, and the clamour of the rain filled the ears of the watching, listening girl.

They were talking about the chess world.

"A good strategist concentrates on what he can change." The sculptress's hands paused at their work while she spoke as seriously as if she were talking about events in the real world. The sound of the rain rose to a crescendo and then faded. "The king, now, he cannot change everything.

Of course," now a smile crept into her voice, "he has to find out first, what it is he can change, and what he can't."

The boy said something inaudible and they both laughed.

The next afternoon, when the sculptress passed the children's room on her way upstairs, she smiled at them both as usual but her eyes lingered in a kindly way on Urmila. So Urmila knew that Aparna Bhuvan had been aware of her watching and listening the night before. After that she stayed in her room in the evenings.

Then one day she noticed a small clay soldier on her brother's desk. It was unpainted, an earthy orange-red, so real that it startled her. The end of the soldier's turban flapped behind him in a permanent breeze; one hand shaded his eyes from the sun, and in the other he held a spear. When (in her brother's absence) she touched the figure with a tentative finger, it felt almost warm, as though it had only lately emerged from the kiln.

After that she began to notice a difference in her brother. Som still didn't talk to her — he would lie on his bed, staring at the giant chessboard, glancing up to look at the soldier on his desk, swinging his crippled leg rhythmically over the edge of the bed as he planned the next move — but there was a lightness about him now, as though his centre of gravity had mysteriously shifted. He seemed to lean more easily on his crutches; his shoulders no longer hunched defensively against the world. Urmila began to sense that the mysterious and troubling barrier between them was dissolving, and that she was being forgiven for some lapse, some insensitivity of word or deed that she had been trying to remember for a year.

But what finally turned hope to certainty was the object that she discovered on her desk one evening. It was a terracotta figurine of a young woman standing with her arms outstretched before her, in a gesture of greeting or release. Her long skirt swirled about her in a gust of intangible wind, and her hair streamed out behind like a banner.

Urmila stared; she picked up the little figure and turned it slowly in her hands.

The Room on the Roof

"It's for you, Didi," her brother said. He looked hopefully at her. She took a deep breath, feeling light-headed with relief and delight. They smiled tentatively at each other.

"Aparna-di made it. She says will you come up and see her in the evenings?"

So Urmila came to understand that there was magic in the world, even if it worked at its own pace, in its own way. Certainly there was something magical about the room on the roof: here the rain was no longer dismal — it sang to them, sometimes loud and wild, sometimes a lullaby. A fine spray often blew into the room from the open window, but no mold grew on the walls as it did in the other rooms. The light in here was warm and yellow, the air smelled earthy and wonderful, and the sagging bed was the most comfortable thing to sprawl on while the children watched the clay take shape under Aparna's hands. They would try to guess what each lump was destined to become and laugh at each other's guesses. The sculptress would laugh at them both.

"I never know what shape the clay will take," she'd say. "Clay has dreams too. When I mix earth with water, I feel the clay move under my hands; all I do is guide it."

"You must be the best sculptress in the world," Som said, once, eyes wide. She shook her head, smiling.

"I'm only a junior instructor at the institute. You should see some of the really good people at work."

She showed them the institute's yearbook; they leafed through glossy photos of paintings, sculptures in clay, stone and metal, vast studios filled with sunlight. So this was her other world. Here was a picture of her, in one of those sunny rooms, bending over a student's work. Now a full-page photograph of a man caught their attention: tall, slender, with round fanatical eyes under shaggy black eyebrows, his longish graying hair combed back like one of the more flamboyant movie stars. "Ah, the genius," Aparna said, glancing up from her work. Her tone was curiously flat. The nationally recognized artist, Vardhaman Mitra, the article said, in his beautiful home, surrounded by his work. His sculptures were abstract, fluid, suggestive.

"That's his wife, Renuka." Aparna pointed with a grimy finger at the picture of a smiling, statuesque woman in a glittering sari standing at the top of a marble staircase. "My friend. She used to be a sculptress too, a good one."

"Why doesn't she sculpt anymore?" Som lifted curious eyes from the page.

"Because she's forgotten who she is," the sculptress said harshly, turning away, slapping water on to the clay with unnecessary violence. "Now she is content to inspire him, or so she tells me."

"What's he like?"

She was quiet for a second or two.

"Vardhaman? Difficult," she said. "Ambitious. Arrogant."

It was some time before she smiled again.

The children finished looking through the yearbook and as Urmila closed it and set it on the bed beside them, she had the disturbing realization that the sculptress inhabited, for the better part of the day, a world completely unfamiliar to them, centered around Vardhaman Mitra and his glittering wife — a world of mysterious adult tensions, with no place for Urmila or her brother.

Their collection of her work grew. On Urmila's desk was an eagle, a dolphin and a creature that was half-bird, half-woman. For Som there was a long boat complete with tiny men bearing oars, a rectangular vase for his pencils and, incongruously, a life-size pair of clay shoes. They were amusing, those shoes, with their floppy laces, the frayed cuffs, the well-worn shape. For a boy who had to use crutches and wear special shoes this would have been a cruel gift from anyone else, mocking his deformity, but from Aparna Bhuvan it was a happy, amusing present.

About this time Urmila began to have vivid dreams that were sometimes disturbing in their intensity. In these dreams she knelt in pools of wet clay, her hands cupped, pouring the silken, liquid mud on to her legs and arms.

Snakes rose from the clay pools and slid into the undergrowth with sinuous grace, and once a bird emerged, wet and earth-coloured, and took flight. Always, the sculptress was a subtle presence in her dreams, no more tangible than a shape in the distance, an awareness behind the trees. Sometimes she dreamed of her brother; lately it had been the same dream: the rain had stopped and moonlight came through the window, falling on the bare floor in a wash of silver light. Som was dancing in the middle of the room without his crutches, his clay shoes making a comical, hollow sound as he turned and dipped and whirled. When she woke and sat up in bed after one of these dreams, the moonlight was real, but her brother was fast asleep in his bed, in the dark shadows at the far end of the room. In the rainless stillness his breathing seemed to fill the space between them. She lay back, lulled to sleep by the rise and fall of his breath.

The next evening, as she watched Aparna at work, Urmila found herself wondering about her. The sculptress liked to talk as she worked but she never spoke about herself, the way ordinary people did.

"Tell us about yourself," Urmila said abruptly. She wished she could be more graceful in her speech, but lately her words emerged without warning in awkward, staccato bursts. The sculptress looked startled for a moment. "Tell us — tell us about your home — where you come from. How you came here."

"I come from rather far away — a place where nothing ever happens. The kind of place you leave to see the world…"

"Is it as far away as Bengal?" Som said. "My nana and nani live there, in a village by the sea. We've only been once."

Urmila looked at him, surprised. He had been so little on that visit — was it possible he remembered?

"My mother never goes back home," he continued. "She's Bengali, you know, but my father isn't. They married… for love," he said shyly.

"We saw the sea only once," Urmila said. "But my father couldn't speak Bengali. He didn't like it. And he doesn't like fish. And my mother was supposed to marry someone else who still lives there. So we don't go there any more."

She paused, thinking about the trip. Som said, "We're talking about ourselves again. Tell us about your family, Aparna-di. And how you came to Delhi."

Her strong hands worked vigorously for a second or two. She picked up a round-tipped wooden tool and began to shape the clay. She looked at them through the hair falling over her face.

"Nothing much to tell. I grew up with Renuka, the lady you saw in the yearbook. We were closer than sisters. Then almost exactly two years ago she got the fever to see the world. She came here, joined the art institute. Never came back, only kept entreating me to join her. I've seen some of her early work — she could make the clay sing! But by the time I got here she was married and no longer working. I stayed with them for a while, then I wanted my own place. And here I am…"

She was speaking lightly, but her eyes were careful. Behind them lurked some unidentifiable emotion, Urmila thought, feeling her own eyes fill unexpectedly with tears, feeling shut out, stupid, ashamed.

"You'll stay here now, won't you?" Som said.

Aparna smiled ruefully.

"I'll go home some day, maybe sooner than I thought at first,' she said. Urmila gripped the edge of the bed. 'One must always go home, you know. It's like music. You start with a theme. You wander from it, using a *raga* or mode as your guide and constraint. You play around, but at the end you come back to the beginning. The beginning is the end."

"If you never go home," the sculptress said, bending over the clay, her hair a monsoon cloud on her shoulders, "you are like a kite whose string has been severed…"

Urmila thought of the sitar in the drawing room, and the village by the sea. Perhaps there was no magic, she thought with a pang. If the sculptress also knew pain in her life, if there were things she could not fix, why, she too was as human and helpless as any of them. There was nothing anyone could do. Then the rain started up again; Aparna began to sing as she worked, and Urmila's sudden gloom lifted as quickly as it had come.

As the rain-filled days passed Urmila was aware of a subtle change in herself. She had always thought of herself as quiet and steady, the kind of person people rely on to be responsible and stable, but now she was aware that there was a wildness in her, as though something inside was responding to the rain. She was filled with a desire to run out into the street, to fly up in the clouds. The world itself seemed more interesting and mysterious than it ever had before; it was rife with secrets, a place where so many other worlds intersected, and she wanted to discover and explore everything. In the circle of children that attended the grandmother's storytelling sessions every week she was gregarious, happy and not at all shy. But sometimes a hopeless melancholy possessed her, and she thought the rain would never end, and that she and her brother and parents would never be happy or free, that beyond one wall there were others, an infinite concentricity of walls. Up in Aparna's room every evening, she felt joy and yearning like a fever, and underneath it the fear that all she had gained was temporary, that one day the sculptress would leave them and the magic would go out of their lives. Sometimes she caught herself holding her breath, waiting for the change.

But the change that came was not the tender, sorrowful parting she had been dreading. One evening Urmila was waiting for Aparna on the landing. It seemed to her that the sculptress was later than usual, and her brother too got to his feet on one crutch and limped over to join her. As they stood together, leaning against the banister in the semi-darkness, with the TV going on below them, they saw Aparna coming in at last. Her hair was more dishevelled than usual and her face was terrible and grim. Her eyes were like hot coals, furious, red-rimmed, bleak. She did not look at them. She ran past them up to her sanctum; they heard the door slam. The air around them still quivered with the swiftness of her passing, and there was the faint, familiar smell of moist clay.

Vandana Singh

Urmila put out an arm to steady Som, whose frightened breathing filled the darkness. She led him into the room and sat with him on his bed, putting an arm around him as she used to when he was younger.

She did not know how long they sat waiting, but the sculptress did not appear at their door. After a while she got up. "I'll be back," she said. She went like a ghost up the stairway. The door was shut. From within came the sounds of things breaking: baked clay statues shattering against the wall, unfinished clay thudding wetly on the floor. And guttural curses in an unfamiliar language, punctuated by howls of anguish. She imagined the sculptress whirling around the room in a dance of destruction, her hair whipping about her face, her eyes pouring forth tears of rage and loss. Urmila had never felt more a child, useless, helpless, shut out by mysterious storms in grown-up lives. She crept back down the stairs, trembling, uncertain what to tell Som, but he was standing at their door, looking up at her, listening. He had been crying. She blinked hard and took his arm, but they did not go into their room. It was all they had to offer, their silent, unacknowledged presence on the landing. They stood there until the sounds from above ceased and a dreadful silence took its place.

For three days the children stayed in their room in the evenings. They did their holiday reading, talked quietly to each other and did not speak of what had happened. But each glanced at the open door of the room when Aparna passed by on her way up.

Then one morning Urmila was sent to the milk booth, the servant maid having been taken sick. Walking away from the booth with the steel container cold and heavy in her arms, she looked towards the noisy main road. Beyond it lay the sodden cricket field and then the river, and on the other side, the specters of tall, grimy buildings, all boundaries smudged in the haze of slow rain. And there, in the park by the river, stood Aparna Bhuvan. Urmila watched, squinting in the rain. Then she trudged home.

The next evening the children heard voices at the bottom of the stairs. Urmila went to the door of their room. Downstairs her mother was holding a large fold of newsprint before her, talking to the sculptress. She pointed to something in the paper. Over the murmurs from the TV, Urmila heard Aparna say,

"Yes, that's her... Yes, from my home town."

"So very sad," said her mother.

There were more words exchanged that Urmila could not catch. Her mother's tone was curious, wistful, as though she wanted to continue the conversation, but at last she went back into the drawing-room. Urmila watched Aparna come up the stairs; at the landing the sculptress looked at her with bright, sorrowing eyes, paused, and reached out one hand as though to touch Urmila's cheek. Urmila stood very still and stiff, and Aparna turned and continued up the stairs.

In the drawing room the TV was going on about unrest in the Northeast. Her mother was shaking her head, muttering to her husband.

"...a fall, from a balcony. Vardhaman Mitra was away, the servants at the other end of the house... broke her neck..."

"Hmm..." said Urmila's father, leaning forward into the TV's glare.

"...imagine what a shock I got, the same Mrs Mitra who sent us that nice reference letter. What a tragedy!"

"Shh... I am trying to listen, for God's sake..."

Urmila picked up the newspaper from its basket near the door. Up in their room they spread it out on her bed. It took them some time to find the article. It was in the obituary pages. There was a picture of the deceased, the same one they had seen in the yearbook.

The sculptress's door was open. She was working on something; she looked up at them and at the newspaper, then she sighed and smiled all at once, and made a gathering gesture with one arm. They went in and sat on the bed, glancing around as though they had never been in the room before. She had cleaned up, but there were still faint marks on the walls. It had stopped raining — a moist breeze blew in through the window, but the street below was full of watery sounds, the splash of cars passing, the plink of pebbles thrown in a ditch by anonymous children. On the table there were two new pieces: a woman dancing, holding a two-headed drum, her skirt billowing out around her legs, and a boy with a kite in his arms, looking up at an imaginary sky. "For you," Aparna said, handing the figurines to the children, her eyes bright, tender, sorrowful. They held the gifts with careful, reverent fingers. Urmila wished she had a gift for Aparna that would ease her pain, but she felt crushed by the magnitude of the loss, and her own poverty.

"We've never given you anything," she said.

"Never say that," said the sculptress. She indicated the lump of clay on which she was working. "Can you guess what this is going to be?"

They watched as the clay began to transform under her fingers.

"It's a hand!" Som said after a while. "Two hands!"

Two hands with the fingertips pointing upwards, the palms facing each other. The wrists were slender, the fingers frozen in an exquisite mudra. A dancer's hands.

"Your hands...?" Urmila said.

"This is my last piece," the sculptress muttered, as though to herself. "Everything I have made has been a gift. Thus I keep a promise, repay a debt..."

They looked uncomprehendingly at her, and after a while she looked up from her work.

"I'm going away," she said at last. The words hung in the air, and Urmila heard them echo slowly in her mind. "Home," said the sculptress, smiling sadly and tenderly at them. "I've given notice to your mother. It will be about a week I think."

They could find nothing to say. This was the moment Urmila had been waiting for, but nothing had prepared her for it. It seemed to her that everything had suddenly slowed: the sounds in the street below, the drip-drip of the rain from the roof of the house, the beating of her heart. Through a numbness that was spreading rapidly through her, she heard Som say something, and Aparna replied, shaking hair out of her face. Urmila looked quickly at him; he was quite composed, but she thought he would cry later, his face turned to the wall by his bed. A lump formed in her throat then, and she felt a great stirring of blind emotion, hot as lava, surging inside her.

She knew without asking that when the sculptress left there would be no forwarding address, no letters exchanged. The room would be empty, as it had been before. But the world would have changed. She wasn't sure how she would live in it.

Aparna began to clear out her room. She took her last sculpture to the dessicator and kiln at the institute, as usual, but she did not bring back the finished work. She packed her few clothes and sundry belongings away in her suitcase. For Urmila time seemed to pass quickly and confusingly; she could not keep up with it. Her chest felt full of butterflies.

Two days before Aparna left, the news came. It was in newspapers, on TV, in glossy magazines: the terrible, violent demise of Vardhaman Mitra. He had been found in his marble bedroom by the servants, strangled to death by an unknown assailant. The guard at the gate had heard nothing, nor had the servant polishing the banisters a few feet from the bedroom door. There had been no visitors, suspicious or otherwise. The newspaper had a picture of the great artist after his wife's death, looking shrunken, with desperate, hungry eyes. "I cannot work," he had said then. "She gifted me her dreams. I gave them shape in clay…" Now he too was dead, and his murderer had left no clues apart from the indentation of fingers around the neck of the corpse. There was no sign of a struggle, but for a clay sculpture that lay smashed beyond recognition on the floor.

Aparna did not comment on the tragedy. She answered Urmila's mother's questions willingly enough, shaking her head sorrowfully, nodding at all the right places. She went out to the *dhobi's* stand on the next street with the bedclothes and curtains and had them washed and ironed. It seemed as though she had already washed her hands of the affairs of the institute, that her mind was on the journey home.

Finally there came the evening of the last day. The sculptress had sent her suitcase on already. The table was clean and unfamiliar, the sheets on the bed smelled like the coal iron of the *dhobi*. It was raining again in a slow, sulky way, perhaps the last rain of the monsoon. Aparna Bhuvan was wearing her red-and-ochre *salwaar-kameez*, defying the grayness outside. Around her neck was a silver necklace Urmila had given her (a gift from some forgotten relative when Urmila had been small), and in her hand she held Som's queen from the chess set. She thanked them with bright eyes.

Urmila said, "Are you taking the train?" and did not understand when Som and Aparna both laughed gently at her. Of course, she would take the bus first, Urmila thought. Her mind felt thick. Aparna embraced first Urmila, then Som, enveloping them briefly in the fragrance of moist earth. Now she was making her way down the stairs, Som following, thumping on his crutches. The boy and the sculptress said something to each other at the landing, then he went into the room and she continued down the stairs, getting smaller and smaller, like a bucket being let down into a well. She paused at the door to the drawing room, limned for a moment in the garish light from the TV, and said something to Urmila's parents. Then she was gone.

The sound of the front door shutting woke Urmila from her stupor; she began to run down the stairs, two at a time. Som called out to her but she didn't stop. The streetlight outside the house was out but she saw Aparna several paces ahead, walking quickly and gracefully through puddles and over potholes. The narrow street was lined with cars, and the rain cascaded gently off them. Urmila followed quickly, not knowing what compelled her, or what she would tell Aparna when she caught up with her. On the main road, with the crowds, the cacophony of car horns and the glare of headlights, she lost her quarry for a moment and stood looking frantically about, soaked to the skin, her hand shading her eyes from the rain. A man nudged up against her, leering, and she gave him a fierce, indignant look and joined a group of people with umbrellas crossing the street to the bus stop on the other side. But Aparna was not there. Urmila looked behind the bus stop at the soggy cricket field, and the dark river beyond it, and the wavering city lights on the other side. There she was, standing on the riverbank, staring away at something. What was she doing there? There was a bus coming now, it would go most of the way to the railway station. People dropped off the bus as it lurched, belching, to a stop; now the crowd surged towards it in a body. Urmila slipped away into the darkness behind the bus stop and plunged ankle-deep into the mud of the cricket field.

The sculptress was standing, stretching her arms before her, bending her body as if in obeisance to the rain. She lifted her face and let the rain fall on it. Only a faint wash of light from the street fell on her; she was a dark silhouette against the murky, glimmering river. Urmila stumbled towards her, dragging one foot, then another in the mud. Aparna must surely have seen her by now, she paused in her stretching and swaying, and perhaps she smiled. Urmila stopped. Aparna knelt, rain falling on her in thick shawls. Now Urmila saw that she was naked, except for the gleam of the silver necklace around her neck; somehow her clothes had rolled off her, or had been dissolved in the rain. She was holding something — the chess queen? — in one hand. Rain fell on her bare shoulders, formed a thick rivulet between her breasts, cascaded over the dimple in her belly, pooled in the hollow below, flowed smoothly over her thighs. Her hands dug into the mud; she bent her head, her hair falling in a wet, tangled mass over her face. Now a forest of hands rose from the mud, clay hands, loving hands, drawing the woman down into the earth. Her body seemed to become molten; a ripple ran over her. Before she sank completely, before her shape had altogether lost form, she raised her head and looked at the girl standing in the rain. Then there was nothing there but trampled mud, and the rain falling on it, smoothing it.

Urmila felt it then: a lightness spreading inside her, not joy, not pain, but something more complex, a kind of effervescence. She began to walk home in the rain. On her street the house lights shone warmly; open windows let out the sounds of conversation, laughter, plates in the sink. In Charu's house the grandmother would be tucking the smallest ones into bed, telling them a story about the monsoons. Urmila understood at last that what the monsoons brought was nothing less than the possibility of dissolving barriers between worlds.

Inside her gate she paused. She could hear the babbling of the TV; the blue light flickered in the window. She stood in the rain, feeling reluctant to go in. It fell on her like a benediction. Over the sound of the rain, the cackle of the TV, she heard it, so soft and tentative that she must have imagined it: the hollow clunk of clay shoes on the floor of the room upstairs, dancing, dancing to the rain.

VANDANA SINGH
A Speculative Manifesto

IN THE DAWN of time, the first humans told tales about ten-headed demons, flying chariots, and gods wielding thunderbolts. The earliest writings in almost every tradition are part of what we call imaginative literature or speculative fiction today. The modern descendants of the *Epic of Gilgamesh* and the *Mahabharata* are the genres of science fiction, and fantasy, including various sub-categories like magic realism, alternate history and slipstream. They are all stories about what cannot ever be, or what cannot be as yet. Such are tales set on other planets, or on rocket-ships; such are stories filled with impossibilities like faster-than-light drives and magic wands, and women who turn into snakes.

But humanity has grown out of its childhood, as each of us grows out of it as individuals. Why not discard the old myths, legends, tall tales, and their modern counterparts, as we discard other childish things? Why not leave them for the children? Aren't grown-ups supposed to read realistic fiction? What good are these wild tales, anyway?

Let us begun with myth. Speaking entirely from a non-religious perspective, what good are these impossible stories? In our times mythology is often dismissed as a hodge-podge of incorrect explanations for natural phenomena. But the role of myth is much more than an attempt to explain thunderstorms or eclipses. In ages past, mythical and fantastical stories recounted people's hopes and fears in relation to the vast universe they inhabited. This universe included animals and plants and forces of nature that seemed magical indeed. Perhaps that is why these old tales are imbued with so much wonder. It seems to me that in modern times we have lost connection, not only with each other but with the natural world and its wonders, and so perhaps it is not too surprising that so much of imaginative literature has been relegated to children's fiction, and that even when it is written for adults, it is not taken seriously by the literary establishment. That is, of course, the literary establishment's loss, but it is also ours. Unless teachers in schools and colleges include speculative fiction in their course work, how will students discover and delight in it? This neglect is a great pity because both children and adults need the literature of the imagination. So much modern realist fiction is divorced from the physical universe, as though humans exist in a vacuum devoid of animals, rocks, and trees. Speculative fiction is our chance to rise above this pathologically solipsist view and find ourselves part of a larger whole; to step out of the claustrophobia of the exclusively human and discover joy, terror, wonder, and meaning, in the greater universe.

But also, speculative fiction has a revolutionary potential that is perhaps unique.

Why do I say this? Because imagination—that faculty that expands the human mind to the size of the universe, that makes empathy possible (you have to have some imagination to put yourself in another's shoes)—also allows us to dream. Science fiction and fantasy posit other paths, alternative futures, different social arrangements as well as technologies, other ways that we could be. Before we do, we must dream. So Rokeya Sukhawat Hussain, dreaming of the liberation of women back at the start of the twentieth century, writes her utopia, *Sultana's Dream*. So Ursula K.

Le Guin, imagining a peaceful anarchic community, writes *The Dispossessed*. As Sahir Ludhianvi said, *"Ao ki koi khwab bune, kal ke vaste"* (Come let us weave dreams for tomorrow's sake). The so-called Third World is undergoing vast and unpredictable changes, and the world at large—for we have only one world, after all—is beset by war and environmental catastrophe. Through engaging our imaginations and making up ingenious thought-experiments, through asking 'what-if' questions and attempting to answer them, speculative fiction allows us to question the path we are on today, to live out possible futures before we come to them. What if books were banned? asked Ray Bradbury, and gave us one possible answer in *Fahrenheit 451*. Walter Miller penned a bleak account of a post-nuclear-holocaust world in *A Canticle for Leibowitz*. While speculative fiction has not yet fully realized its transgressive potential, dominated as it has been by white, male, techno-fantasies— Westerns and the White Man's Burden in Outer Space—there is still a strong undercurrent of writing that questions and subverts dominant paradigms and persists in asking uncomfortable questions. No other literature, to my knowledge, has written with so much passion about technological and social issues, nuclear war, or genetic engineering.

Yet there is another aspect to speculative fiction, which is also the place where the two distinct sub-genres of fantasy and science fiction meet. Part of the appeal is that while the literal story has its own charm and interest, the characters or tropes in the story often have symbolic or metaphoric value. Symbol and metaphor, according to such thinkers as Carl Jung, are part of the language of our unconscious minds. So good imaginative literature, in being many-layered, appeals to us at many levels, including the deepest tiers of the human mind. (Perhaps this accounts for the persistence of myth across the ages.) I had said earlier that speculative fiction is about what cannot ever be, or what cannot be as yet. But it is also true that when it uses symbol and metaphor in certain ways, speculative fiction is about us as we are, right now. This may be the case even if the story is set on another planet, in another age, and the protagonist is an alien. Because haven't we all felt alien at some time or another, set apart from the norm due to caste and class, religion and creed, gender and sexual orientation?

Underneath all this is the fact that good speculative fiction is fun. Of course much of what is 'merely' fun is dismissed by the establishment, as though 'fun' is necessarily synonymous with 'frothy and shallow'. But good speculative fiction can be fun and meaningful at the same time. I'm not talking about the acres of garbage that constitute 90% of science fiction and fantasy (and probably 90% of mainstream realist fiction as well). I'm talking about the grain in the chaff. Here I mean 'fun' not only in the sense of enjoyable, but also in the sense of play: both in the sense of playing like children, and in the sense of theatre, with the universe as a grand stage. This might result in an intellectually satisfying play of ideas, whether scientific or philosophical, or a hilarious exposé of human nature, or both—think of Premendra Mitra's Ghanada tales, for instance. Art as play-time, in its deepest and most literal sense, all at once—the Sanskrit term *Leela* comes to mind.

Emily Dickinson famously said: Tell all the truth but tell it slant. Reality is such a complex beast that in order to begin to comprehend it we need something larger than realist fiction. Enter speculative fiction, with its aliens and magic and warp drives, set against the backdrop of the universe itself. At its bedrock, despite the strangeness of the setting, we recognize familiar things: love, rage, struggle, wonder—our selves, disguised, but there. After all, the *Mahabharata*, for all the wonderful storytelling, is also the battle that rages within each one of us.

Vandana Singh
Framingham, MA
2008

ACKNOWLEDGEMENTS

NO SIZEABLE PIECE OF work is due to the author alone; underlying it are the inspiration, support and influence of others. My first debt is to the vast clan that is my family: my eternal gratitude to my parents, Leela and Priyaranjan, for inculcating in all three of us siblings a love of books and learning, for encouraging us in our ambitions and for bringing us up to think freely; to my brother Ashok, companion of my childhood, fellow reader, conspirator and supporter as well as an invaluable inspiration for ideas; my sister Ruchika, who turned me into a story-teller by demanding stories from me when she was small, and whose friendship and wisdom are more important to me every day; my grandparents, Ranchor and Sharda Prasad, now deceased, whose love and inspiration continues to keep me going; my husband Christopher who is first editor and sounding board, for his faith and patience; his dogged belief in my writing helped me get past numerous blocks to where I am today; my daughter Joya for taking over of my sister's role in demanding stories every day and thus honing my writer's skills and—through her eyes—allowing me to experience the world in new and wondrous ways; my sister-in-law Ramaa for reading many of my stories before they were published and giving me useful comments filled with her trandemark wit and insight; my parents-in-law, Melanie and Russ, for reading and appreciating my work and encouraging me by delighting in my successes; the family at large: aunts, uncles, cousins, for indulging and encouraging me in my various eccentric pursuits, and for giving me that most precious of gifts, a wonderful childhood. My nieces and nephews, including the youngest joyful additions, Trisha, Dhruv, Rushil, Rahul and Anunay, give me a reason to keep writing and to remember what it is like to look at the world through the eyes of a child.

My endless gratitude goes out to Shariann Lewit, Renu Namjoshi, Pam Schossau, Sarah Smith, and Karen Soorian for their warm friendship, for sharing their wisdom and saving my sanity on multiple ocasions; to Carol Russell for her support in difficult times and for her vigour and greatness of heart; to Swati Singh for her affection and generosity; to Michele Gutlove for her inspiration as a person and an artist; to Margaret

Krell for shared laughter and writing discussions; to Smita Kundu for her indomitable spirit; to my long-lost college friends as they once were, in the far country of our youth, with fond memories of Delhi University.

I am indebted to my dogs, Jhankar, Jasper and Bandit, the first two gone, for their loving companionship, humour and kindness.

India is one of the deepest sources of inspiration to me, and being Indian is a very large part of the kind of writer I am. When I say 'India' I mean less the man-made political entity than a certain set of philosophical attitudes toward the world, a palimpsest of memories and impressions, the tastes and sounds and rhythms of an entity that evolved from the mingling of many sub-cultures. Much of my writing and indeed, much of who I am is grounded in that India.

I am indebted also to writers of past and present who continue to inspire me through their work: the great Hindi novelist and master of the short story, Premchand, the Urdu poets Ghalib and Faiz, the Bengali writer Premendra Mitra, the nameless authors of folk songs and folk tales in India, the Latin American magic-realists Borges and Garcia Marquez, the masters of English writing from Shakespeare to P. G. Wodehouse and Terry Pratchett. While I take all responsibility for any shortcomings, errors or omissions in my own work, I acknowledge the deep and abiding influence these writers have had on my world-view.

Of modern writers in the realm of imaginative literature, I owe the greatest debt to Ursula K. Le Guin, who, through her pioneering work, made this once exclusively white-male domain open to such aliens as women and non-whites. For me, she has been the kindest teacher and mentor: the inspiration of her writing and her personal encouragement mean more to me than I can say. My thanks go out also to Molly Gloss for giving me critical encouragement when I was green and vulnerable, and to Kurt Kremer, Pam Schossau and Steve Shervais, my oldest writer friends. Many thanks also to the Cambridge Science Fiction Workshop, the most venerable science fiction and fantasy workshop in the United States, whose current and former members welcomed me into their midst (after a tough entrance exam) four years ago, and helped me become a better writer through their ruthlessly intelligent critiques and sound advice. So thank you: Shariann Lewitt, Sarah Smith, Theodora Goss, Kelly Link, Gavin Grant, F. Brett Cox, Jim Kelly, Steven Popkes, Alex Jablokov, Alex Irvine,

Jim Cambias, David Alexander Smith. My gratitude also to Anil Menon, friend and writer extraordinaire, for giving me something to celebrate in new Indian imaginative fiction, indeed, in imaginative fiction in general.

For help with specific stories I'd like to thank Saleem Kidwai and Danish Husain for their generosity in agreeing to read my story "Infinities" and for their very useful feedback. Also thanks to Michele Gutlove and Anil Menon for their useful comments, and to my mathematician friends for indulging me. For the story "Thirst" I owe inspiration to my husband Christopher, who first suggested I write a modern story about the Naga-people of legend. The story "Conservation Laws" is an inadequate tribute to that genius of Bengali science fiction, Premendra Mitra, and is inspired by his Ghanada tales.

Finally I'd like to thank the visionaries at Zubaan, in particular, Anita Roy, and Jaya Bhattacharji (formerly at Zubaan), for their invaluable support and friendship, for discovering and publishing my work, and for bringing it to the audience that is most crucial to me: India. Indeed I am grateful for all that Zubaan does to publish fine, off-mainstream writing from a variety of voices that may otherwise have been lost or forgotten. Thank you.

Grateful acknowledgement is made to the following for permission to reproduce the stories:

'Hunger' from *Interfictions* (Delia Sherman and Theodora Goss eds), Small Beer Press (USA), 2007

'Delhi' from *So Long Been Dreaming* (Nalo Hopkinson and Uppinder Mehan eds), Arsenal Pulp Press, 2004

'The Woman Who Thought She Was a Planet' from *Trampoline* (Kelly Link ed.), Small Beer Press (USA), 2003

'Thirst' from *The Third Alternative Magazine* (UK), 2004

'Three Tales from Sky River' from *Strange Horizons Magazine*, 2004

'The Tetrahedron' from *Internova Magazine* (Germany), 2005

'The Wife' from *Polyphony*, Volume 3 (Deborah Layne and Jay Lake eds), Wheatland Press, 2003

'The Room on the Roof' from *Polyphony*, Volume 1 (Deborah Layne and Jay Lake eds), Wheatland Press, 2002